Also by Marie Nicole Harper

For Best and Worst

February 2015

Available at Amazon and most online booksellers.

Also available at certain "brick and mortar" shops.

SUNSETS OF FIRE AND ICE

MARIE NICOLE HARPER

SOUTHLAND BOOKWORKS

http://www.southlandbookworks.com

SUNSETS OF FIRE AND ICE

ISBN 978-0-9991685-0-9

Published by Southland Bookworks, LLC.

Cover art is from iStock by Getty Images, stock photo number: 531551204. Cover design is by Southland Bookworks, LLC.

Printed in the United States of America
August 2017

ACKNOWLEDGEMENTS

While I have been inspired by many people, many places, and many things, all the credit goes to my Lord and Savior, Jesus Christ. With him all things are possible. The following is a list of the many things with which my Heavenly Father has blessed me.

First, he gave me the privilege of being made by Woodrow Graham and Gladys Ruehl Graham. Mama and Daddy loved me, nurtured me, disciplined me, and sacrificed greatly for me. I love them and miss them.

God couldn't have done any better than to set me down where he did, Cullman, Alabama. Though I didn't always appreciate Cullman; as time passed, I came to realize that it's a place, a community of individuals, although they may not show it in day life, who genuinely care about others and continually strive to make not only Cullman a better place to live, but to make this world a better place for all of us.

God has given me so many great friends through the years, and blessed me with a great extended family. I love them all. And yes, God has put individuals in my life I probably could have done without. While I will probably never look upon these individuals fondly, they made me strong.

PROLOGUE

A crowd of twenty-five to thirty gathered close to the funeral tent on a cold January day. Gunmetal colored clouds were forming in the western sky around a fiery sun. In a couple of hours, the folks of Wentworth, Alabama would be able to witness what some called a sunset cf fire and ice.

Most of the graveside attendees were huddled close to the tent, to catch a glimpse of the family, and listen to the minister read scripture, while weaving into his message, accolades of the deceased. Approximately twenty yards from the crowd stood two lone figures. One was a tall gentleman, and standing about ten feet to his right was an attractive woman. The tall man had wavy blond hair and a beard, the woman had chestnut colored hair mixed with strands of gray. It would be obvious to anyone that she had once been a beautiful lady. In fact, she still was.

As the minister was talking about the deceased's dedication to the Lord Jesus Christ, to family, to work, and to Alabama football, the man, handsome in his own way, appeared to be somewhat nervous, shifting his weight from one leg to another. He had his cell phone in hand, checking the screen every ten or fifteen seconds. Also, straining to get a glimpse of the folks seated in the tent, the woman appeared as nervous as the gentleman standing to her left.

While the woman was not able to view the folks sitting on the front row, she spied someone in the second row who looked familiar, a woman with gray hair woven in with her dark hair. Being unable to see her face, she couldn't be sure if this woman was Anabelle Martin.

The chestnut-haired woman and the blonde gentleman nodded to one another as the message continued. Neither had any idea who the other one was.

When the graveside service concluded, both lone figures slowly made their way to the tent. The woman saw Barry Tidwell staring at the casket. Then she saw him look toward one of the people still sitting in a chair on the front row. Barry didn't look happy, but was anyone supposed to look happy at a funeral. The chestnut-haired woman and the blond stranger arrived at the front of the tent at the same time, both had tears in their eyes.

CHAPTER 1

Eric Channing glared at the TV. Pounding his fist into the tray, he turned over his glass of iced tea, spilling it onto his plate of meatloaf, mashed potatoes, green beans, and cornbread. There stood Kristie, his ex-wife of several months, on the red carpet at the Bridgestone Arena in Nashville. And with her was none other than country music's most famous unknown, Jake McPherson. The dress Kristie was wearing looked like a replica of the dress she wore when the two of them were married last year in June. This dress, though, was solid black and floor length; whereas the wedding dress was light blue and street length.

Eric knew Kristie liked Jake McPherson, and he also felt that Jake had a thing for Kristie. But Kristie had professed to love him and only him, even telling him on the day their divorce was final, throughout all the drama, she had never stopped loving him.

It didn't take Mr. Jake McPherson long to swoop in, nor did it take Kristie long to find someone else. Forget it! Eric flipped the TV back to his favorite cable news channel as he got up out of his recliner to get a towel to clean up his ruined dinner.

After preparing another plate, and sitting down on the sofa to watch the last thirty minutes of his favorite opinion journalist, his phone rang. It was Jimmy Harpo. "Hey, old man, it didn't take "Little Miss Perfect" long to find someone else, did it? And someone famous at that? Who would have thought that fat Kristie Tidwell would one day be attending the CMA awards with a celebrity?"

"Look, Jimmy, I'm just not in the mood right now, and don't start up with the fat thing. That was decades ago."

"Are you still carrying a torch for her? I suggested you give Kristie her marching papers after Ruthie and I ran into her in New Orleans; where she informed us that she hated our whole family. Talk about a hypocrite."

"Kristie's not a hypocrite. She was hurt by the way some of our old Wentworth gang treated her when we were in high school, and I can't say that I blame her. She's one of the finest people I have ever known. The fact our marriage didn't work out hasn't changed that."

"Suit yourself, but there's still plenty of women around that would love to be with you. In fact, there is one right under your nose, and she wants you."

"Anabelle? Get real."

"What's wrong with Anabelle? She's loaded, plus she's like you and the rest of us. She fits in, unlike Kristie."

"Look, Jimmy, I'm not attracted to Anabelle in the least. She has wrinkles and varicose veins. Plus, her hair is faded and dry. Just the other day, I saw her scalp."

"So, we've all aged. Just think about the knock-out Anabelle was when she and Wiley married."

"That was then, and this is now. Anabelle doesn't hold a candle to Kristie, and I am not attracted to her in the least."

"You're going to be sorry you wasted so much time pining away over that snobby bitch."

"That's enough Jimmy. I'm beginning to think Kristie was right about y'all. You're narrow-minded and cliquey. Kristie's friends were always kind to me, but I can't say the same about the actions of my friends toward Kristie. I have to go, bye."

Later that evening, Eric was still sitting on the sofa in Anabelle's basement watching some re-runs on TV Land, when he heard Anabelle coming down the stairs. When the door to the basement suite opened, there was Anabelle wearing a see-through nightgown. Eric could only stare. It was the first time he had seen a naked or nearly naked woman since Anita, the waitress at the run-down fish place in the Florida Keys.

Eric stood up as Anabelle began moving seductively toward him. The two embraced while Eric ran his hands up and down Anabelle's body. The next morning, Eric found himself upstairs in Anabelle's king-sized bed alongside her.

What would Kristie think, Eric chuckled to himself? His mind wandered back to Kristie and the dream she claimed to have had on the night before their wedding. A dream in which she caught the two of them in bed together the same afternoon that Anabelle's late husband, Wiley Martin, died at Wentworth Medical Center.

Jimmy Harpo was Eric's best friend, but he could be difficult at times. Jimmy, along with Eric, was a part of a group that smoked, drank, and had sex while they were still in high school. This crowd had no interest in attending college anywhere, preferring to hang out in Wentworth for the rest of their lives. It wasn't until Jimmy was almost thirty that he decided he needed to grow up and make something of himself.

Reluctantly, he attended the now defunct St. Randolph College on the east side of Wentworth. He could get a decent education and still remain in his beloved town of Wentworth,

Alabama. Jimmy was the youngest of the Harpo children, having an older brother named Sam and an older sister named Jan. Jan had married high school sweetheart Jeremy Franklin and Sam had married Wentworth native, Kathryn Campbell. After earning his degree from St. Randolph, Jimmy met and married Russellville, Alabama native Ruthie Williams who was a nurse at Wentworth Regional Medical Center.

Since moving back to Wentworth with Anabelle Martin, Eric had been miserable. He was content to live in the Florida Keys and have Anabelle as a friend. He fished and swam in the warm shallow waters almost every day. While there was no desire on his part to pursue a relationship with Anabelle, he did enjoy her company.

Anabelle soon grew tired of the leisurely island life and wanted to return to Wentworth where she had been a matriarch of the small town's close-knit society. She missed her clubs, her charity work, and her friends, notably Jan Harpo Franklin, Kathryn Campbell Harpo, and Ruthie Williams Harpo. She didn't meet any of these ladies until after she and Wiley began seeing one another. But after the wedding, the four of them were inseparable.

Even though she would keep her house in the Keys, Anabelle talked Eric into moving back to Wentworth with her. It would be great having the gang together again, after his ex-wife, Kristie, almost split them apart.

Having sold all of his Wentworth County property except for a lot on Jones Lake, Eric agreed to move into the fully furnished basement of Anabelle Martin's spacious house in Summerdale, an upscale subdivision, until he could build something on his lake property.

After Eric Channing divorced his first wife, Gina Hanover Channing, it was the mission of the Harpo couples to find the perfect girl for Eric. They tried and tried, but Eric didn't seem interested in any of the women they paraded in front of him.

Then, one New Year's Eve, Eric brought Kristie Tidwell, a former classmate at Wentworth High, to a party the Harpo women were hosting at Jan's house. Because of childhood weight problems, Kristie was not popular with the gang, even though she lost the weight and became one of the best-looking girls in school. This didn't bode well with most of the group because the girls who thought they were the best-looking ever, now had competition.

After high school graduation, Kristie left Wentworth to study at the University of Alabama, and subsequently became a successful career woman. After leaving her hometown, she returned sparingly, and only then to visit family. A few years ago, Kristie decided to show up at a high school reunion. Eric Channing, single and available, was there also. That night, the two of them started a relationship which led to marriage.

While Kathryn Campbell Harpo had graduated in Kristie's class and hung out with her a bit, she had no desire to be friends with Kristie now. Eric was part of their group, and Kristie was taking him away from them.

CHAPTER 2

When Jake McPherson asked Kristie to go to the CMA Awards' ceremony with him, she was on cloud nine. Jake McPherson wanted to be with her, wanted her to be his date, and perhaps wanted the millions of people who would be watching the ceremony on TV, to see her with him.

Upon arrival at Jake's Nashville condo, Kristie was greeted by the maid, who instructed her to put her things in the guest room. She then told Kristie that Jake was still at the recording studio, but would return shortly to shower and dress for the ceremony.

When Jake arrived, he greeted Kristie, who was dressed and ready to go, with a quick hug, and went off to his master suite to get ready. He didn't even tell her how beautiful she looked.

For this event, Kristie had chosen a black crepe gown fashioned similar to her wedding dress. Unlike the wedding dress, which was street length, the gown was floor length, with the same puffed sleeves, and a plunging neckline. Kristie accessorized the dress with a pearl choker, a dainty pearl bracelet, pearl drop earrings, and black high heel shoes.

After Jake had left to shower and dress, his two daughters arrived to accompany her and Jake to the event. While they were waiting, one of the daughters let it slip that Jake and his girlfriend were having a spat. So, that was the reason for his asking Kristie to be his date for the CMAs. He obviously had no interest in her.

Feeling like someone had taken a knife and stabbed her in the stomach, Kristie no longer wanted to go to the ceremony, no longer wanted to talk to the daughters, and didn't want to see Jake. The next few hours were going to be some of the worst in her life.

When Jake emerged from his bedroom, he kissed his daughters, and announced that the limo transporting them to the awards' ceremony should be arriving in five minutes. Then he sat down on the sofa beside Kristie, casually put his arm around her and said, "I'm so glad you could come and go with us. However, I have to be up early tomorrow. But I want you to stay for the big party being thrown afterward. I'll have the limo run me back here. Then the driver will go back to pick you up. You can stay as long as you want to, though.

I'm sure it'll be fun. You're all settled in the guest room, I assume?"

"Yes, thank you."

"Since I have to go to Boston tomorrow morning, take your time and leave when you're ready. Melba will be here, and she'll be happy to fix you some breakfast, lunch, or whatever."

While riding in the limo, Kristie loosened up a bit. This was an experience not many people get to have. Would Eric be watching? Probably not, he was more into rock than country. Would any of the Harpo's be watching?

The limo pulled up to the curb outside the Bridgestone Arena where a uniformed security guy opened the vehicle door. Jake got out first and then helped Kristie and the girls out. Jake took Kristie's arm and steered her toward the entrance of Bridgestone, with the girls following behind. Even though he was not scheduled to be interviewed on the red carpet, onlookers behind the barricades yelled at Jake, and he waved back to them as he, Kristie, and the girls entered the large facility. They were escorted to their seats by an attractive young lady in formal attire.

Kristie, not a big fan of awards' shows, did find herself enjoying this one. The music was great, and Jake won an award.

Afterward, Jake escorted Kristie and the girls next door to the Renaissance Hotel where the main party would be held. He left them at the party and headed to the waiting limousine that would return him to the condo.

Kristie had a magnificent time at the party, and immensely enjoyed talking to the girls, who knew many of the stars, and introduced Kristie to them. After a couple of hours, they decided to leave, and the limo dropped them off at Jake's where the girls got into their vehicle and left. Kristie unlocked the door and let herself in. The door to Jake's bedroom suite was closed.

While Jake told her to stay at the condo as long as she wanted to, Kristie was up early and left about 8:30 am. Even though she had a great time at the party, and Jake had treated her like a queen when she was with him, Kristie wanted to get away as soon as she could. Jake had used her to make someone else jealous.

She knew severe weather was forecast for parts of north central Alabama later in the day, but wasn't concerned. The inclement weather was supposed to hit between 4:00 pm and

10:00 pm. She would arrive at her Helena, Alabama home well before hand.

Stopping in the trendy suburb of Franklin, Tennessee may have been a mistake. After having breakfast of pork tenderloin, scrambled eggs, biscuits, gravy, and grits at the renowned Puckett's Grocery, Kristie hit just about every boutique in the quaint little downtown area. After purchasing sweaters, boots, skirts, and some original artwork, she headed south toward her home in the Birmingham, Alabama suburb of Helena.

CHAPTER 3

The severe weather warning for North Central Alabama had not been lifted. In fact, the warnings from the weather service sounded more ominous, calling for possible long-track violent tornadoes in an area south of a line from Red Bay to Russellville, to Hartselle, to Guntersville; and north of a line from Moundville, to Centerville, to Jemison, to Alexander City. This was the area in which Kristie would be entering and traveling through during the peak severe weather hours.

Should she stop somewhere, maybe in her old hometown of Wentworth, and spend the night? Wentworth was a severe storm and tornado magnet, having experienced numerous violent twisters ever since records were kept. Should she stop in the Decatur/Huntsville area which was north of where the severe weather was predicted to hit? What should she do?

Unable to make a decision, Kristie kept on driving south into the forecasted dangerous area. It was just after 4:00 pm, and she was getting hungry, the Puckett's Grocery breakfast was long gone.

On a whim, she exited I-65 at the northern most Wentworth exit and pulled into the parking lot of a well-known chain restaurant. Maybe she would get something to eat here, then head toward Birmingham.

As she got out of her SUV, Kristie had some butterflies in her stomach. Even though Wentworth was where she was born and raised, it was also the town of her ex-husband, Eric Channing. When their divorce was final, he was living somewhere in the Florida Keys, but she had since heard from some former classmates he had moved back to Wentworth, and was building a house on some property he owned on Jones Lake. Kristie had no clue as to where, in Wentworth, Eric was living while his house was being built. She wasn't sure she wanted to know.

The air was heavy, and the clouds were dark and low-hanging. As Kristie headed for the restaurant entrance, a gust of wind kind of blew her hair up. She didn't like the way it looked outside, but entered the restaurant anyway. Even though it was not quite 5:00 pm, some of the diners were already having their evening meal. Guess folks wanted to eat and get home where they would tune their TVs to the station where the Birmingham area's legendary weatherman would be broadcasting live if there was a tornado warning in the station's market area.

Deciding to get something to eat at the bar, Kristie sat on a vacant bar stool and asked the bartender to bring her a Bud Light and a menu. The TVs set up at the bar were tuned to the station where the weather legend himself, in his standard TV outfit, was already delivering the news of a supercell thunderstorm showing definite signs of rotation, making its way from Mississippi into Alabama. While the timelines for the storm did not extend to I-65, Kristie guessed it would cross the interstate in about two hours. Maybe she should leave now without eating, and head toward Birmingham and her Helena home.

After the bartender brought her the Bud Light, she ordered one of the entrée salads thinking that would be quicker, and she could be on her way. While she was sipping on her beer and watching the closest TV, a gentleman, who looked to be about Kristie's age, approached her and asked if she had everything she needed. He was tall, thin, and had a faint mustache. His name tag read Jake. Last night she was with a blonde Jake, now she meets a dark, kind of smarmy looking Jake.

This Jake was the manager on duty this evening, and started making small talk with Kristie. She told him she was from Birmingham and had attended the CMA Awards last night and was on her way home.

"You should get a room at one of these hotels for the evening since the weather is supposed to be bad."

Folks in this part of the state of Alabama were very aware of the dangers of tornadoes, having recently experienced the tragedies of April 27, 2011. A large, violent tornado had ripped through Wentworth and went on to wreak damage in the Alabama towns of Arab and Guntersville. Kristie and Eric got engaged a few weeks before that terrible day.

"I might do that," Kristie said, even though she had no intention of spending the night in Wentworth. "My ex-husband lives here, and Wentworth doesn't give me warm fuzzy feelings. But I definitely don't need to be on the interstate heading south."

"Some good people live here. I bet you would change your mind if you spent some time with us. In fact, why don't you drive up here some evening in the next couple of weeks and we can have dinner together."

This smarmy Jake was coming on to Kristie, but she wasn't particularly attracted to him.

Her salad had just been placed in front of her when Jake excused himself to greet a group of folks who had just entered the restaurant. He apparently knew most of the folks in the group because there was some good-natured, small town ribbing taking place between Jake and the newest restaurant patrons. From where she was sitting, Kristie could not see these people as they entered, and were seated at a table in one of the sections where the bar would not have been visible to them.

As Jake left the table where his friends were seated, he thought to himself, that lady is hot-looking. The ex-husband must be mighty stupid. He definitely wanted to talk to her before she left, thinking maybe he could get her to stay for the night.

While Kristie was eating her salad, another gentleman approached the bar apparently, checking the TV for the storm situation. He walked toward the area where Kristie was seated, but said nothing to her. Less than a minute later, Jake sauntered up and stood beside him while they discussed the weather.

As the guy turned around to return to his friends, he noticed the striking dark-haired woman who was eating a large salad and drinking a beer. OMG, that's Kristie Tidwell,

Eric's second wife. What if Kristie sees Eric and Anabelle Martin together and causes a scene? The man, Dean Abercrombie, was part of the same gang in which Eric belonged. He remembered the somewhat uppity Kristie from Wiley Martin's funeral. Even though she had attended Wentworth High School at the same time he did, he didn't remember her. And it was just as well because she refused to socialize with any of the folks attending the reception after the funeral, choosing to sit off to herself in a remote corner of the Martin house. He also remembered how she walked out the door with Eric, not acknowledging anyone.

Dean went back to join his wife, Marianne, and friends, Ruthie and Jimmy Harpo, Eric Channing, and Anabelle Martin. Anabelle and Eric were embarking a relationship, and the members of the gang were overjoyed for the widow Anabelle and the twice divorced Eric.

Kristie finished her salad, signed the credit card receipt, and looked up at the television for a last-minute weather check before heading out the door, to her vehicle, and then back to her home in Helena. The tornado that had crossed from Mississippi into Alabama when Kristie first arrived, was approaching Jasper and traveling in a northeasterly direction. It was scheduled to cross I-65 in about an hour near Dodge

City. According to the weather forecast legend, it was a strong tornado that was leaving extensive damage in its wake. If Kristie left now, she could be past Dodge City in ten to fifteen minutes. Furthermore, if the twister was headed toward Dodge City, in a northeasterly direction, Wentworth would be in its crosshairs. Time to "get the hell out of Dodge," no pun intended.

Quickly heading toward the door of the restaurant, Kristie, not paying much attention to her surroundings ran into one of the customers.

"Kristie!"

"Eric!"

"Kristie, what are you doing here?"

"It's a free country, and this is a public place. I have just as much right to be here as you do. Haven't we acted out this little scene before?"

Kristie was referring to a scene, which took place before they were married, in the famous Panama City, Florida eatery, Captain Anderson's. Kristie had decided at the last minute to spend the weekend in Panama City with some of her friends, and Eric was planning to go deep sea fishing off the Alabama Gulf Coast with some of his friends. The guys' plans changed, and they ended up in Panama City. On the

Thursday night before the weekend began, Eric and Kristie ran into each other in Captain Anderson's lounge.

Their meeting didn't go well, with Eric accusing Kristie of stalking him. Because she was so upset, Kristie left Panama City the following morning and drove home to Helena.

"I thought you would still be in Nashville, I saw you on TV last night with Jake McPherson."

"Yes, I attended the CMAs with Jake, but I'm on my way home, now."

"Well, I wondered how long it would take you to hook up with 'ole Jake.'"

"What! I have not hooked up with 'ole Jake.' I attended with him as a friend, and slept in the guest room of his condo. This morning, he had an early flight to Boston. After the ceremony, we went to one of the parties, but he had to leave early because of his flight. But he arranged for me to stay at the party as long as I wanted. I didn't see him this morning and don't know when I'll see him again."

Hearing loud voices near the front of the restaurant, manager Jake Stanley, went to see what was going on. At that moment, Jake realized the woman was Kristie Tidwell, Eric's second wife. Until now, he hadn't seen Kristie since they were in high school. She had changed some, but still had her thick curly dark hair. He hadn't thought about her since high school. As a part of the bad boy trio, he, Wiley Martin, and Johnny Morton had given Kristie a hard time because she, at one time, was overweight. Even though she lost the weight, the three of them continued to give her a hard time. He didn't like Kristie then, but that was then, and this was now. Jail time had not made him a perfect, God-fearing person, but he had grown up. Jimmy Harpo, Dean Abercrombie, and some of the others had often commented about what a bitch Eric's second wife was. She had grown into a beautiful woman and knew it. She had also experienced some successes in life which had gone to her head.

Jake approached the arguing couple, put his hand on Eric's shoulder, and said, "What's the matter, buddy? Is this lady bothering you? I'm going to have to ask you to take your little fight elsewhere."

By this time, customers in the front part of the restaurant had become quiet. Dean Abercrombie and Jimmy Harpo, sensing something was wrong, left Anabelle, Ruthie, and Marianne at their table to see what happening up front. Dean and Jimmy were startled to see Kristie with Eric and Jake.

"I'm obviously not welcome here, so I'm leaving," said Kristie.

When Kristie was opening the door to go outside, she heard a woman's voice behind her saying, "Well, hello Kristie."

Turning around, Kristie looked into the eyes of Anabelle Martin, who had her arm linked with Eric's arm. Eric grinned and nodded as Anabelle leaned against him.

"Eric's staying in my basement until his lake house is finished. Well, actually, he's not staying in the basement anymore," smirked Anabelle as she stroked Eric's arm.

"You bitch, you whore. Eric's always had a thing for you. I hope both of you and your cliquey friends rot in hell."

With that, Kristie left the restaurant, got into her SUV, and headed toward Birmingham, not taking into consideration the time that elapsed during the restaurant drama, and that a violent tornado was heading northeast from Jasper.

Completely forgetting the weather, Kristie continued to listen to CDs in her vehicle instead of trying to get some updated weather information. All that was on her mind was seeing Eric and some of his Wentworth friends, along with Anabelle Martin, who was now in a relationship with Eric. Kristie was in shock, and couldn't think of anything else. The past two days would surely go down as some of the worst in her life. Right up there with the day Eric had unexpectedly left her this past December 23.

CHAPTER 4

First, Kristie finds out that Jake McPherson has no interest in her, and was just using her to get back at his girlfriend. Then, this other Jake seemed to be coming on to her, but after learning she was Eric's ex-wife, he ordered her out of his restaurant. Could this man be Jake Stanley, one of the guys who gave her a hard time in high school?

Overwhelmed, Kristie started crying. Why not? There was no one to hear her and no one to care.

Kristie came back to reality when she saw the Dodge City exit sign. This was where the tornado was projected to cross the interstate. It was dark, and some light rain was falling. Other than that, it was calm. She'd better try to find some weather updates on her radio, her phone, or her tablet. Large and maybe violent long-form tornadoes were in the forecast for this area, but an outbreak like the one on April 27, 2011, was not supposed to take place. When she was a few miles past the Dodge City exit, she breathed a sigh of relief.

Meanwhile, back at the restaurant in Wentworth, Eric, Anabelle, and their friends were enjoying their meal. Manager

Jake Stanley indicated he was ready to throw Kristie out of the restaurant had she not left voluntarily.

Anabelle, Jimmy, Ruthie, Dean, and Marianne were making fun of the way Kristie acted when she learned Anabelle and Eric were now a couple. Eric sat in silence. While he had hurt Kristie deeply because he didn't like being married, he still had feelings for her, and an intense physical desire for her. Last night, Eric had to imagine Anabelle was Kristie to get through their sexual escapades. He would never refer to what they were doing as making love. Now, Kristie was the subject of his friends' jokes. She didn't deserve that.

Because everyone at the table knew the tornado coming from Jasper would be headed toward Wentworth, though it shouldn't affect the areas where they lived, Dean got up and said he would go back to the bar to check on things. When he returned, he said the tornado had picked up strength, taken a right turn, and was headed almost due east. It would be soon crossing I-65 south of Dodge City, missing Wentworth County entirely. While a couple of tornadoes had also crossed into Alabama from Mississippi, and there was a tornado warning for a supercell near Gadsden, Wentworth was in no immediate danger.

"Kristie!" yelled out Eric.

"What about Kristie," asked Jimmy?

"She's on I-65 heading south right now."

"Oh, bother Kristie," said Anabelle.

"She's a human being, she was at one time my wife, she was a classmate of ours, and she could be in danger. Do y'all have no shame?"

"Oh, she'll be alright," said Dean. "Maybe having her out of the way would calm you down a bit."

"Dean, that was uncalled for, I'm leaving."

Eric stood up and walked toward the front of the restaurant. He found Jake and asked him to get his check so he could pay for his and Anabelle's dinners. "Don't worry about it," said Jake. "Your dinners are on me tonight. I'm sorry for the drama."

Eric walked out the door followed by Anabelle. "Eric, why do we have to leave now? I was thinking about having dessert."

"If you want dessert, go back and get dessert, I'm headed to the house. My marriage to Kristie may not have worked out, but Dean's flippant remarks were classless. We're not in high school anymore."

"Okay, okay, let's go home and snuggle up together and watch TV."

Anabelle and Eric got in Eric's truck, and the couple rode to her house in silence.

Back at the restaurant, Dean, Marianne, Jimmy, and Ruthie finished their dinner, not saying anything until Dean broke the silence by asking the group how well they remembered Kristie. Dean indicated he barely remembered her since she was two years behind him. Jimmy also barely remembered her and really didn't get to know her until after she and Eric married. "Jan and Jeremy knew her better than we did. Although, I never heard Jan say anything about her until the New Year's Eve party of 2010."

Even though Kristie had driven past the Dodge City exit where the tornado was forecast to cross over the interstate, she knew that she needed to get some weather information in case there were additional problems as she headed toward Birmingham. Luckily, she was able to get the legendary weatherman's station and his broadcast on a low FM frequency on her car radio. He was discussing a new tornado coming out of a supercell thunderstorm that was in the Hackleburg, Alabama area. Hackleburg was a town which was almost destroyed on April 27, 2011. Those poor people, thought Kristie. Maybe the tornado will skip over the small community quickly, causing no damage.

Next, the legend started talking about the tornado that was due to cross I-65 at Dodge City. This storm was a violent one that had a history of being on the ground for miles, leaving extensive damage in its wake.

Uh-oh! He indicated the tornado had made a right turn, heading almost due east, as large, dangerous tornadoes often do. He also said that it was forecast to cross I-65 near the Hayden/Corner exit. Oh crap, thought Kristie. I'm almost to that exit. Should I pull off the road and wait until there is confirmation that the storm is east of I-65? It was dark now, and a steady rain was falling.

CHAPTER 5

Suddenly, Kristie's SUV was enveloped by what appeared to be a light gray fog. She lost control as the car began lurching. Even though she was wearing her seatbelt, she was being slung back and forth and round and round for what seemed like an eternity. If not for the seatbelt, she would have undoubtedly gone through the windshield. Was this it? Was she going to die right here in her SUV on I-65? She could feel her chest hitting the steering wheel and her head hitting the left front window, but no airbag was inflating, and the window didn't break. Also, there were loud noises, and red/blue flashes of what appeared to be lightning surrounding the vehicle. At one point, Kristie felt the SUV being lifted up in front, and she thought it might flip over.

Then her vehicle was still. The motor was running, the headlights were on, but the vehicle was in park and sitting still on the highway. Did she put it in park? She certainly didn't remember doing so. There were no other cars in sight, and the light gray fog that had enveloped her vehicle disappeared.

Kristie's heart was racing, and she started taking deep breaths to calm down. In addition to the motor running and the lights being on, the radio was still playing, and the weather guy was still broadcasting, saying the tornado should be in the vicinity of I-65 and the Hayden/Corner exit. No one should be on I-65 between the Mulberry and Locust Forks of the Warrior River. That was where she was.

The rain was coming down hard, and Kristie thought she saw some pea sized hail hitting the windshield. Had she been in the tornado? She put the car in drive and stepped on the gas. The car began moving forward. She then put it in reverse, and was able to back up. Because of the torrential rain, thunder, and lightning, Kristie didn't want to get out of the car to see if there was any damage to the vehicle's exterior. She would try to drive it home, then have it checked out tomorrow. The car drove fine, and even though the hard rains continued, she drove at 65 mph with no apparent problems.

Uh-oh, she was coming upon the Hanceville/Arkadelphia exit. She was driving north, and her vehicle compass confirmed it. The storm must have turned her car around. Kristie started shaking again, but kept on driving toward Wentworth. Guess she would spend the night there, and have her vehicle checked at the town's Chevrolet dealership the next day.

Kristie exited I-65 at the same place she had exited earlier, pulled into the parking lot of the Holiday Inn Express, got out of her car, and went into the lobby to inquire about a room for the evening. The manager, noticing Kristie's disheveled look, asked her if she was all right. Not wanting the manager to think she was crazy, she said, "Yes, just a bad day." And it had been.

As she was initialing forms, the door opened and in stepped Jake Stanley, the manager of the restaurant where Kristie had eaten earlier, where she had run into Eric, with Anabelle Martin, Jimmy Harpo, Ruthie Harpo, and some other guy and his wife. Jake, carrying what looked like takeout from the restaurant, nodded to Kristie.

When Kristie had the key, she left the two men in the lobby to go out to her car and retrieve her bags. As soon as the door shut, Jake Stanley informed the hotel manager, whose name was Jodie, that Kristie had been in his restaurant earlier and caused a scene with some of his best customers. Had she not left when she did, he would have thrown her out. Jodie replied that the lady did have a wild look in her eyes when she first entered the lobby.

"I'd keep an eye on her while she's here. I thought she was headed toward Birmingham when she left the restaurant, but I guess she thought better of it, due to the weather, and decided to head back up here and spend the night."

Jodie took his supper out of the bag that Jake had brought him and sat down on the sofa in the lobby to eat. Jake also sat down, and further informed Jodie he and the lady had attended Wentworth High School together, but now she lived in the Birmingham area. She had been in Nashville for the CMA Awards last night and stopped off at the restaurant earlier to eat. While she was there, her ex-husband, Eric Channing, came in with a group of friends including his new girlfriend.

"Remember Wiley Martin?"

"Yes."

"His widow."

"Oh."

"Well, after seeing Anabelle and Eric together, little Miss Kristie threw a small hissy fit. She distracted the diners, and I was going to throw her out had she not left."

"When she came in here, she looked like she might have been crying or had seen a ghost."

"Again, I'd keep an eye open while she's here."

"Thanks, buddy."

With that, Jake left and headed back toward the restaurant. After finishing his supper, Jodie retrieved Kristie's registration. Kristie Tidwell-Channing, Kristie Tidwell? She was Mary Tidwell's daughter and a second cousin or first cousin, once removed, of his step Mom. Kristie's Mom and Judith's Mom were first cousins. In fact, he had attended a small family gathering with Kristie and some other cousins shortly after her Mom died. Maybe he should check on her. Jake Stanley didn't have the best reputation in town, having served time for sexually assaulting a minor when he was in his late teens or early twenties. Then he served additional time for dealing drugs. Even though Jodie liked Jake, he knew Jake wasn't exactly pure as the driven snow. But he remembered Kristie being a lovely and gracious lady.

Jodie called Kristie's room, and when she answered, he told her that he was Charlie Vickers' son and Judith Stansbury Vickers' stepson. I think we may be related.

"Well, I guess we are," said Kristie.

"Kristie, are you all right?"

"NO!" cried Kristie.

"Okay, want to come down here?"

CHAPTER 6

The sun was sinking low in the west, and daylight was almost gone, as Anabelle Pickens lay on the dock outside her family's Guntersville lake house. She had graduated from Vanderbilt University with a Bachelor of Arts in Education two weeks ago, and was taking it easy this weekend while her parents were in Montgomery, attending the wedding of one of her father's business associates.

In a couple of weeks, she would be off to Europe for a month, a graduation present from her Mom and Dad. Afterward, who knows? Would she try to get a teaching job or work in some capacity in her father's Huntsville-based computer consulting business? While Anabelle barely knew how to create a Word Perfect document, Daddy would give her a job and perhaps make her an officer. Daddy's employees would resent her, but she didn't care. Even though Anabelle failed to find a husband while attending Vanderbilt, surely someone rich and as beautiful as she was would be able to find a suitable husband in the next few years. There would be babies, and she would live out her life as a rich and pampered wife.

The once vacant lot next to the Pickens house had been purchased a few months ago by a guy from Wentworth. At present, only a small clapboard cabin had been erected by the new owner. Anabelle hoped he would soon build something more suitable to the other lake houses in the area. Except for the clapboard house, all the other houses were expensive vacation homes built by old wealth Alabama families in the nineteen fifties.

In the late fifties/early sixties, with the construction of the Jones Dam near Jasper and Wentworth, many home owners sold their properties on Lake Guntersville and moved to Jones Lake. Her family didn't. While Guntersville did go through a slump in the sixties, and seventies, it did appear to be making a comeback. Property values had declined, but were starting to rise again.

The Jones Dam was built on the Sipsey Fork of the Warrior River in Walker County, creating a large finger lake extending into Walker, Wentworth, and Winston Counties. The area was wild and treacherous, consisting of wooded, mountainous countryside inhabited by poisonous and non-poisonous snakes, mountain lions, panthers, and bobcats.

While some of the wooded areas were cleaned out, many were not, leaving the water to back up and cover thousands of trees and acres of underbrush. The dam was almost 300 feet tall, making the pool above it over 200 feet deep. Other parts of the lake were much deeper because the water backed up into slews off of bluffs. At almost any place on the lake's shoreline, you could walk out from the shore for about ten or so feet still touching bottom. Then suddenly you couldn't touch bottom anymore.

Hearing a motor boat in the slew, and forgetting her bikini top was undone, Anabelle raised up. The top fell, exposing her ample breasts. Quickly realizing this, Anabelle immediately hooked the top, looked up, and saw a nice looking outboard with three, twenty something guys riding in it.

When the driver saw Anabelle fiddling with her bikini top, he slowed the boat and drove it up to the dock where Anabelle was collecting her stuff to go inside. The guys were drinking beer and held up their cans to her and asked her what was up. While her top was now intact, she remembered that she had rolled down her bikini bottom to where only the essentials were covered. She didn't feel comfortable standing until she rolled the bottoms back up.

Anabelle, not exactly a virgin, played it cool and asked the guys where they had been and where they were headed. The driver indicated he was the owner of the property next door. The three of them had been fishing and were going to have a fish fry and spend the night. The front passenger was the cutest of them all, having dark wavy hair and a crooked smile. The other two were nice looking, but couldn't hold a candle to the guy who said his name was Wiley. The driver introduced himself as Jimmy, the other passenger as Eric.

Starting up the motor, Jimmy asked Anabelle to come over and have a drink with them.

"Okay, just as soon as I shower and change. It will probably be about forty-five minutes."

"See you then," yelled Wiley.

Anabelle laid back down, pulled up here bikini bottom, stood, scooped up her things, and headed to the house. Naturally, the guys were staring, and their hearts skipped a beat until they realized her swimsuit was a light tan color, about the same as her skin.

"What a looker," said Eric. "If you want, Jimmy and I'll disappear, then you can have her all to yourself." Both Eric and Jimmy were married. Jimmy was happily married and

Eric, though he and Gina had their problems, was okay with his marriage.

Wiley, rubbing his chin, said, "That might be a possibility. Let's work out some signals."

When the guys got their catch into the cabin, Eric suggested Wiley hit the shower first since the girl would be over soon. He and Jimmy would clean the fish, and then thy would take their showers. Finding a woman for their friend Wiley had been a project of theirs for several years.

One of the best-looking guys at Wentworth High when they were in school, Wiley, a womanizer, had yet to meet the right girl. After graduating from high school, the same year as Eric, Wiley attended the University of Alabama. Then he returned to Wentworth to take over the family's lucrative appliance sales and service business. While at the University, Wiley never went out with any of the cute coeds. Instead, he insisted on dating only girls from Wentworth. Even though he had married a girl from Wentworth, Eric's first fiancé, who he had met through one of Wiley's former girlfriends from Wentworth, was from Birmingham.

Wiley, just out of the shower, was freshly shaved and smelled manly and clean. For the evening, he dressed in a pair of white shorts, a green polo shirt, and brown topsiders. The girl had not arrived, so he decided to go out to the dock and check on Jimmy's and Eric's fish cleaning. Both, being seasoned fish cleaners, were almost finished. From the dock, they could see the girl when she walked from her house to the cabin. So, Wiley decided to stay with the guys.

When the fish were ready to fry, Eric and Jimmy took them into the cabin, then proceeded to take their showers. Now that he was cleaned up and smelling good, Eric would prepare his famous batter. They would cook the fish in a large pot placed on the barbecue grill behind the cabin. Things were still a little primitive, but Jimmy had big plans to turn it into a cool hunting and fishing camp.

While Eric was mixing the batter and coating the fish, there was a knock on the door. It was the girl with a beer in her hand. She was indeed beautiful and sexy. Her long, straight dark brown hair was still slightly wet. She wore denim short shorts and a skimpy white halter top. As she entered the cabin, she said, "I'm Anabelle Pickens."

"I'm Wiley, and this is Eric and Jimmy."

"Nice to meet y'all again," replied Anabelle.

"I'd offer you something to drink, but I see you already have something," said Wiley.

Looking around the sparsely furnished room, Anabelle said, "Why don't we move all of this over to my house. We have a large deep fat fryer where we can fry these fish."

"You sure you're okay with that? Fish stink," said Eric.

"Sure, my parents have fish fries all the time."

"Are your parents here?"

"No, they went to a wedding in Montgomery. We live in Huntsville where my Dad owns a computer consulting firm. This is just a weekend retreat."

Wiley could hardly contain his excitement. With Eric and Jimmy offering to disappear, he might get lucky this evening. The swimsuit Anabelle had on earlier didn't leave much to the imagination and her outfit tonight covered slightly more skin.

The guys moved everything the short distance to the Pickens house where Anabelle set up the deep fat fryer on the spacious patio where the fish and the hushpuppies would be fried. The rest of the meal would be potato salad and coleslaw. Eric asked Anabelle if she liked jalapeno hushpuppies and she replied yes.

While the guys had brought only beer, the Pickens' had a fully stocked bar, and Anabelle told them to help themselves. It had been decided earlier that after dinner and cleanup, Eric and Jimmy would excuse themselves and go back to the cabin. Wiley would, of course, remain with Anabelle.

With the Pickens' huge fry pot, the fish and hushpuppies were ready in no time. Anabelle and Wiley set the table with the everyday china and flatware which belonged to the family, while Eric scooped up the fish and hushpuppies onto two platters, and Jimmy, not seeing the need to dirty up any more dishes, placed the plastic containers of potato salad and coleslaw on the table.

After finishing the main course, it was discovered that there was nothing for dessert. However, Anabelle said there was vanilla ice cream in the freezer and some chocolate cookies in the pantry. So, that was dessert. As promised, after everything was cleaned up, Eric and Jimmy indicated they were getting sleepy and left Wiley alone with Anabelle.

When the two were alone, Anabelle poured two shots of Bailey's Irish Cream into cordials, and suggested they go sit on the dock. It was a beautiful summer night, and Wiley put his arm loosely around Anabelle's shoulders as they walked down the path to the dock. They both sat down, and Wiley took her hand in his. In a few minutes, they were lightly kissing.

As their kisses got deeper, they both stood up and walked to the house where they sat down on one of the plush living room sofas. Suddenly, Anabelle said, "I don't even know your last name. Are you from Wentworth like Jimmy?"

"How did you know Jimmy was from Wentworth?"

"I had heard that the buyer of the lot next door was from Wentworth."

"Yes, all three of us are from Wentworth, and my last name's Martin."

"Nice to meet you, Wiley Martin."

"Nice to meet you, Anabelle Pickens."

Wiley pushed Anabelle back on the sofa and unhooked her halter top.

"Let's go to the bedroom," whispered Anabelle into Wiley's ear.

They got up and walked to the bedroom where Wiley finished removing Anabelle's clothing and Anabelle removed Wiley's clothing.

Sans any clothing, Anabelle and Wiley stood beside the bed kissing passionately while running their hands up and down each other's bodies. When Wiley couldn't take it anymore, he pushed Anabelle onto the queen-sized bed and took control.

For someone who was either twenty-one or twenty-two years old, Anabelle was experienced in love making. In fact, Wiley felt like she was much more experienced than he was. Even though he was almost thirty, his experience was much more lacking than that of a typical twenty-nine-year-old good-looking bachelor. Could Anabelle sense this?

Anabelle and Wiley made love for hours before Wiley said he had better go back to the cabin. The guys were leaving to go back to Wentworth first thing in the morning.

"Why don't you go back to the cabin and tell the others that I will drop you off at Wentworth tomorrow on my way back to Huntsville."

"You don't mind?"

"Not at all."

"But it's out of the way."

"That's okay, I don't have anything better to do."

"Okay, I'll be right back.

Wiley got dressed and went out into the darkness to the cabin to retrieve his overnight bag and tell Eric and Jimmy to drive to Wentworth without him. While Eric and Jimmy kidded Wiley about getting lucky, they were both pleased he had maybe found himself a woman, having almost exhausted the supply of available women in Wentworth.

Anabelle and Wiley did manage to get a few hours of sleep before an intense late May sun, streaming into Anabelle's bedroom, awakened them. After another round of lovemaking, the two took a steamy shower together and got dressed.

Anabelle had come to the vacation home this weekend to retrieve some luggage for the family trip to Europe. There was no breakfast food at the cabin, so after loading the car with the luggage, and hers and Wiley's weekend bags, the two left the lake house, stopped at a local restaurant for breakfast, then headed toward Wentworth.

Wiley thought Anabelle was probably the most beautiful woman he had ever been with. However, she was early twenties and hardly a virgin. Was she someone he wanted for a relationship or was she going to be a one-night-stand?

During the forty-five minute drive to Wentworth, Wiley could sense a sadness about her that he didn't detect last night. She was a pampered little rich girl, but something was bothering her.

When Wiley asked her what she, a recent college graduate, was going to do, Anabelle replied she was debating between teaching school, utilizing her education degree, or working for her father in some sort of capacity.

"Where did you go to school?"

"Vanderbilt."

"Eric's high school sweetheart attended Vandy, but that would have been after your time."

Anabelle and Wiley were a gorgeous couple, and both came from well-to-do families. Wiley, upon college graduation, had gone to work for his father in the family's appliance sales and service business. Since Wiley had been a part of the operation, two new stores had been opened, one in Fultondale, a northern suburb of Birmingham, and one in Hartselle, a small town fifteen miles north of Wentworth.

When Anabelle dropped Wiley off at his condominium just off Main Avenue, he got her phone number and said he would call her in the next few days. Would he? That remained to be determined. Of course, he kissed her, telling her he had a fabulous time last night.

When Wiley and his older sisters were children, the family attended the First United Methodist Church in Wentworth. Now that his sisters were both married and living out of state, and Wiley had his own place, he and his parents rarely attended church. In fact, his parents usually spent Saturday night at one of Wentworth's two country clubs, drinking and dancing until late into the evening. Thus, all of Wiley's friends thought his parents were cool.

Sunday dinner of either roast beef or fried chicken was a tradition at the Martin home, and Wiley usually went over there for Sunday dinner at 1:00 pm. He would have time for about an hour's nap before driving five minutes to see the folks.

Not being able to get the strikingly beautiful Anabelle off his mind, Wiley called her on Tuesday and asked her out for the following weekend. He drove to Huntsville and met her parents, finding them to be much like his parents; older, but cool socialites. After taking Anabelle to dinner at one of Huntsville's upscale restaurants, they spent the rest of the evening making love in the fully furnished basement of the Pickens' Huntsville home. After that, they saw each other once a week until Anabelle and her family left for the month-long vacation in Europe. Following the trip to Europe, Anabelle and Wiley resumed their relationship, which consisted mostly of Anabelle driving to Wentworth, where she and Wiley would spend endless hours making love at Wiley's condo.

While Wiley was enjoying having little more than a physical relationship with Anabelle, Mr. and Mrs. Martin liked Anabelle, and encouraged Wiley to marry her.

Football season was approaching, and the Martin's had season tickets to the Alabama football games. Generally, Wiley would ask various friends to attend the games with him and his parents. This season, it was planned that Anabelle would be using the extra ticket. During the final minutes of the third quarter of one of the Bama games they were attending, a small airplane flew over Bryant-Denny Stadium with a banner reading, "Anabelle, will you marry me."

As Anabelle shrieked, Wiley pulled a small velvet covered box, which contained an expensive diamond ring, from his jacket pocket and placed the ring on Anabelle's left ring finger. The folks sitting in the seats surrounding the newly engaged couple cheered for them.

Wiley and Anabelle married the following April at the First United Methodist Church of Huntsville. There were nine brides' maids and eight groomsmen, including Jimmy Harpo and Eric Channing. Following the wedding ceremony, an elaborate reception took place at the Huntsville Country Club. After honeymooning in the Hawaiian Islands, the couple moved into their new home in one of Wentworth's upscale residential areas. Wiley continued working with his father in the family appliance business, and Anabelle quickly became the pillar of Wentworth society. Two prominent North Alabama families were joined.

Because she was exceptionally smart, Anabelle's parents sent her out of state to attend the academically acclaimed Vanderbilt University in Nashville.

In high school, Anabelle won the school beauty pageant for two years in a row and was homecoming queen her senior year. She lost her virginity to a senior football player the first weekend of her freshman year when she was only fourteen. Afterward, she made it with almost every football and basketball player while she was still a freshman.

One day after school, the assistant principal caught her with a six foot five basketball star behind some lockers. Neither were sporting a stitch of clothing. While the basketball player grabbed his clothes, and ran behind some other lockers, Anabelle got the assistant principle, a happily married man with a new baby girl, to begin touching her. They were soon rolling around on the tile floor behind the lockers, with the basketball player nowhere to be found. This was on a Friday. On Sunday, at the First United Methodist Church of Huntsville, Harriet Dorsey, baby daughter of Amy and Oliver Dorsey was christened, with Anabelle Pickens looking on from the balcony.

Anabelle and Oliver continued their affair until the end of the school year, and she and her Mom traveled to Martha's Vineyard to spend the summer months. Meanwhile, Oliver Dorsey worked on his doctorate in academic administration at the University of Alabama, and accepted a position with the Tuscaloosa City School System. He moved Amy and Harriet to Tuscaloosa, and never returned to Huntsville.

During her sophomore year, Anabelle became the most popular girl in the school, but had settled into a dating relationship with the president of the student body, a senior, who had previously played football, but had to drop sports because of his other responsibilities. During her junior year, Anabelle continued to see Rick while he was a freshman, attending the University of Tennessee. After his freshman year at UT, Rick was awarded a scholarship to study abroad, and ended his relationship with Anabelle. As a senior, Anabelle was up to her old tricks, and made the rounds through the football and basketball teams.

By this time, Anabelle's reputation was well known throughout the city of Huntsville and surrounding areas. Thinking that their daughter would never find a suitable man to marry, who didn't know about her reputation, in the state of Alabama, her parents sent her to study at Vanderbilt University in Nashville. Thank goodness, she had been able to maintain a high-grade point average with minimal studying.

Anabelle continued her wild ways at Vanderbilt, but this time she didn't have parents looking over her. During freshman orientation, she met a guy and slept with him at the men's dorm for both nights.

When the fall term began, she immediately visited the student infirmary, telling the rather naïve nurse practitioner she was having severe cramping and bleeding. The nurse practitioner, without blinking an eye, gave her a prescription for birth control pills.

During sorority rush, she was wooed and pledged the best sorority on campus, as a legacy, since her Mom had belonged to the same sorority while at Alabama. She then spent the night after pledging with her big sister's boyfriend. Anabelle pulled the unsuspecting lad into the house kitchen after the staff had left for the evening and seduced him.

The following week, her big sister announced she was pinned to this guy, and Anabelle watched as the ceremony for pinning took place.

It didn't take Anabelle long to go through the football team and head for the basketball team. Her activities were becoming known across campus. One evening, when Anabelle was at the sorority house, the president, the pledge trainer, and her big sister called her into one of the empty study halls, and informed her that her conduct was unbecoming to the sorority, and was also unbecoming to the Greek System at Vanderbilt. She was being kicked out of the sorority.

After a few days of mourning, Anabelle bounced back, continuing to seduce jocks and frat guys. Being the smart coed, she was, Anabelle also made the Dean's list. She told her Mom and Dad that sorority life was interfering with her studying and she wanted to quit. While her Mom was disappointed, she accepted Anabelle's decision with reservations.

For the remainder of her college career, Anabelle continued to sleep around, but after exhausting the male students and the professors, she started on young professional men living in Nashville.

CHAPTER 7

Kristie didn't know this person from Adam's housecat, but she did recall Judith Stansbury, a second cousin of hers, having married Charlie Vickers, a guy with whom she had attended high school. Jodie did sound like he was concerned, and Kristie needed someone to talk to.

While they were sitting on one of the sofas in the hotel lobby, Kristie told Jodie her story about attending the CMA awards with Jake McPherson the night before, only to find out Jake had no interest in her. Instead, he wanted to make someone else jealous. Then she told Jodie about stopping in Wentworth earlier to get something to eat before heading to Birmingham, and seeing Eric, Anabelle, and a few of their friends. Anabelle made it clear she and Eric were now in a relationship. She also threw in that Anabelle was the widow of Wiley Martin, who had tormented her about her weight when they were growing up. Then she told Jodie about her vehicle getting spun around during what may have been a tornado crossing I-65. Kristie started to cry. Could anyone have had a more horrible day?

Jodie sympathized with Kristie, but couldn't think of anything to say to her that might make her feel better. Even though he was skeptical about the tornado story, he did advise her to have her vehicle checked before attempting to drive it to Birmingham.

It was getting late, and the tornado threat was winding down. Wentworth had been spared, but there were touchdowns in several other areas, and damages had been reported. While a few people sought medical attention, there were no known fatalities. While Jodie was not a fan of Jake Stanley, the restaurant manager, he did have his cell number. Whenever he was on night duty, he would often call on Jake to bring him something from the restaurant for supper.

After Kristie went back to her room, Jodie called Jake and told him that Kristie seemed disturbed, and thought Eric should be notified. Did he know how to reach Eric? Jake was hesitant about giving Jodie Eric's cell, but did it anyway. While Jake liked Anabelle more than Kristie, he didn't want Kristie doing something stupid that night and perhaps have part of the blame placed on him for what happened earlier in the restaurant. Besides, Anabelle and Eric were probably going at it, and wouldn't hear the phone ring. Anabelle was known as a wild child before she and Wiley married, and while he thought Anabelle had remained faithful to Wiley until he passed away from cancer, summer was a year ago, she was a flirt and seemed to enjoy giving the guys a peek at her goodies while being touchy-feely.

After Eric and Anabelle returned to Anabelle's house, Eric told her he wanted to be alone. It was certainly Dean's and Jimmy's prerogatives to dislike Kristie because she was not part of the group they ran with in high school. But to talk like they did about her, even expressing a desire for her to die in the storms, was uncalled for. Dean and Jimmy had lived in Wentworth all their lives and never matured.

Not happy with Eric's request to be alone in the basement, Anabelle gave Eric fifteen minutes, then she went downstairs not wearing a stitch of clothing. Men were men, and she knew Eric wouldn't be able to resist her. But Eric somehow managed to and ordered her to go upstairs, put some clothes on, and leave him alone. "Come on Eric, don't be silly, no man, including you, can resist me. Remember the time you and Gina and Wiley and I went skinny dipping in Hawaii? You could hardly keep your eyes off me."

"That was then, and this is now. Go back upstairs, and leave me alone."

Reluctantly, Anabelle went upstairs, but indicated to Eric he wouldn't be able to hold out on her for long.

Eric was worried about Kristie heading south on I-65. The weather guy said the large, violent tornado had crossed I-65 just north of the Hayden/Corner exit and that no one should be on the interstate between the Locust and Mulberry Forks of the Warrior River. Knowing how Kristie drove, and the time she left the restaurant, he was aware that she could very well have been driving in the vicinity of the storm.

Eric's phone suddenly rang displaying a number he didn't recognize. When he answered it, a guy identified himself as Jodie Vickers, the manager at the Holiday Inn Express. Jodie apologized for calling at this hour, but told him his ex-wife, Kristie, was at his hotel, and was disturbed about some things. Jody also indicated his stepmom was a second or third cousin of Kristie's. Jodie asked Eric if he would consider coming over there and spending some time with Kristie, at least until she calmed down. Eric agreed to do so.

That was actually an answer to prayer. Eric didn't want to sleep at Anabelle's house. He was almost sure Anabelle was planning to get into bed with him later, and that was the last thing he wanted.

On a whim, Eric quickly packed a suitcase with as many of his clothes as he could stuff in it. He then packed up his toiletries. If Anabelle discovered he had left, she might not let him back in the house, so he did leave some stuff there.

When Eric arrived at the hotel, Jodie called Kristie's room and told her Eric was in the lobby and wanted to see her. He was concerned about her and what had happened earlier this evening. Kristie, still shaken from her earlier experience, said it was okay for him to give Eric her room number. How Eric knew she was at the Holiday Inn Express, didn't occur to her.

Kristie opened the door and motioned for Eric to come in. "Kristie, I know you've had a disastrous day. Can we talk about it?"

While Kristie sat on the bed, and Eric sat in one of the chairs, Kristie told him everything from Jake McPherson rejecting her, to her car being spun around by a possible tornado.

"If you want me to, I'll go with you to the Chevy place tomorrow so we can have the car checked out. If there's damage, we'll notify the police and make a report."

"You don't have to do that," said Kristie.

"I know, but I want to. The scene at the restaurant was unpleasant, and I regret that you had to find out about Anabelle the way you did."

"I hope you and Anabelle will be very happy together. You've always had a thing for her."

"I don't think there's going to be an Anabelle and me anymore. I really didn't like the way she acted in the restaurant earlier. I also didn't like some of the things Jimmy and Dean said about you earlier. I was in love with you at one time, and even though things didn't work out between us, I admire you more than you'll ever know. In fact, I have a packed bag in the truck. When Anabelle discovers I'm gone, she probably won't let me back into the house."

"You're quite good at hurriedly packing bags, aren't you?"

Chuckling, Eric said, "I guess I am. Are you okay? Do you think you can get some sleep tonight? Call me when you wake up, and I'll meet you at the Chevy place to have your car checked for damages."

"That's really kind of you, Eric. Thanks, I will."

"I'll call Jimmy and see if I can stay over there tonight. I may not be going back to Anabelle's again."

Kristie stood up and walked Eric to the door. Before he opened the door, Eric kissed Kristie on the lips. Kristie kissed him back. And, as if the events of this past year hadn't happened, Kristie put her arms around Eric, and he put his arms around her.

"It's a little late to bother Jimmy, would you mind if I stayed here tonight?"

"If you want to."

"I need to run to the truck and get my bag."

When Eric returned, Kristie had put on her nightgown, a soft blue nightgown he remembered from when they were husband and wife. Kristie had lost more weight, and Eric found himself turned on by the outline of her body through the gown. He sat down on the bed beside her, and they lightly kissed and touched for a few minutes. Eric then opened his bag and pulled out a pair of pajama pants, put them on, got in the bed with Kristie, and turned out the light. In a few minutes, the two of them began kissing, and he removed her nightgown and panties, along with his pajama pants, t-shirt, and underwear.

As so often happens after a dark and stormy night, the sun was brilliant the next day, and the air was clear and clean. Eric and Kristie woke up almost simultaneously in each other's arms. Wow, thought Kristie. The night before last, she slept alone in Jake McPherson's expensive Nashville condominium after having been assured by Jake that their relationship would be nothing more than a platonic one. Late yesterday afternoon, she was again shocked to find out that her ex-husband, Eric, her one and only true love, was in a relationship with someone she despised. Then last night, she was caught up in a violent tornado, and only by the grace of God was she spared. Now, Kristie was waking up in the arms of her once loving husband, Eric Channing. Kristie and Eric made love again.

"Want to take a shower?" asked Eric.

"You always hog the water."

"Maybe I've changed."

"I doubt it."

"Come on, give me a chance."

"Oh, okay."

And off to the bathroom, they headed. Afterwards, when Kristie and Eric were wrapped in towels, holding one another, Eric asked, "And how was it?"

"You still hog the water."

"I am what I am. Actually, you knew that before you married me."

"Let's get dressed. I need to get the car to the Chevrolet place, and have the it checked out before I head back to Birmingham."

Eric followed Kristie to the dealership. When they arrived, Kristie told the service department manager everything that happened last night, and he said he would have someone look at her vehicle immediately.

While Kristie and Eric were sitting in the waiting room, Kristie told him she felt stupid about telling the story of what happened to her last night. Eric agreed with her that it sounded strange, but something had to have happened for the car to be heading south and then it was turned around, heading north.

"Are you going to tell the weather folks in Birmingham your story?" asked Eric."

"I hadn't thought about that. Think I should?"

"Why not. I'm sure they hear things all the time that sound just as crazy."

The service manager came into the waiting room, and told Kristie her vehicle checked out just fine, and she should have no problem driving it.

Kristie thanked him and asked about the charges.

"No charge, Ms. Tidwell. We valued your family as customers, and I'm not about to charge you after what you went through last night. We're all thankful you weren't hurt."

Kristie thanked the gentleman and walked to her SUV with Eric.

"It's almost lunch time; want to get something to eat?" asked Eric.

"Sure. Where do you want to go?"

Eric suggested Wentworth's signature barbecue restaurant, and followed Kristie there. After being seated at a table, neither one said anything for a couple of minutes. Then Kristie told Eric she appreciated him going with her to have the car checked out.

"No problem. It's not like I have anything better to do. Well, actually, I do. I have to find a place to stay now that I've decided to leave Anabelle, not that I was ever really with Anabelle."

"Well, y'all seemed pretty chummy last night."

"Night before last, she seduced me. She came downstairs in a see-through nightgown, and I'm a man. Last night after we returned to the house from the restaurant, she approached me and didn't have a stitch on. I rejected her, packed a bag, and left. She's been calling me all morning, but I haven't talked to her."

"Look, Eric, we're divorced now, you're free to do whatever you please. And so am I, for that matter."

The food came, and they ate in silence.

After paying the check, the couple walked outside. As they were walking toward Kristie's SUV, Eric said, "I guess I had better find a place to stay."

"You're really not going back to Anabelle's?"

"No. The lake house is nowhere near completion, so I guess I'm homeless."

After several awkward seconds, Eric asked, "I don't suppose I could stay with you?"

CHAPTER 8

After trying to call Eric multiple times, and pacing from room to room in her spacious house, Anabelle Martin was frustrated, and didn't know what to do next. How had Eric sneaked out of the house last night without her knowing it? She looked through his stuff and found some of his clothes and toiletries missing along with one of his suitcases. How could he just up and leave her? After all, she had given him a place to stay when he needed one.

Anabelle and Wiley had been married for nineteen years, until Wiley died from an aggressive form of lung cancer. When they first married, Wiley had been a heavy cigarette smoker, but quit after several years of marriage. Wiley was also a heavy drinker, and on occasions, used cocaine and marijuana. Anabelle had never smoked cigarettes, but considered herself a moderate drinker, and did smoke pot before and after her and Wiley married. Before getting married, both of them decided they didn't want any children. Wiley's family was well off, and Wiley was one of the best-looking guys to come out of Wentworth High School. In her day, Anabelle was a brunette beauty, and came from a wealthy family as well.

However, two years after Wiley and Anabelle married, her father's IT consulting business failed to keep up with the fast-moving technology industry. Her father was forced into bankruptcy and started drinking heavily. The Pickens' lost their stately home and moved into a three bedroom, two bath ranch style house in a middle-class subdivision. One night, in a drunken rage, her father snapped, shot Anabelle's mother in the head, and then turned his own cold hand.

Shortly before the tragedy, Anabelle found out she was two months pregnant. She had somehow messed up in taking her pills. Wiley was unhappy and screamed at Anabelle, "How could you have been so stupid."

Before they were married, Anabelle changed her mind about wanting children, and Wiley was agreeable. She didn't want anything to come between her and Wiley that might destroy the relationship they had created and nurtured, including their fabulous sex life.

After having discovered her daughter had slept with practically the whole town of Huntsville before she was sixteen, Anabelle's mother saw to it that she always had birth control pills. It was much too late to teach her daughter any morals, and a teen pregnancy would destroy her reputation as a prominent socialite. Anabelle was never very astute when it came to taking her pills. For years, she was just lucky.

Wiley soon got used to the idea, and hoped to have a boy as good looking as he was. When the time came, his son would take over his family's lucrative appliance sales and service business.

Anabelle was almost three months along when the murder/suicide happened. Already being distraught over her parents' financial status, Anabelle then had to endure the murder/suicide and all the gossip that went along with it. A week after her parents were buried, Anabelle miscarried. Things were bottoming out for the beautiful couple.

The Martin appliance business did prosper through the years, and Anabelle was never in a financial bind. When he died, Wiley was worth about seven million dollars, and all of it went to Anabelle.

After the miscarriage and the deaths of her parents, Anabelle immersed herself into Wentworth society, and found some of the women quite uppity, even more so than some of her Mom's contemporaries in Huntsville. Even though she was an outsider, being the wife of one of Wentworth's prominent businessmen, Anabelle was eventually accepted by the crème de la crème of Wentworth. Her life became one of charity events, bridge luncheons, and travel. Being totally immersed in herself, Anabelle couldn't care less about charity events and helping those less fortunate. She did, though, enjoy the many luncheons and dinner parties her charity work allowed her to attend. She also loved having her picture in the papers, even if it was only in the Wentworth papers.

Anabelle soon became best friends with Jan Harpo Franklin, Ruthie Harpo, and Kathryn Campbell Harpo. Ruthie Harpo's husband, Jimmy, was a good friend of Wiley's, along with Jeremy Franklin, husband of Jimmy Harpo's sister Jan, and Sam Harpo, Jimmy's brother, who had married Wentworth native, Kathryn Campbell. Another good friend of Wiley's was Eric Channing. Eric, however, was married to an aspiring career woman, Gina Hanover. Gina, although she was born and raised in Wentworth, had no use for "high society," and had nothing to do with Anabelle and the Harpo women. During the last few years of Eric and Gina's marriage, Gina spent most of her time in Birmingham, building her rehab business. Whenever the group got together, Eric was usually the odd person out.

According to Wiley, Eric had been a good football player in high school. He was awarded a scholarship to Georgia Southern University, but incurred a career ending injury on the second day of summer football practice. Eric returned to Wentworth where he later enrolled at a junior college, then enrolled at the University of North Alabama and earned a Bachelor of Science in Business Administration. His career took him to Nashville and Dallas. Then after a near fatal automobile accident on a stormy evening near the Oklahoma/Texas state line, a severely injured Eric spent time at Baylor University Medical Center. Upon his release from Baylor, he did most of his rehab at UAB where he met Gina Hanover Channing. He then came back to Wentworth and took a job in one of the banks as a loan officer.

Eric was ruggedly handsome with thick straight brown hair and chiseled features, and although she loved and was in love with Wiley, Anabelle was physically attracted to him. She often thought about the time when she, Wiley, Eric, Gina, and the Harpos were visiting the Martin beach house in Navarre Beach, Florida. She, Wiley, Gina, and Eric were the only ones up late one night. All of them had had a little too much to drink, stripped down, and went skinny dipping in the pool. While no fooling around took place except between the couples, Anabelle couldn't help but notice how Eric was staring at her Marilyn Monroe shaped figure. Gina, on the other hand, was flat chested and had an ample derriere.

Later, after the four went inside to smoke some pot, Anabelle got up to go to the bathroom. When she came out, Eric was standing at the door waiting to get in. The two, both still unclothed, touched front to front. She doubted Eric remembered, but she certainly did.

CHAPTER 9

"Oh, my goodness," exclaimed Kristie. "Eric, I don't know."

"Well, why not?"

"Eric, you come, and then you go. You hurt me, then you come back on your hands and knees begging to be forgiven. I take you back, then it's the same cycle again."

"Look, I'm not asking you to marry me again or make anything permanent, I just need a place to stay until the lake house gets built. Then I'll be moving there, and resume my life as a bachelor, like I was before you and I got together."

"I don't know if I can handle that, considering we were once so much in love, or at least I was in love with you."

"Okay, I'll see if I can stay at Jimmy's or maybe Dean's. It shouldn't be but just a couple of months before I can move into the lake house."

"Why don't you stay with Anabelle? I'm sure she would welcome you with loving arms."

"I'm not attracted to Anabelle, and besides, I really didn't like the way she treated you last night."

"You could have fooled me."

"Look, she was the one who latched onto my arm when the drama started, not the other way around."

"But you have been with her?"

"Yes, she's not that bad from the neck down."

"I think I need to go."

"Come on, Kristie, I really need a place to stay. While Dean or Jimmy would probably be okay with me bunking at their houses, I'd rather not intrude."

"Eric, if I let you stay with me, you'll talk me into letting you sleep with me. Then, you'll tire of me, leave, and who knows, get a hankering for Anabelle and go back to her."

"Kristie, listen to me. I'm not talking about moving in permanently or getting back together. It'll just be until I can move into the lake house."

"Eric, I just couldn't handle it."

"Okay, I'll go to Jimmy's or to Dean's."

With that, Kristie thanked Eric for lunch, for being with her at the Chevy dealership, then left.

CHAPTER 10

Anabelle came back to reality when her phone went off. It was Eric. "Honey, where in the world are you? I'm about to go crazy."

"Can I come by and get the rest of my things?"

"Eric, what in the world is wrong? Yesterday, at this time, we were basking in our lovemaking, and now, you want to come and get your things, and move out."

"Kristie was my wife, and she's really a wonderful person. I love her, and I guess I always will. Be that as it may, we have our differences. She won't accept, nor attempt to be a part of my group of friends, and I don't blame her. Those folks were rough on her when we were in high school. Wiley was mean to her and so was Jake Stanley. Dean admits he barely remembers her, but didn't like her for no other reason than at one time she was chubby. I don't want to be back with Kristie, I made my choice to be with y'all instead. But that doesn't change the fact that I still care about her."

"Okay, come over and get the rest of your things. I'll make sure the basement door is unlocked."

Eric drove to Anabelle's house, quickly gathered up the rest of his clothes and other things, and left, not seeing or talking to Anabelle. Driving out of Anabelle's subdivision, Eric thought to himself, I'm homeless.

He didn't want to stay with Jimmy Harpo or Dean Abercrombie.

Eric thought about going over to Jake Stanley's restaurant. Maybe he could stay with Jake. After getting out of prison, Jake had moved into his parents' house. They were both deceased, and had left the house to Jake. But he really couldn't deal with Jake because of some bad things which happened years ago. Jake had tried to befriend him, but Eric just couldn't come around.

There was Eric's sister, Sandy, who lived in Trussville, a northeastern suburb of Birmingham, with her husband and their two teenaged sons. He would be closer to Kristie if he moved to the Birmingham area. Then, there was his first wife, Gina. Gina and their teen-age daughter Tanya were living in the Birmingham suburb of Chelsea. That was even closer to Kristie's house than Sandy's house.

Gina's physical therapy business was thriving, and the partners had just opened their third branch in the Hwy 280 corridor between Greystone and Chelsea. Eric's relationship with Gina was one of "just send the checks." Of course, he loved Tanya and wanted to develop a closer relationship with her. Tanya was seventeen going on thirty and Gina was way too lenient with her. Maybe he could stay with the two of them.

When Eric called Gina, she told him that his moving in with her and Tanya was out of the question. After a few minutes of Eric trying to convince her it would be temporary, Gina then admitted she was seeing a guy, and while he maintained a residence of his own, he spent most nights at her house. Oh great, thought Eric. Tanya is wild as buck and Mommy's boyfriend sleeps over. Sheesh! Eric buried his head in his hands. If he had stayed with Kristie, maybe they could have had some influence on Tanya; maybe they could have convinced Gina to give them custody of Tanya. Kristie had wanted so much to be a great stepmom, and wanted to love Tanya and be there for her.

Sitting in the parking lot of Wentworth's oldest shopping center, Eric had nowhere to go, literally nowhere to go. There were some apartment complexes in Wentworth. Maybe he should see about renting an apartment until the lake house was completed.

Eric started his truck, put it in reverse and began to back out of his parking place. Two women, one about his age, and an older woman were right behind the truck. Eric slammed on the brakes to keep from running over the two. Can't people watch where they're going?

As the two women made their way to the left side of Eric's truck, he immediately noticed the woman about his age was incredibly beautiful. Oh my God, it's Rita McDonald, and that other woman is her mother.

CHAPTER 11

Kristie arrived at her Helena home mid-afternoon. Oh, what a couple of days it had been! Even though she had a great time at the CMA awards, she had been rejected by Nashville insider, Jake McPherson. Because Jake and his girlfriend were having problems, he had asked Kristie to be his escort to the awards' show to make her jealous. This was like something out of high school or even college. Then her SUV was apparently flipped back and forth and turned around in what was an apparent tornado that crossed I-65 last night.

Afterward, she and Eric somehow managed to end up in bed together. Earlier today, he asked if he could stay with her for a couple of months while his lake house was under construction. Then to top everything off, Eric had apparently hooked up with Anabelle Martin, the widow of Wiley Martin, a guy who had tormented her when they were growing up in Wentworth. Eric had told her he was through with Anabelle, but she didn't believe him.

Kristie was the only child of Mary and Bobby Tidwell, both deceased. Until the second grade, Kristie was thin and picked at her food. This displeased her Mama and Daddy, and they were always fussing at her about her eating. When she did over-eat, she would often get sick. However, something kicked in between the first and second grades, and Kristie began to eat because she thought it made the grownups happy. However, poor Kristie ate too much and became a chubby little girl. Because this didn't please anyone either, she was the subject of ridicule by the other children at school, and even some adults. When Kristie began high school, and found herself attracted to the opposite sex, she went on a diet and subsequently lost the weight. Some of her classmates were supportive, but some were not, especially Wiley Martin, Anabelle's deceased husband.

Kristie attended her last high school reunion, a little over two years ago, and so did popular jock, Eric Channing. Both single, Kristie and Eric began a relationship. Even though the relationship was tumultuous at times, Kristie and Eric did marry. The problems arising in their relationship were mainly because Eric and Wiley Martin were good friends and Kristie had a difficult time with that. Also, Eric was friends with a group of folks who were in high school with them who never left Wentworth after high school graduation. These were the wild kids who also gave Kristie a hard time about her weight, and never recognized that after her weight loss, she had become a beautiful teenager.

Kristie left Wentworth two days after high school graduation to attend the University of Alabama. In leaving, she vowed to never go back there except to see family. After Kristie graduated from the University, she continued to avoid Wentworth, while making friends and having a reasonably good life. Kristie stayed true to her vow to avoid Wentworth, until receiving a phone message from a classmate indicating this was a reunion year. She decided to grow up, and attend the reunion where she sat by, and talked to Eric.

Last night at the restaurant, Kristie had run into, of all people, Eric, who was with Anabelle Martin. Eric and Anabelle were with some folks who had never accepted her when she and Eric were dating, and after they were married. After six months of marriage, December 23, to be exact, Eric left Kristie after a fight with his gay younger brother and his brother's significant other.

A private detective, hired by Kristie, tracked Eric to a sleazy motel in the Florida Keys. Subsequently, Kristie filed for divorce. The proceedings went smoothly with Eric telling Kristie she had done nothing wrong in their marriage. He just didn't want to be married anymore.

Kristie's business was going okay, as she was making some money from her political blog and her political writings. She was also blogging about workplace issues, an area in which she was extensively experienced. The occasional designing of websites for third party clients was also generating some income.

Kristie was fatigued all the time, though. Having experienced heart failure two years ago she would probably need a heart valve replacement in ten or so years. Her Dad had always said, when you own your own business, you never get to take a day off. And that was so true. While Kristie enjoyed the freedom of having her own business, she felt that day jobs did have their advantages. Maybe she should start looking for a "real" job. Immediately after she and Eric had returned from their honeymoon, Kristie quit her job as an IT Manager. But did she want to go back into management? Did she even want to go back into IT? IT was a hard field, and Kristie realized her short-term memory wasn't as good as it once was. Short-term memory is a necessity in software engineering. Maybe she could get a job as a project manager or a business analyst.

Sitting in her living room, and attempting to watch the news proved impossible. All thoughts were on Eric. Maybe she should have agreed to let him stay with her until the lake house was built. He might be sitting beside her right now. Kristie was depressed, and the walls seem to be closing in on her. Should she call Eric and tell him she had a change of heart?

Since she was not able to concentrate on the news, Kristie went to the kitchen and decided to straighten up in there. Clean dishes that needed to be put away were in the dishwasher, and the floor needed sweeping. Tomorrow was garbage pickup day, and she needed to empty some waste baskets that were scattered through the house. She also needed to clean out the refrigerator. After finishing these tasks, she unpacked her suitcase from Nashville, and put some dirty clothes in the washing machine.

Kristie wanted to go to bed and stay there, but it was much too early. She didn't want to watch TV, or read, or sleep. She didn't want to do anything. Kristie had been used by two men who didn't care anything about her, Jake McPherson, and her ex-husband Eric Channing. Thank goodness, she didn't tell many people that she was accompanying Jake McPherson to the CMA awards. Kristie was a loser at love. There was no other way to put it.

Maybe she could do some writing, write some blog posts
and queue them up to be published over the next several
days. After finishing three blog posts that were to be
uploaded to her political blog, Kristie couldn't hold out any
longer. She decided to call Eric and tell him she had a change
of heart, and he could stay with her. It was a little after 8:00.
He would have eaten dinner by now, and would probably be
watching the news. The phone rang and rang, then the voice
mail kicked in. Kristie shut off her phone without leaving a
message.

CHAPTER 12

Eric heard his phone ring, but the phone was in his pants pocket on the other side of Rita McDonald Fisher's bedroom.

"Are you going to answer that?" asked Rita.

"No," said Eric, as he pulled Rita closer to him. "I have better things to do with my time."

Rita's king-sized bed was a far cry from the single bed in the farmhouse many years ago. Her chestnut colored hair was still long, but it now contained a few gray streaks. Like everyone else, Rita had gained some weight, but her body was just as pleasing to him as it was when they were in high school. In fact, the ever so slight aging made Rita more appealing to him.

After seeing Rita and her Mom in the parking lot of the shopping center, Eric called out to Rita, who he hadn't seen in decades. Rita was taking her Mom, who was now in assisted living, out to lunch and shopping. There were enthusiastic greetings and hugs. Eric had not seen Rita since the summer after he graduated from high school. Mrs.

McDonald, who had always liked Eric, was happy to see him also. Rita and Eric exchanged phone numbers, with Rita telling Eric she would call him after she and her Mom finished shopping.

During the time between seeing Rita and her call to him, Eric looked at a two-bedroom apartment to rent until his lake house was ready for occupancy.

Rita called him shortly after he left the apartment complex, and asked him to come over to her house. She had purchased the McDonald home from her siblings when their Mom went to assisted living, about a year after her Dad died. Since then, she had worked hard on fixing the place up, and had done an excellent job with it.

Rita, a year behind Eric in school, had broken up with him shortly after Eric had graduated from high school, and went off to play college football at Georgia Southern University. Before the actual break-up, Rita was seeing a guy who attended Crystal Springs High School in southwest Wentworth County. Upon graduation from high school, Rita received a partial scholarship to Vanderbilt University. While an undergraduate at Vanderbilt, she met a handsome medical student who was from Woodbury, New York, on Long Island. Hampton Fisher, III turned out to be the one for Rita, and they were married at Hamp's parents' estate. It was a fairytale wedding where the Fishers paid for Rita's family members and her bridesmaids to fly to New York and stay during the days leading up to the wedding. Dr. and Mrs. Fisher accepted Rita's middle-class small-town Alabama family and friends, and they loved their new daughter-in-law.

Rita had completed her undergraduate studies receiving a Bachelor's degree in early childhood development, and Hamp had graduated medical school with honors. After honeymooning in Italy, the newlyweds moved to Philadelphia where Hamp did his internship and residency at Temple University Hospital. After successful completion of those programs, Rita and Hamp moved to Woodbury where Hamp was to begin work at his Uncle Sam's already established practice. Hamp would eventually buy Uncle Sam's practice and continue the family tradition.

Even though Rita had graduated with honors from Vanderbilt, she was not to work outside the home except for charity functions, which were mandatory for the crème de la crème wives living in upscale Long Island. Rita loved every minute of her life. Two years after moving to Philadelphia, while Hamp was doing his residency, she bore the family a son, Hampton Burbank Fisher, IV. Little Hamp would follow in the steps of his father and become a doctor.

After Hamp finished his residency, the young couple, with little Hamp in tow, moved to Woodbury, N.Y. into an estate home with a full-time staff to attend to the needs of the family. Two years later, Rita had a baby girl they named Maggie Elizabeth.

While there was a nanny to care for the children, Rita played a significant role in their upbringing, finally getting to use some of the degree she worked so hard to earn while at Vanderbilt.

While Hamp IV followed his father to Vanderbilt for undergraduate work, he chose to attend medical school at Columbia University. Maggie was attending Yale University in New Haven, Connecticut.

What more could a small town, middle-class girl from Wentworth, Alabama desire? Rita had a more glamorous life than any of her classmates.

Her happiness would not last forever, though. While Maggie was a junior at Yale, and Little Hamp was still in his second year of medical school, a routine examination uncovered large tumor in Hamp's chest. After all tests were performed, he was diagnosed with non-Hodgkin's lymphoma.

While the survival rate for this cancer is quite high, and Hamp had the best care you could possibly get in the United States of America, he only lived six months after the devastating diagnosis. Rita and the children inherited millions, enough for them to do anything they wished to do for the rest of their lives.

Rambling around in that huge Long Island house, Rita soon became bored. Hamp IV had married a lovely girl, who was a recent graduate from the exclusive mid-town Manhattan liberal arts college, Barnard, and was from Sag Harbor. Because both families were wealthy, Hamp would continue medical school while Shari established herself in the New York/Long Island social strata. When Hamp finished his training and began his practice, the couple would already be crème de la crème. After graduating from Yale with a degree in finance, Maggie accepted a job with HSBC (Hong Kong Shanghai Banking Corporation) in their midtown Manhattan offices. For a graduation present, Rita purchased a luxury condominium for Maggie in mid-town Manhattan.

CHAPTER *13*

Rita had fallen asleep in Eric's arms, and his head was spinning. In the last three nights, he had been with three different women. He hadn't experienced this since he was a twenty-something. Anabelle, Kristie, and now Rita.

Anabelle was the widow of one of Eric's best friends in high school. His and Wiley's friendship had continued after high school and college graduations. Anabelle, once one of the most beautiful and sensual women Eric had ever laid eyes on, was a victim of aging. Her hair was rust colored and her body, while slender from having lost weight after Wiley's death, was saggy. Plus, her legs were streaked with varicose veins. But she was worth millions.

Kristie was his second wife for about eight months. She didn't fit into his Wentworth crowd, even though the two of them had been in the same class at Wentworth High School. Kristie wouldn't accept his friends, including the Harpo family, Dean Abercrombie, and others. She claimed she didn't remember Dean, even though Dean was one of the most popular guys in the class two years ahead of them.

Maybe it was because Dean was a bad boy and may have said mean things to her. Kristie was beautiful and she knew it, even with her weight problem she sometimes controlled and sometimes didn't control. Also, Kristie was middle class. While she was no pauper, she didn't have the millions of Anabelle or Rita.

Then there was Rita, his first love, the woman to which he had lost his virginity. Rita was still beautiful, and her body still appealed to him. Also, Rita was worth millions, many more millions than Anabelle. How would Rita fit into his Wentworth group of friends? Rita was in the same high school sorority as Jan Harpo Franklin, but Kathryn Campbell Harpo had been in a different sorority. Because that was so long ago, Rita should fit in with the Harpo women by the fact she was in a high school sorority. That apparently still mattered in Wentworth society, because Jan and Kathryn both held it in high esteem. In fact, Jan had indicated she couldn't possibly be friends with Kristie because Kristie had not been in a high school sorority.

But what about Anabelle? Anabelle wanted him, and apparently so did Rita. Could Rita fit in with the Harpo women, and Anabelle? Would it be awkward because he had rejected Anabelle, and chose to be with Rita?

As far as a love interest goes, Kristie was out because she wasn't wealthy enough, and Anabelle was out because she wasn't physically appealing. He was going with Rita, his first love.

Rita woke up in Eric's arms. After stretching and yawning, she kissed Eric good morning, and he kissed her back. Then they made love again. After finally getting out of bed, they took a long steamy shower together and got dressed.

After calling her Mom, Rita and Eric prepared a late breakfast at the house. When breakfast was over, they went to bed and made love until late afternoon. Then it was time to talk. Eric was having a house built on his Jones Lake property, and he needed a place to stay until the house was completed. That might be two to three months away. His options were renting an apartment in Wentworth, or finding some well-to-do widow to stay with. And it looked like he had found one.

"Rita, do you remember when I was a stud football player, and you were a cheerleader when we were in high school? We were such a cool couple, and everyone thought we would get married and live happily ever after. We really loved each other until we parted ways, and life didn't bring us back together until now. We lost our virginity to one another. That should mean something. Now that fate has brought us together, let's start over again. It's never too late."

"Eric, I loved you once and wanted to marry you, but it didn't happen. Our lives took different turns. You were married to Gina Hanover, and had a daughter. Then you married Kristie Tidwell. Kristie was the last person I thought you would end up with. I was really shocked when I heard about the two of you."

"What's wrong with Kristie Tidwell?"

"Nothing."

"Did you know she was Jake McPherson's date for the CMA Awards in Nashville three nights ago? Yeah, Jake McPherson, winner of many awards, and a mover and shaker in Nashville music business."

"The only thing I remember about Kristie Tidwell was she was first runner-up in the Miss Wentworth beauty pageant the year I was a junior. I didn't place, and that sucked. She was not a part of our crowd either."

"Look, sweetie, why are we sitting here arguing about Kristie Tidwell? I want us to start over again and be together. Please say you want that too."

"Eric, I do care about you, but I'm just overwhelmed right now. Can you give me a little time?"

"Rita, I need a place to stay. If you don't let me stay here, I'll have to rent an apartment. So, I need to know something now."

"Eric Channing, you're despicable! Let me get this straight. You need to know right now if I'll agree to take up where we left off decades ago, so you'll either have a place to stay, with me, or you'll have to rent an apartment until your lake house in finished?"

"Yes, it's up to you, my sweet one."

"Can't we just start a relationship by seeing each other socially? Why don't you rent an apartment, and we'll see what happens?"

CHAPTER 14

It had been twenty-four hours since Kristie had called Eric, and he had not bothered to call her back. However, she didn't leave a message. But Eric should have called her just as soon as he checked his phone. Maybe she should have left him a message.

Eric was a master at dodging folks, including her. Steve Conley, the married guy, and the biggest mistake of her life, was that way too. He never returned phone calls, and never called when he said he was going to. It seems she was attracted to guys who treated her this way.

Should she call Eric again? They had been married for eight months, and for six of those months, they were exceedingly happy. Then something snapped. Eric decided to leave her on December 23, 2011, after having a fight with his gay brother at their house. After walking out on her, Eric would not answer her phone calls or her texts to him. In early January 2012, she tracked him down in a rather cheap motel in the Florida Keys. It was then he told her he didn't want to be with her anymore, and wanted to end the marriage.

Kristie and Eric's divorce was straightforward and amicable. They owned a few investments together which they split according to the percentage each had contributed. Because they each had their property to which they had not added the other, there was none to divide. A few days before the divorce was final, Kristie was taking a week's vacation on the Alabama Gulf Coast, and was staying at an Orange Beach hotel. Eric, also visiting the Alabama Gulf Coast, was staying with a friend and his wife who lived there. The two ran into one another at one of the area's traditional establishments one evening and decided to have lunch the following day. After lunch, they went back to Kristie's hotel where they walked down to the beach and remained there until the sun set. It was indeed a beautiful sunset. The clouds were gunmetal gray, and the sun was a deep coral, almost red. It was one of the most beautiful sunsets Kristie had ever seen.

When the sun disappeared, the two of them stood, gathered their belongings, and walked back to the hotel, through the lobby, and out to the parking lot where Eric's truck was parked. They both leaned against the truck for a few minutes, then Kristie began to cry.

"Eric, what did I do to make you hate me?" Kristie asked.

"Nothing, Kristie, nothing at all."

Eric got into his truck and drove away.

The two did not have any contact with each other until two nights ago, after the tornado had supposedly flipped Kristie's SUV around with Kristie in it. A concerned Eric spent the night with her at the Holiday Inn Express where they made love. It was almost like things were when they were married.

There had been two class gatherings since the divorce, and while Kristie had attended both, Eric did not show up for either one. While the women at the socials seemed to support Kristie, and were shocked Eric would do something like that to her, some of the guys were stand-offish, especially a couple of the guys who had played sports with Eric.

Alabama was playing LSU in Baton Rouge, and it wasn't looking good for the Tide at half-time. Kristie knew Eric would be watching the game from somewhere, maybe even Auburn fan, Jimmy Harpo's house.

CHAPTER 15

It was Saturday morning, and Eric asked Rita to go apartment hunting with him. She hadn't changed her mind about letting him stay with her at her Wentworth house, and indicated she couldn't go apartment hunting, since her Mother was visiting her that day. Eric wanted to spend the day watching football, but that wasn't going to happen.

He wanted an apartment which was already furnished, so he could just move his clothes in, and not have to worry about furniture. Alabama was playing LSU that night, and Eric knew if he couldn't go back to Rita's, he could probably watch the game at Jake Stanley's restaurant.

Eric did find something suitable in a complex just off Graham Street. There was a Graham girl in his and Jake's class at WHS, her first name was Nancy. She was another classmate he didn't know very well. Wonder what ever happened to her? He thought Graham Street may have been named after her family.

The apartment wasn't furnished, but the leasing agent did give him the name of a furniture and appliance rental company in town. Eric drove over there, and picked out furniture, including two flat screen TVs. The company representative indicated they could deliver everything by 5:00 pm. The power and cable were turned on, so Eric could watch the game at his new place if he chose to do so.

Furniture was delivered, and the TVs were setup. Eric wanted to call Rita to see what she was doing. Where was his phone? He hadn't needed it for a while. Then he remembered it was probably in the pocket of the pants he had worn last night, the pants he hurriedly got out of when things started happening between him and Rita. Eric found the pants and the phone. He had missed a call, and that call was from Kristie, but she didn't leave a message.

Eric called Rita and found that she and Mrs. McDonald were having dinner at a local seafood restaurant. Rita was an Auburn fan, and could be rooting for LSU, but he still wanted to watch the game with her. It wouldn't happen, though.

"Okay, I'll call you tomorrow."

"Okay."

Well, this was going to be the first time in three nights he didn't have a woman with which to bed down. What was he

going to do? Get something to eat since he was hungry. He
also needed alcohol.

He called a local pizza place and ordered a pizza. Then he
went out and picked up some beer, and picked up the pizza.
By the time he got home, it was getting close to kick-off.
Kristie would probably be watching the game from Mojito
Grille. That's where she watched many of the Alabama games
when the team was playing out of state. Should he try to call
Kristie? No. Rita was his girl now. She was beautiful and
wealthy, and he wanted her, even though she was an Auburn
fan. Kristie was a mistake of his past, and that's where she
would stay, in his somewhat checkered past.

It was half-time, and the Tide was struggling in Baton
Rouge. Surely Rita would be home by now. Maybe he would
call her. Even though he now had a bed, and a roof over his
head, he didn't want to sleep alone tonight, especially now
that Rita was his girl.

His phone rang, and looking at the screen, he saw it was
Kristie. What did she want? He immediately hit the end
button transferring the call to voice mail. After several
seconds, he heard the notification that he had a voice mail
message. He didn't play it back, though. He didn't want to
hear from her ever again. He and Rita belonged together.

With no timeouts and minimal time left on the clock in regulation, Alabama had the ball and could tie the game with a field goal, sending it into overtime. However, T.J. Yeldon caught a screen pass from quarterback A.J. McCarron, and sprinted into the end zone, giving Alabama a win. Eric was ecstatic. Without thinking, he grabbed his phone to text Kristie.

This time last year, LSU had beaten Alabama in overtime at Bryant-Denny Stadium. It had been dubbed the game of the century. Kristie was there, while he was watching the game at their home. He remembered her being disappointed and in tears.

But wait, he didn't want to see Kristie ever again. He was with Rita now. Maybe he should text Rita and say "Roll Tide," knowing it would make her mad. No, they were just beginning for the second time; he didn't want to take any chances.

He decided to play back Kristie's voicemail, and was surprised when she told him, that after thinking it over, he could stay with her until the lake house was completed. Shit! Did he have women problems or what? He wanted to leave town and forget everything, but had just signed a lease on this apartment, plus he had rented all this furniture.

Leaving Anabelle in a huff, making love to Kristie, and leaving her with the possibility of getting together again, had certainly put him between a rock and a hard place. He was almost in a relationship with Rita, choosing Rita because Anabelle was not good-looking enough and Kristie was not rich enough. Rita was rich and beautiful. With droopy eyes, Eric texted Kristie, saying only "Roll Tide." Then he texted Rita saying he was thinking about her and would call her tomorrow.

Immediately, Rita texted back saying she was taking her mother to church and out to lunch the next day, a Sunday. Then she would be spending the afternoon with her, and wouldn't be available until late tomorrow evening.

A text is a text, and no one should try to read feelings into a text, but this one from Rita sounded antiseptic.

CHAPTER 16

Eric was leaving her, and wanted to come over and get the rest of his stuff. "Eric, what we had was great. I'm sorry I gloated in front of Kristie, but I was so proud to be with you, I care about you so much."

"Anabelle, it won't work. In fact, I'm considering severing my friendship with Jimmy and Dean. What they said about Kristie last night was unfathomable. It was worse than high school. Imagine wishing someone would die?"

"I don't think it was meant like that. They just want you to get Kristie out of your system, and get on with your life."

"Look, I need to get my things. I'll be over there in about ten minutes. Will you leave the basement door open for me? I won't disturb you."

"Yes."

With that, the conversation ended. Not wanting to be at the house when Eric arrived, Anabelle grabbed her purse and car keys and left the house. When she was out of the subdivision, she called Jan, and asked if she could come over to her house for a while. Jan, who was also a rich and pampered wife, said sure.

"Eric left you just like that," asked Jan when Anabelle arrived at the Franklins home?

"Yes. After we had returned from dinner, he said he didn't want anything to do with me because I had gloated to Kristie about being with him. He was also upset at some comments Dean and Jimmy had made about Kristie."

"I'm sorry things didn't work out between you and Eric, but at least this happened before you got too emotionally involved, or fell in love with him."

With that, Anabelle burst into tears. "I think I've been in love with Eric for a while. It may have started a couple of months after Wiley died. Eric was so kind to Wiley while he was sick, even though he and Kristie were in a relationship and Kristie didn't care for Wiley. You remember, Wiley died about the time Kristie and Eric returned from their honeymoon. Eric was so noble and sweet to me at the viewing and the funeral. Then, nothing. I didn't hear from him or see him until he left Kristie, drove to the Keys, and looked me up."

"Look, sweetie, I wish there was something I could do."

"I don't guess there's anything anyone can do. Eric is collecting the remainder of his stuff from the basement. I think I'll ride around for a while to clear my head."

"Don't leave. Jeremy will be home soon, and I'm making the chicken casserole we love so much for dinner. Please stay. Would you like a glass of wine?"

"I really don't feel like eating right now, but a glass of wine sounds nice, thanks."

Jeremy Franklin arrived at his home about 5:30 and found Jan in the kitchen preparing dinner, and a loopy Anabelle sitting on the sofa watching the news.

"How much wine has Anabelle had to drink?" asked Jeremy.

"I don't know. I gave her a bottle of merlot with a glass, and said help yourself."

"Well, she's certainly in no shape to drive home."

"I asked her to stay for dinner. Maybe some food will sober her up. She told me she hadn't eaten all day, so I guess the wine went right to her head."

"Anabelle's always been weak, and a cheap drunk to boot. She was a spoiled little rich girl. Then after meeting and marrying Wiley, one of the best-looking guys to graduate from Wentworth High School, she became even more spoiled. She can't deal with imperfection."

"Give her a break, Jeremy, she and Eric were getting along so well."

"I heard something interesting today at lunch. Some of us went to Jake Stanley's restaurant. He was the manager on duty, and said he had talked to the manager on duty at the Holiday Inn Express last night. Kristie appeared at the hotel, after supposedly leaving for Birmingham. She was disheveled and scared. After she had booked a room, the manager got Eric's number from Jake. He called Eric and told him that Kristie was there. Eric drove to the hotel, and then went to Kristie's room. The next morning, the two of them left together."

"Well, Eric can get very defensive where Kristie's concerned. He left her after six months of marriage and said he didn't want her anymore, but if someone says something bad about her, he gets mad. I talked to Ruthie today. At dinner last night, Dean made a comment that Eric might be better off with Kristie out of the way, after Eric expressed concern about her driving down I-65 with one of the tornadoes headed that way."

"Did Dean really say that? Did Dean imply that Eric would be better off with Kristie dead?"

"According to Ruthie, he did. Eric then told Dean he was out of line."

"Honey, you have to admit that was brutal."

Jeremy Franklin, who had attended Willow Lake High School in Wentworth County, didn't hang out much with Jan's two brothers and their friends. He also didn't care for the late Wiley Martin, always saying he thought Wiley was corrupt to the core.

"Supper's almost ready, go tell Anabelle to come to the table."

Walking into the den, Jeremy found Anabelle passed out on the sofa. When he tried to nudge her awake, Anabelle opened her eyes, sat up, and hurled red wine all over the Franklins' cream-colored sofa.

"Oh my God! Jan!"

"Oh dear. Get a face cloth out of the powder room and dampen it with cold water and put it on Anabelle's head. I'll start cleaning this mess up."

The sofa would have to be cleaned, plus the oak coffee table and the hardwood floor would most likely have to be refinished due to the acidity in the wine.

"Why did you give her a whole bottle of wine?"

"She was so distraught."

Anabelle, in a stupor, groaned about her aching head.

"I think I'll take Miss Anabelle home right now. Why don't you drive her car behind me? That way we'll be rid of her and her car for the night."

"She hasn't had anything to eat all day. We really need to try to get her to eat something."

Jeremy followed Jan into the kitchen.

"You gave her this much wine, knowing she had an empty stomach?"

"Poor Anabelle, Eric dumped her earlier today, and she was devastated."

"I'm really getting sick of poor Anabelle. Wiley left her millions. She can go anywhere, and do anything she wants. Frankly, I wish she would move out of town for good. I've never liked her, nor did I like your high school buddy, Wiley. If you ask me, they were both spoiled brats, who demanded to be the center of attention at all times."

"I'll never forget that morning we found Wiley and Anabelle with Eric and his first wife in the living room of their beach house butt naked after they had been smoking pot. We all could have been arrested. When the four of them awoke, and realized they were naked, everyone but Anabelle tried to cover themselves. But what does Anabelle do? She just gets up and walks to their bedroom, naked, like she was fully dressed."

The timer went off, and Jan pulled the casserole from the oven. Then she retrieved a can of chicken soup from the pantry and heated it.

"Let's see if we can get some soup down Anabelle."

Jeremy went to the den to get Anabelle, but she had fallen asleep again. Not being pleased with things at the house after having a hard day at the office, Jeremy shook Anabelle, telling her to wake up and come to the kitchen and have some soup. She groaned and held her head, but got up and went to the kitchen with Jeremy.

"Anabelle, I heated some soup for you. You can have some casserole if you want, but I think you had better eat this soup instead."

"Thanks, Jan. That was mighty sweet of you," said Anabelle.

Anabelle did eat a small amount of the soup, and said she had better get back to the house. "I don't want to intrude on your dinner."

"Anabelle, you're not intruding. We care about you, and want you to know that anytime you need to talk, just let us know. We're sorry things didn't work out between you and Eric, but we're here for you."

When Anabelle arrived at her house, none of Eric's stuff was there. He was gone.

CHAPTER 17

ROLL TIDE? Was texting "Roll Tide" all he could do after she left him a message that he could bunk at her house until construction on his lake house was finished. He could have at least called her and thanked her for the offer, and told her he had already made other arrangements. Was he going to stay at Jimmy's or was he back with Anabelle?

Since Kristie had started dating, she seemed to be attracted to guys who treated her poorly or ignored her when it suited them. There was Steve Conley. She didn't think anyone could have treated her as bad as that SOB had. Now Eric was treating her shabbily. What was wrong with her? Why couldn't guys just treat her with some semblance of respect?

Alabama won the game on a last-minute drive with no timeouts. For that, Kristie was thrilled. But she was still upset about Eric. Should she call him and hash things out? But where was he tonight? Was he at Jimmy's? Or maybe he went back to Anabelle. Anabelle was a champion at putting on a helpless act when she wanted something. Memories of Wiley's funeral came flooding back to her.

Kristie knew there was no chance of sleep until she talked to him, or at least tried to talk to him. She called him, half expecting him not to pick up. When he did, she didn't quite know what to say.

"Eric?"

"That's me."

"Eric, I've been trying to get hold of you."

"Been busy."

"Look, Eric, I know I was hesitant about letting you stay with me until your house was finished, but it caught me off guard. In fact, Thursday and Friday were both rough days for me. I was in the middle of a tornado, then my ex-husband and I spend a romantic night together. Then he asks me if he can stay with me only for a while. Could you possibly understand?"

"You're a little late. Earlier today I signed a lease on a two-bedroom apartment just off Graham Street, not far from Ancestry Park. I've already had furniture delivered. The power is on, the cable is connected, and I was able to watch the game on my flat screen TV."

"You didn't waste any time."

"I had to get out of Anabelle's. I just couldn't take that woman any longer."

"Aside from the fact she was rude to me Thursday at the restaurant, what made you change your mind about Anabelle? You used to be so crazy about her."

"Used to be is right. Anabelle's beauty has faded, and now that she has Wiley's millions, she acts like a spoiled little rich girl."

"I thought she was always a spoiled little rich girl."

"You know about her family and the family business, don't you?"

"No, I haven't said more than ten words to Anabelle Martin in my life. And remember, your little clique would have nothing to do with me when we were dating, and Wiley was still alive."

"Kristie, don't start."

"Okay. You now have an apartment and don't need a place to stay any longer. I won't keep you."

"Wait a minute. Let's not end this call on a sour note. I had a good time with you Thursday night. I had forgotten just how good you were in bed, and what we did have together at one time. Not just the sex, but everything else. I did love you."

"And I loved you too. Can we talk soon?"

"Sure, I'll call you in the next few days."

After the phone call, Kristie was smiling. Did she want to get back together with Eric? Did she still love him? The answer to both questions was yes, unfortunately, yes.

Eric had said something about Anabelle's family and their business, what happened? She let Eric get off the phone without asking him about that. Guess she will have to find out about it later.

With that, Kristie crawled in bed, and went to sleep thinking about Eric and Alabama's great win.

As Eric was falling asleep, he decided to see how things would work out with Rita. She was still his first choice. If she rejected him, he didn't have any problem falling back on Kristie, even though Kristie wasn't wealthy and Rita was.

Now that he and Anabelle were through, was it going to be awkward with Jimmy and the gang? Anabelle was best friends with Jan Franklin and her sister-in-laws, Ruthie Harpo and Kathryn Harpo? Ruthie was Jimmy's wife, and Kathryn was Sam's wife. What if he and Rita started a relationship? Rita and Jan were in the same high school sorority, but it could get dicey with Anabelle in the picture. And, what if he ended up with Kristie? The Harpos vehemently disliked her.

He wasn't aware of that until after their divorce when they said some unflattering things about Kristie. They apparently still disliked her because she was overweight until her early high school years.

Eric was screwed. No matter which girl he chose to be with, there would be problems. Maybe he should drop both Rita and Kristie. Maybe he should leave town for a while, and try to meet a woman who didn't have Wentworth connections.

Eric woke up in bed alone and wanting a woman. Rita was taking her Mom to church, then out for lunch, and then she was spending the afternoon with her. Anabelle was probably available, but he had no desire to be with her. Kristie was probably getting ready to go to church. But maybe she would be agreeable to driving up from Birmingham after church to be with him for a while. Forget that. By the time she could get up here, Rita might be through with her Mom, and they could get together.

As he was flipping channels on his bedroom TV, Eric admitted to himself that he was a jerk. He really wanted Rita because she was rich, but he would settle for Kristie because she was beautiful and good in bed. As far as Anabelle was concerned, Eric wanted nothing more to do with her. He was willing to ask Kristie to drive up to see him just to have sex. I'm definitely a jerk, thought Eric. But who cares.

CHAPTER *18*

On her way home from church, Kristie stopped to pick up something for lunch, and take to the house. After eating, she did some research on some articles that she was expected to write, as a guest, for some political blogs. She had her own blogs, but they were generating miniscule income. She really needed to publicize them more in hopes of getting more hits. Should she pursue a day job, one where she would have a steady paycheck and benefits? Kristie was enjoying her freedom, but was not making enough money to live without dipping into savings, and those funds were depleting fast.

What did she want to do? She could get back into IT management, but the stress could be unbearable. She could go back into software developing, but technology had moved so rapidly, and there were new methodologies out there with which she had no experience. To get experience with those disciplines, you had to have a job, and she didn't have a job. Besides, she had no desire to get back into software developing. Like IT Management, the stress could be unbearable. To be successful, you needed to have good recall, and Kristie could already tell her short-term memory wasn't as good as it was when she was younger.

She really enjoyed researching and writing political articles. In fact, she really enjoyed writing. Maybe Kristie should step outside of her comfort zone, and try to get her blogs noticed by some major political websites. If she could get some of these well-known sites to link to her site, she might be able to make enough money to live on, ending the depletion of her savings, at least for now. But how?

She had to add some bells and whistles to her current blogs, which could be done in the next couple of days.

Jordan Vann, yes, Jordan Vann! Kristie had known Jordan for over ten years. He had a local political radio talk show, and often spoke at local events. Surely, he had some good contacts. Maybe Jordan could help her get more traffic for her blogs, or steer her to someone who could.

In the next few hours, Kristie determined how much money she could invest on publicizing the blogs. She also began making changes to the websites so their appearances were more professional looking. Then she sent a Facebook message to Jordan telling him about her blogs and asking if he had time to have lunch with her to discuss some things. Jordan, though, was a minor local celebrity, and probably wouldn't have time for Kristie. But she had to try. Eric was all but forgotten.

Eric spent Sunday morning reading about Bama's victory on the Internet, along with skimming the results of the other SEC and nationally important football games. Lunch was leftover pizza and Diet Coke. After showering and getting dressed, he went to the grocery store to stock the apartment with food staples. By the time he returned and put everything in its place, it was after 4:00. Would Rita be finished with her Mom? The apartment needed a woman's touch, and maybe Rita could give him some pointers on making it look homier.

When he called her, Rita answered promptly and said she had just returned from dropping her mother off at her assisted living apartment.

"Well, would you like to come over and see the new place? It's not very impressive, but it just might be livable with a few feminine touches."

"Sure. Where is it?"

After taking down the directions, Rita said she would be over there in fifteen minutes.

Eric hung up, and strutted around the apartment. He was going to have a woman visitor. When Rita arrived, Eric gave her a hello kiss, and she kissed back. After a tour of the apartment, she told Eric the place did need a few additional items to make it look like home, and she would be glad to go shopping with him, and make some suggestions.

"Are you hungry? I bought some steaks, and some chicken this afternoon. I also picked up some ham and turkey for sandwiches."

"Mom and I had a big lunch, so I'm not hungry. But if you're hungry, go on ahead and fix yourself something."

"You know," said Eric, we've never been domestic together. I've been through two wives, one fiancée, and too many girlfriends to count, but this is the first time I've ever been domestic with you, and you were my first love."

"I think you're right."

"Want to get domestic?" asked Eric, as he pulled her close to him and steered her toward the master bedroom, forgetting about food.

After making love, the couple fell asleep in each other's arms. When Eric woke up, it was daylight outside, and Rita was still asleep. Her long chestnut colored hair, streaked with gray fanned out on the pillow. Eric thought she looked like a princess. The bed sheet was wrapped around her in such a way that the top of her ample cleavage was visible, along with one pink nipple. While he was still gazing at her, Rita opened her eyes and smiled. Eric took her head in his hands and began to kiss her gently. Soon they were making love again.

Afterward, Rita and Eric, both famished from having no supper, took a shower together, got dressed, and decided to go out somewhere for breakfast. Then they would go shopping for apartment furnishings.

CHAPTER 19

For breakfast, Rita and Eric went to a quaint little eatery across the street from the First United Methodist Church of Wentworth.

The church was hit head on by the April 27, 2011 tornado, blowing out the beautiful stained-glass windows for which the church was known. Even though the roof was ripped off, and the sanctuary was extensively damaged, the solid stone structure was left intact. The only item in the sanctuary not damaged was a large wooden cross which hung in the back of the choir loft. An elderly church member in the early 2000s had built the cross. Kristie had grown up in that church. In fact, Eric remembered taking Rita to their Christmas program when he was a senior in high school. Kristie sang in the choir, and he remembered her looking like an angel.

Before the tornado, the place where they were having breakfast had belonged to a retired couple. Except for the basement, the house was taken out. The couple took the insurance money for the house, and sold the land to an out of town investor who opened a quaint little restaurant on the property. Breakfast and lunch were served Monday through Saturday.

Wiley Martin was a member of the Methodist church also. To the best of Eric's knowledge, Wiley never attended.

"Mind if we walk over to the church?" Eric asked Rita.

"No, but why?"

"I attended a funeral there several months before the tornado, and I'd like to see the new sanctuary."

They entered the church through a side door which was unlocked, walked up some side steps and into the sanctuary. A good job was done repairing and replacing because the sanctuary looked very much like Eric remembered it.

They walked to the front, and stared up at the back of the choir loft, and saw the beautiful hanging cross.

"Let's go up in the choir loft and see if there's a plaque somewhere that will tell us who built the cross."

"Why are you so interested?"

"I don't know, I just am."

There was indeed a plaque at the base of the cross that read, "Inspired by God and constructed by his faithful servant, William Robert Tidwell."

Eric gulped.

At first, Rita didn't make the connection, and then asked, "Was that Kristie's father?"

"Yes."

"Ready to go?"

Rita and Eric hit several interior decorating shops in Wentworth where Eric purchased a centerpiece for the dining room table, several lamps, some framed prints for the walls, and other miscellaneous items for the apartment. He also purchased some everyday china and stainless-steel flatware, some glassware, and some cooking utensils.

Before he and Kristie married, he had all of this stuff, but either sold most of it or gave it away before the wedding. When he moved in with Kristie, they used her stuff. Having none of these things after the divorce, Eric chose to purchase quality items so he could take them with him when he moved into the lake house.

Eric and Rita returned to the apartment late in the afternoon, and began to put away the purchases, but found themselves too tired to complete the tasks at hand. They were also hungry, so Eric suggested they drive up to the restaurant that Jake Stanley managed on Highway 157.

Jake was happy to see the couple. He hadn't seen Rita since they were in high school, and the three of them enjoyed talking about old times while they were having drinks, and waiting for their food to arrive. Jake, however, was a bit confused. Eric was with Anabelle four days ago. Now it seems he is back with his high school sweetheart, Rita McDonald. While Anabelle was a looker in her day, her looks had all but disappeared. Rita was beautiful when they were in high school, and she was beautiful now.

CHAPTER 20

Jake Stanley had no doubt lived a colorful life. He barely graduated from Wentworth High School, and stayed in trouble during his high school years. He drank heavily and smoked both cigarettes and marijuana. In fact, he started dealing marijuana when he was a senior in high school. His Mom and Dad owned a little café in town, and both stayed busy with the business, leaving Jake to his own devices. As a result, Jake became "street smart" to the extent anyone could be street smart in Wentworth. His father had served time in jail, and felt that boys would always be boys, never taking the time to discipline Jake when he got into trouble.

Jake was part of the so-called "bad boy trio" of his class at Wentworth High School. He palled around with his bad boy trio counterparts, Wiley Martin and Johnny Morton. Both Wiley and Johnny's Dads were wealthy, prominent Wentworth business owners, but they accepted Jake into their little fold. While not a member of the bad boy trio, Eric Channing often hung out with them when he wasn't hanging out with his girlfriend, Rita McDonald. Another guy, Jim

Winston, was also a part of their group, and hung out with the bad boy trio when he wasn't with his girlfriend, Hannah.

During his junior year, Jake had started dating a girl from Tremont, a small rural town close to the northern Wentworth County line. Jake was faithful to this girl until after he graduated. The couple eventually parted ways. Paula was a smart girl, and was planning to attend Auburn when she graduated. Jake, however, had no plans to go to college. He wanted to do nothing but drink and smoke his life away. Having no career ambitions, Jake took a job at one of Wentworth County's factories after high school graduation. Johnny Morton was smart, and went off to Auburn to college. He dated lots of girls in high school, but there were no particular standouts. Wiley's grades and college test scores were barely enough to get him accepted to the University of Alabama. While at Alabama, Wiley continued to date Wentworth girls.

Jim Winston attended a local college, and married his high school sweetheart, Hannah. Eric went to Georgia Southern on a football scholarship, but on the second day of practicing in pads, he suffered a devastating knee injury which ended his college football career. Eric dropped out of Georgia Southern, and returned home to Wentworth. He was then accepted to Calhoun Junior College near Decatur. After completing his studies at Calhoun, he attended the University of North Alabama, where he received a business degree. Rita broke up with Eric after his injury occurred. By the time he graduated from North Alabama, he was seeing a girl from Birmingham. He would later get engaged to Rhonda, but they eventually broke up.

Jake moved into his parents' basement, and turned it into a nice bachelor pad. He moved furniture from his bedroom downstairs, purchased some additional furniture for the living room, and some kitchen appliances. A full bathroom was already in the basement.

Jake's parents didn't care what he did, so he spent much of his free time drinking and smoking pot. He also started seeing a twenty-one-year-old woman who lived in a house trailer in the western part Wentworth County. After their relationship began to develop, Jake would spend most weekends at her trailer.

After dropping out of Georgia Southern, and coming back to Wentworth, Eric lived with his parents, but would spend most evenings at Jake's apartment. Jake was glad to have him back, and even tried to fix Eric up with some of the women who worked at his plant.

One Saturday evening after Christmas, Eric had a date with a girl who was a senior at Wentworth High. She was a beauty and Jake had previously told Eric he could bring girls over to his place if he was staying at Deborah's trailer. On this particular evening, Eric brought Julie Yarborough to Jake's place to see how much he could get.

Jake arrived at Deborah's trailer a few minutes early, finding Deborah in bed with one of her ex-boyfriends. Jake had already downed a couple of Jack and Cokes before arriving, and was enraged at what he saw. Jake pulled the ex-boyfriend out of bed, and punched him in the nose. The old boyfriend grabbed his clothes, and left the trailer before Jake had a chance to hit him a second time. He ran to his truck with his clothes in hand, and scratched off as he was leaving.

Jake then snatched Deborah out of the bed, and after slapping her across the face a few times, he threw her back on the bed. Deborah begged him not to leave her, and said she still wanted him, and would be up to a threesome with him and the ex. Jake had always fantasized about having two women, but he wasn't about to share a woman with another man.

Jake ran out the door, got in his car, and left, also scratching off. On his way back to Wentworth, he retrieved his bottle of Jack Daniels from the glove compartment, and chugged on it while driving. In addition to being well on his way to getting drunk, Jake was desperate for sex. He was looking forward to getting some this evening, and that wasn't happening, at least not with Deborah.

When Jake arrived at his basement apartment, he found Eric in his bedroom with his cute little high school date, Julie Yarborough. Julie was fully dressed from the waist down. Eric had managed to get her sweater off, but not her bra.

When Jake came into the bedroom, Eric rose and sat on the bed, trying to hide Julie, so she could get her sweater back on. Still wanting a woman, Jake pulled Eric off the bed, and forced Julie to lie back down. He then began to sexually assault her.

Eric hit Jake over the head with a ceramic lamp, pinned him to the floor, and put a couple of pieces of furniture on top of him. Eric then managed to call the police, who came and took Jake off to jail. He was tried, convicted and sentenced to six months in the Wentworth City jail. There was no penetration, and Julie had no injuries except a red mark across her face where Jake had slapped her.

Julie Yarborough went on to graduate from Wentworth High School. Following graduation, she enrolled at Emory

University in Atlanta, where she graduated with a degree in Sociology. During her college years, there were rumors she was into drugs and the Atlanta party scene. After graduation, Julie took a job counseling troubled teenagers at a half-way house, but was still into drugs and nightlife. One Saturday night, approximately one year after she graduated from Emory, she was out clubbing and left one of the clubs with a young man. They went to his apartment and shot up heroin. The next morning, the young man woke up next to a dead Julie Yarborough.

After Jake's assault on Julie, Eric would have nothing to do with him. While most of his other friends, particularly Johnny and Wiley, were just teenage boys getting into trouble like teenage boys do, there was something dark about Jake. He was real trouble, one of those types you knew would never amount to anything.

After serving his sentence in the Wentworth city jail, Jake was released and got a job at the same factory where he had worked before his incarceration. Because there were no women in Wentworth County who would have anything to do with him, Jake got his supply of women from the Huntsville area. He continued to smoke pot, and after a while, he began dealing it again.

With the money he made from his day job, plus the money he made from dealing, Jake was able to purchase a 2,000 square foot house in Blount Springs, Alabama, a small Blount County town south of Wentworth. In addition to dealing marijuana, he began dealing cocaine. While Jake dealt cocaine, he never used it because he had seen how it had destroyed other lives, and he didn't want that to happen to him. He also dealt barbiturates. Soon, he was making enough money to quit his factory job and deal full time.

Jake was now spending time with women who were living and working in north Jefferson County. With the advent of Video Cassette Recorders, Jake got into filming himself with his women friends. During a recording session, he almost always had two women with him. When he was in the movie, he would set the VCR on a tripod and could only shoot from one angle.

One afternoon when his drug supplier was paying him a friendly visit, and they were sitting around watching Jake's movies, the supplier commented that the movies were quite good, and suggested they start a porn movie business together. George had, at one time, acted in porn movies in New Orleans, and wouldn't mind being the man in the films.

That way Jake could hold the recorder, moving around to get the best shots.

George was about ten years older than Jake, and had the perfect looks for a porn star, dark wavy hair and a thick mustache. George, though, liked women much younger than the ones in Jake's films.

Because George had been with several girls from the local high school, he wanted to put them in the movies. Even though Jake was uneasy about using underage girls, George convinced him they could make more money. All the rich old perverts out there wanted to see young girls.

The first night of their new, money-making adventure, George brought two fifteen-year-old girls over to Jake's house. After several hours of filming, it was 4:00 am, and everybody stopped. After all, tomorrow was a school day. George left with the girls, leaving Jake to wonder what kind of parents they had.

Per their agreement, George got 60% of sales and Jake got the other 40%. After all, George was in the films, and was also marketing them. Jake was only doing the filming, per their agreement.

This went on for several years, with George never failing to supply fresh teenage girls from various high schools in the area.

One stormy night in the spring, Jake was scheduled to meet a drug purchasing client near a well-known Blount County restaurant. It had just begun to rain as Jake was pulling into the restaurant's gravel parking lot. Because the surrounding area was wooded, the client always parked his vehicle in a small clearing about a quarter of a mile southwest of the establishment. The exchange always took place on the southwest side of the restaurant, which had closed several hours earlier.

As Jake handed the bag of marijuana to his client and took the cash, two Blount County deputies came from the woods behind the restaurant, grabbed, and handcuffed both Jake and the client.

One of the girls, Katie, who was in some of the films had gotten pregnant. When she was about to be sedated before having an abortion, she told the medical personnel in the room with her to stop. She then got up and walked out of the clinic, choosing not to have the abortion. After the baby was born, she found Christ and he forgave her sins. Even though the child's father had deserted her, she had Jesus, an adorable baby girl, and needed nothing more.

Being aware of the exploitation of adolescent girls by Jake and George, Katie had notified the authorities. The sheriff's department had been watching the two. Not only were they aware of the porn ring, but they also discovered the drug ring. While they arrested both Jake and George on dealing, they couldn't get them on exploiting underage girls, but both would be off the streets, and the porn ring would disappear. Jake was sentenced to 20 years in prison, and so was George. Both got off for good behavior, after serving 15 years.

Jake returned to Wentworth about the time Kristie and Eric's divorce was final. Doing hard time had straightened him up to the extent that he wanted to stay away from doing anything illegal. With Wentworth County having recently voted to allow the sale of alcohol, and the opening of new restaurants, Jake was able to get hired as a manager for one of the national chains that was opening a place just off the northern-most Wentworth I-65 exit. The home office guy with whom Jake interviewed was an ex-con himself. Jake was honest about the mistakes he had made in life, and came across as sincere about never going back to a life of crime.

Jake began going to church, and contacted Julie Yarborough's family, asking for their forgiveness. Mr. Yarborough, who was in poor health, let Jake know he had destroyed not only Julie's life, but those of her family as well. However, it wasn't his place to judge Jake, the judging would take place in front of the Almighty.

Jake was saddened to hear of the death of his high school friend, Wiley Martin. When he contacted his other good friend, Eric Channing, he was surprised to find Eric had just divorced his second wife, the former Kristie Tidwell. Jake didn't like Kristie, and remembered the time he, Wiley, and Johnny Morton planned to kidnap Kristie, and force her to drink straight bourbon. When she was close to passing out, they were going to tie her up and throw her into some woods close to a local creek, in hopes that poisonous snakes would bite her to death. Were they really thinking about doing something like that? He was glad Johnny Morton, at the last minute, refused to participate.

While Jake was sure, like everyone else, Kristie had changed, he didn't plan on being friends with her, and he was glad she and Eric were divorced. Eric was cool to Jake when he called, and while he was glad Jake was ready to begin a new life, he still planned to keep his distance.

While in prison, Jake heard that Johnny Morton was living in Vancouver, and had come out of the closet. He wasn't surprised when Johnny turned out gay. While Johnny dated girls in high school, it was more of a social thing. He never talked about wanting to go all the way with any of his dates, or boasted about getting to any of the bases.

Jim Winston was living happily with his wife, Hannah, and their children. When Jake contacted Jim, Jim let him know he didn't want anything to do with him. Jim and Hannah had a teenage daughter, and they didn't want Jake anywhere around her.

Jake became a successful, well-known restaurant manager, and after a few months, Eric did warm back up to him, thinking he had changed.

CHAPTER 21

Rita and Eric had dinner at Jake's restaurant, then returned to the apartment. After setting up some of the new purchases in the apartment, Eric, assuming Rita was going to spend the night with him, started steering her toward the bedroom. Sensing her resistance, he stopped abruptly, and ask her what was wrong.

"I'm just not sure we should rush into things. Just last week you were living under the same roof as Anabelle Martin. Now you're assuming we're a couple."

"But aren't we? I left Anabelle. I don't think it was a coincidence that we ran into each other in the parking lot at the shopping center. We were meant to be together."

"Do you really want to start up where we left off decades ago, or do you just want someone to sleep with? And, by the way, why did you leave Anabelle? She would have been perfect for you. You and Wiley were good friends. I think it's only fitting that you and Wiley's widow get together. By the way, how's Tanya?"

"Tanya is seventeen, going on thirty. She's beautiful, doing well in school, but still wild as a buck. It's my hope she will attend the University, graduate, and get a good job. Then she can look for a man, but until then, I want her to study hard and become a successful career woman. How are your children?"

"Hamp is busy with his practice and his wife is busy with her social obligations in Woodbury. Maggie is busy climbing the corporate ladder at HSBC. They're on their own now and don't need their Mama, so when I was needed down here, I decided to come and stay for a while. Besides, I have yet to get used to the winters up there."

"Welcome back down south where all of us belong. I hope you'll stay awhile. Have you ever thought about encouraging Hamp and Maggie to move down here? We have banks, and we always need doctors."

"I don't think there's a snowball's chance they would pull up roots and move to Alabama. They're dyed in the wool New Yorkers."

"Come on, let's go to bed. We've had a long day, and we're both tired."

Rita was tired, and allowed Eric to steer her into his bedroom, and out of her clothes, and into his bed. After making love, she fell asleep in his arms.

After waking up and making love again, Rita, not having a change of clothes, wanted to get back to her house as soon as possible. She wanted to shower, put on clean clothes and feel human. Rita dressed in what she had on yesterday and left. Eric showered, dressed, and went back to the grocery store to pick up some items he had forgotten to get earlier. For the first time in a while, he felt happy and content. He loved Rita when they were in high school, and he was falling in love with her all over again.

Eric hadn't talked to Rita regarding how long she was going to be in Wentworth. He knew her life was on Long Island. She had married into a wealthy family, becoming a sophisticated New York socialite, and he was just a rube. While Eric would never consider moving to New York, maybe he might change Rita's mind about moving down south. As she said, her children were grown and doing just fine without her. She could visit them whenever she wanted to. He might even be talked into a short visit up there.

By the time Eric returned from a second trip to the grocery store, and put everything away, it was almost noon, and he hadn't eaten all day. He called Rita and left her a message, asking her to come over to his apartment for dinner. Having the ingredients to make his famous beef stew, Eric thought that would be a good first meal in the new place. While he was eating a ham and turkey sandwich, the phone rang, and it was Jimmy Harpo. He hadn't talked to Jimmy since the night they dined at Jake's restaurant, almost a week ago, the night of the tornado outbreak.

"What's going on with you, man?"

"I've rented an apartment until the house is ready, and I'm just about settled in."

"Why didn't you let us know you left Anabelle's house. You could have stayed with Ruthie and me?"

"Not knowing how long it would take for the contractors to get the house ready, I didn't want to intrude. So, you know about Anabelle and me; that we're no longer a couple?"

"The whole town knows you moved out of her house. On Friday, she went over to Jan's, got blubbery drunk on red wine, and threw up all over Jan's cream-colored sofa."

"Yuk. I didn't realize Anabelle had such a thing for me."

"Apparently she did."

"Well, guess who's back in town? Rita McDonald, Rita McDonald Fisher, that is."

"Your old flame?"

"Yep."

"Didn't her husband die not too long ago?"

"Yes, a little over a year ago."

"Ugh, are you two?"

"Yep," Eric said enthusiastically.

"Well, congratulations old buddy, that's awesome."

"Where's she staying?"

"At her home place. She purchased it from her siblings, and fixed it up. Her late husband left her millions."

"And she's loaded too, perfect."

"Rita was my first love, and I hope to make her my last love."

"If you two love birds can tear yourselves away from one another, let's go out and celebrate tomorrow night. What would you say to dinner at The Coach?"

"I'm in. I'll check with Rita and let you know."

"Okay, great!"

"I'll get back to you as soon as I talk to her."

When Eric finished eating his sandwich, he went back to the second bedroom which was going to serve as his home office. One of the amenities of his apartment complex was

Wi-Fi. Eric got his laptop set up, and was on the Internet in no time.

To earn a living, he did some freelance writing for a couple of hunting and fishing magazines. He had two articles due this coming Sunday, and he was going to have to spend some time in the next few days completing the articles. Thankfully, most of the research was done.

He still hadn't heard from Rita about dinner at his place tonight, but went on ahead and put the stew together. It needed to cook several hours before it would be ready to eat. Then he headed back to the computer to work on the articles. After a couple of hours, he still had not heard from Rita, and Eric wondered where she might be. He really needed to talk to her, and let Jimmy know if they would be able to go out to dinner with them tomorrow night. He'd give her another hour to return his call, then he would call her again. He was acting like a school girl and he knew it, but damn, he was in love.

Eric decided to check his Facebook page, and saw a post from Kristie linking to one of her political blogs. Should he unfriend Kristie, and Anabelle too? He didn't plan on seeing either one of them ever again. He had Rita now. She was far ahead of Anabelle in the looks department, and far ahead of Kristie in the net worth department.

CHAPTER 22

Kristie was clutching the bed sheets and sweating profusely, though she typically didn't sweat, even after vigorous workouts. It's just a thunderstorm, she said to herself; it's not even severe. November was secondary tornado season in the South. November was also her birth month, and it was an important month in college football. The weather could be anything from sub-freezing temperatures, to mid-80s, with tornadoes and strong thunderstorms not uncommon.

Kristie's heart was now racing. Should she get to an emergency room? What was happening to her?

Last week was bad for Kristie. Thinking she and Eric might be on the way back to getting together, she had texted him, asking for his thoughts on the Alabama – Texas A&M game. With football, he usually got back to her right away, but she never heard from him. She also had a birthday on November 8 which Eric failed to acknowledge.

After an emotional win over LSU at Baton Rouge, the Tide suffered a heart-wrenching four-point loss to SEC newcomer Texas A&M, and their hot-shot freshman quarterback, Johnny Manziel. The Tide's national championship hopes took a nose-dive, while Manziel was now being talked about as a viable Heisman Trophy candidate.

The day after her birthday, and the Friday before the game, she logged onto Facebook, and was greeted with a post that Eric was now in a relationship with Rita McDonald Fisher, his high school sweetheart. He didn't go back to Anabelle Martin, but moved on to Rita. But wasn't Rita married to some millionaire doctor, and living the life of a Long Island socialite?

Navigating to Rita's Facebook page, she saw that Rita listed Woodbury, New York as her current town. No marital status was listed. Next, Kristie decided to try tracking down a Dr. Fisher in Woodbury, New York, and found an obituary for a Hampton Fisher, III. His surviving spouse was Rita McDonald Fisher. Okay, she and Eric have hooked up again, but how? Was she back in Wentworth? Kristie was crushed and spent most of the next few days crying.

Maybe she would finally sell the property in Wentworth, and never go back. She could then take some of the money and buy a place on the Alabama Gulf Coast. Kristie had grown up with the old adage, "Don't make decisions when you're down, wait until things level out." She was going to sell the property one of these days, though. So, she might as well work on getting everything in order.

Kristie decided to spend part of Thanksgiving week in Wentworth where she would separate out the items still in the house that she wanted to keep and the pieces she would either sell, give away, or leave at the house. The house itself wasn't that valuable, but the acreage was. She would probably sell the property to an investor that would level the house and construct a shopping center or a parking lot on the property. Kristie didn't care. While she did have some good memories of growing up in Wentworth, there were some bad memories also. Now that Eric Channing and all of his gang were back together in Wentworth, it was certainly no place for her.

Jan Harpo Franklin and Rita McDonald Fisher were in the same graduating class at WHS, and Kristie thought they were also in the same high school sorority. Could things get any worse? But wait! What was going to happen to Anabelle Martin? Anabelle and the Harpo women were thick. Now that Rita was in the picture, things could get dicey, but that wasn't her problem.

On the Wednesday before Thanksgiving, Kristie's SUV was loaded with items she was taking to her house in Helena, along with stuff she was going to donate to charity. After Christmas, she would get rid of some of her old furniture and move her mother's charming antiques into her Helena home. In fact, Kristie was considering redecorating her whole house in antiques. She stayed Monday and Tuesday nights at the infamous Holiday Inn Express, and one of those nights, she had dinner at Jake Stanley's restaurant. He wasn't the manager on duty that evening, though. The other night, she had dinner at the popular upscale eatery, the Coach.

The Coach was well known throughout North Alabama. Having been operational since before Kristie was born, it was in its third location, and the food and service were better than ever. Since alcohol sales were now legal in Wentworth, the town was becoming a happening little place.

The entire time Kristie was in Wentworth, she failed to run into anyone she knew. She did have family and friends up there, and needed to see some of her older relatives, but not on this trip, just not in the mood. As she drove through the area, on the way up and on the way back, where her SUV was engulfed by the tornado, shivers ran up and down her spine, and she became tense. Was this something for which she would have to seek professional help, or would these feelings go away in due time?

Kristie spent Thanksgiving, her favorite holiday, with Natalie and Tim Rolland, a couple with whom she was close friends. After her Mom died, Kristie started this tradition, and really enjoyed her Thanksgivings, even though they were not anything like what they were when both her Mom and Dad were alive. Last year, when she and Eric were husband and wife, Eric went hunting with Jimmy Harpo, and some of the other guys, near Jimmy's place in Guntersville. In the early afternoon, she drove to Wentworth to have dinner with Eric and his only living aunt. It was okay.

On Saturday, the Iron Bowl, the annual Alabama vs. Auburn football game, was played in Tuscaloosa with Alabama winning easily. Cross-state rival, Auburn, was having a difficult season, and there were few Auburn fans in attendance. A big Bama victory usually made Kristie forget her problems, but this time, she couldn't get her mind off Eric and Rita. The thought of them making love every night made her nauseous. She prayed every day for God to give her strength to get over this, and she was confident, through her faith, that he would.

Kristie knew she needed to put all thoughts of Eric behind her. In January of this year, he had let her know he wanted out of their marriage. She had dwelled on the night she and Eric spent together, but was she just accepting crumbs? Was she trying to make something out of nothing? Men always slept with women who meant nothing to them. Did Kristie not mean anything to Eric? Guess not.

CHAPTER 23

Rita returned Eric's call a little after 5:00 pm, saying she would love to come over to his place for beef stew.

"So, you've become quite the cook since we were in high school?"

"If I do say so myself, I'm pretty good."

"Can I bring anything?"

"No, just your beautiful, sexy self."

"Okay," laughed Rita. "I'll be there around 6:00."

When Rita arrived at Eric's apartment, it was fragrant with the smell of the stew, which was simmering on the stove. After giving Rita a "hello" kiss, he told her he had not fully stocked his liquor cabinet yet, but offered her either Bud Lite, red wine, or white wine. She chose the red wine.

After pouring Rita's wine, Eric grabbed his partially drunk Bud Lite, and steered her toward the living room, where he had put a carton of French onion dip and a bag of potato chips on the rented coffee table. After turning the TV on to the news, and he and Rita sat on the sofa, with Eric putting his arm snuggly around her. The two of them watched TV for about ten minutes, before Eric excused himself to go make the cornbread.

"Are you sure there's nothing I can do to help?"

"Absolutely, I'll be through in here in a minute."

Eric put the cornbread mixture in his brand new cast iron skillet. When he and Kristie split, he got his clothes out of the house, but that was about all. The cooking utensils he added to their home were still at her house. The cast iron skillet Kristie now possessed, belonged to his mother. Maybe he would call Kristie and see if she would let him have it. He would gladly give her the new one if he could get his Mom's skillet back.

After setting the timer, Eric went back in the living room, and sat down by Rita. They talked about old times, and the old gang from high school. This jogged Eric's memory. Jimmy Harpo had invited them to dinner at The Coach for tomorrow night. When he asked Rita about this, she said she would love to go.

"It's going to be great getting back together with the old crowd."

"Weren't you and Jan Harpo, Franklin now, in the same sorority in high school?"

"Yes, and when I was at Vanderbilt, and she was at Auburn, we were in the same sororities. I know Sam married Kathryn Campbell, but did Jimmy marry a Wentworth girl?

"No, he married a girl from Russellville, Ruthie, I can't remember what her maiden name is."

The timer went off, and both went to the kitchen to get dinner on the table. Rita was quite impressed with Eric's beef stew and cornbread. For dessert, Eric cheated, and brought out a key lime pie he had purchased at the grocery store.

After they finished eating, Rita and Eric went back into the living room to watch some more television. After a couple of hours, they retired to Eric's bedroom for the night.

The next morning, Eric finished the hunting and fishing articles, and uploaded them to the magazine's website, while Rita made breakfast of French toast, eggs, and bacon. After eating, both retired to the bedroom for more lovemaking. Then it was ham and turkey sandwiches for lunch. Afterward, Rita left to go back to her house to get ready to go to the Coach for dinner.

"Maybe you should bring some stuff over here, so you won't always have to go running to your house," said Eric.

"I can do that, if you're sure you want me to."

Later that evening, Rita and Eric met Jimmy and Ruthie Harpo, and Jan and Jeremy Franklin, and Kathryn and Sam Harpo at The Coach Restaurant for dinner. There were squeals and tears, as Jan and Rita hugged one another after all these years. Rita and Ruthie met for the first time, and instantly liked one another. While Rita and Kathryn didn't really hang out in high school, they renewed acquaintances. Eric was grinning from ear to ear. He was with his friends, in his town, and with his girl. He hadn't been this happy in a long time.

The dinner was excellent, and the conservation was great. Neither Anabelle nor Kristie were mentioned. After dinner, Eric and Rita returned to her house where she and Eric spent the night making love. The next day was Thursday, and Rita said she really needed to spend the day with her Mom, but asked Eric to come over to her house later, so she could cook dinner for him. Her place was bigger, plus she had a well-stocked kitchen.

When Eric returned to his apartment, he fell into the bed and slept for a while, thinking about nothing but Rita. About 5:00, Rita called him and said she was home from her Mom's, and told Eric to come over when he was ready. This time, Eric decided to take a change or two of clothes with him. He would leave these clothes at Rita's. On the way over, he stopped at the drugstore, and purchased extra toiletries to also leave at Rita's house. He hoped this would prompt Rita to do the same at his apartment.

Rita prepared spaghetti, salad, and garlic bread for dinner. They both drank quite a bit of red wine, and once again, spent most of the night making love. While the two were certainly on the path to a permanent relationship, there was still the problem of having a mixed relationship. Alabama was playing Texas A&M on Saturday. A&M had a hot shot red-shirt freshman quarterback in Johnny Manziel. "Johnny Football" and the Aggies were enjoying their first season as members of the SEC. Also, on that day, Rita's team, Auburn, was playing its big border rival, Georgia. He and Rita would sit on the sofa together and watch football this coming weekend. Rita didn't like Alabama, and Eric didn't like Auburn. When they were kids in high school, it didn't matter, but now that they were mature adults, it did.

Eric spent Friday night at Rita's place. After a quick breakfast of coffee and toast, the two parted ways. Eric went back to the apartment to clean up a bit before Rita arrived to watch football. Rita went to visit her Mom.

The Bama – A&M game kicked off. Things weren't going well for the Tide, with Alabama finding itself down 21 to nothing in the first quarter. Johnny Manziel could do no wrong. Like true champions, though, the Tide began its comeback, but it was difficult. During the game, Eric was constantly squeezing Rita's knee. Then all at once, Eric leaned forward and exclaimed, "Kristie!" There on the TV screen was Kristie with a worried look on her face.

"Was that Kristie Tidwell, your ex?"

"That was definitely Kristie. Her seats are somewhat high up, and I never knew cameras would pan that high, but I guess they can focus on anything now."

"I don't remember much about her from high school. Did she go to Alabama?"

"Huh, what?"

"Kristie, did she go to Alabama?"

"Ugh, yes," said Eric as he picked up his cell phone. "I need to text her and tell her she was on TV, and not looking happy."

Snatching the phone out of Eric's hand, Rita said, "I thought Kristie was out of your system, and you didn't want to be with her anymore."

"I don't, but she was on TV."

"I'm sure someone else will inform her she was on TV. She's not the first person to ever be on television."

After that exchange, Rita seemed a bit upset. Eric put his arm around her, and told her she didn't need to worry about Kristie Tidwell anymore. He was through with Kristie, and all other women. Even though it took decades, the right woman for him had come along, and was sitting beside him.

Feeling what Eric was saying to her was true, Rita snuggled up close to him as the game was winding down. She despised Alabama and wanted them to lose. Alabama had a chance to take the ball into the end zone for the winning touchdown. When they got inside the ten, instead of running the ball, which had worked for them on this drive, they started passing, with quarterback A.J. McCarron throwing an interception at the goal line, thus sealing a victory for Texas A&M.

Eric, unhappy about the game, stalked around the apartment. Rita, secretly pleased, said nothing. Auburn was having a rough year, and lost to Georgia. Like Rita was when Alabama lost, Eric was pleased when Auburn lost to Georgia. No one was happy that day, but the two managed to get over things and spend yet another night making love.

Thanksgiving was the week after next, and Eric wanted to spend the holiday with Rita. Even though he was expected at his Aunt's house, he felt he could get out of that obligation, so he and Rita could spend a romantic day together. He would prepare the turkey and dressing, the sweet potato casserole, and the homemade rolls. Rita could bring desert and another couple of side dishes.

Gina, his first wife, and Tanya, his daughter were traveling to Atlanta to visit some cousins of Gina's. Therefore, Tanya would not be with him for the Thanksgiving weekend, but would be with him at Christmas.

When Eric approached Rita about their romantic Thanksgiving, Rita indicated Maggie, her youngest child, would be flying in the Sunday before Thanksgiving, and returning to New York the following Saturday. Rita was planning on having a quiet Thanksgiving with her Mom and Maggie. Hamp would remain in New York with his wife. Rita would fly back on Dec. 12 to spend some time with Hamp, and to do her Christmas shopping. She had not decided if she would spend Christmas in Alabama or in New York.

Eric was disappointed, and told Rita he thought it was about time she informed Hamp, Maggie and her Mom they were in a serious relationship.

"Ugh, Eric, I'm just not ready to tell Maggie and Hamp about us."

"And why not?"

"It's not the right time, it's just not."

"Are you ashamed of me?"

"Of course not."

"Then why don't you tell them, and tell your Mom too. Your Mom knows me. In fact, she wanted us to get married."

"That was then, and this is now."

Sensing Eric's angst, Rita put her arms around him, and said she cared for him, but things were moving a little fast. Hamp had been dead for only eighteen months. Maggie and Hamp IV were still getting used to the idea that he wasn't around. Maggie, especially, was having a hard time. Also, she had just been informed by "little" Hamp that he and his wife were expecting a baby. Maggie really needed someone to show her some love, and Rita wanted to be in New York for much of the pregnancy, and the birth of her first grandchild.

"Try to understand. I plan to be down here a lot, but I do have a life in New York."

Eric spent Thanksgiving with his aunt, and other family members. His sister, brother-in-law, and their two children were there. His brother, Roger, and friend Henry, who lived together in Hilton Head, flew into Birmingham from Charleston.

The night Eric left Kristie, December 23 of last year, he, Roger, and Henry had a fight of words at Kristie's home in Helena. Roger and Henry left before dinner was served, and Eric followed suit. That episode led to Eric and Kristie's divorce.

Before Thanksgiving Day, Eric's aunt informed Eric, Roger, and Henry there would be no arguing at her house. She was getting too old to put up with such things, and she wanted what few holidays she had left on this earth, to be pleasant.

Eric muddled through Thanksgiving Day. In fact, for the entire week, he had managed to keep himself from calling Rita.

On the Saturday after Thanksgiving, Alabama won the Iron Bowl in fine fashion, beating cross-state rival Auburn, 49-0. Alabama would be representing the SEC West in the SEC Championship game in Atlanta, the following Saturday. Kristie never texted him about the game. Guess she was over him and out of his life.

CHAPTER 24

After returning from church on the Sunday after Thanksgiving, Kristie had lunch, and then decided to take a nap. After returning home from the Iron Bowl, she stayed up late reading the reviews, visiting the various forums, and updating her Alabama sports blog. The game was certainly a great one, with Alabama winning 49-0. The Auburn coach was sure to be fired. The Alabama-Auburn college football rivalry was the most intense rivalry in the nation, with some thinking it was out of hand. It was always great to beat Auburn, but this year, the victory was tantamount to beating a directional school. There were few Auburn fans at the game, and it was obvious Auburn was a poorly coached team. While Kristie didn't like Auburn, and always cheered for whoever was playing them, she never wanted things to get this bad.

After her nap, Kristie went to her office to check her email, and saw one from Jordan Vann, the political talk show host. Because it had been three weeks since she emailed him, and not heard anything, she had given up on the possibility of making contact. In the email, Jordan said he had read her political blogs and found them fascinating. She had a good grasp on political issues, and pointed out many things the celebrity talking heads never mentioned.

He asked her to meet him for lunch the following Tuesday at one of Birmingham's trendy restaurants. At lunch, Jordan reiterated he felt Kristie had an excellent grasp of political issues, and he was willing to help her publicize herself and her blogs. However, he did remind her he was only a minor local celebrity, and couldn't guarantee success. Kristie told him that was fine, she would be appreciative of anything he could do for her.

"I'm traveling to New York City later this week to be a part of a group discussion on a major cable news channel. It's going to be filmed Friday evening, and will be aired on Sunday night. I'm flying up from Birmingham Friday morning, and flying to Atlanta Saturday morning for the game. Suzanne is meeting me in Atlanta. The stars and their folks are always looking for new faces for their group shows. In fact, I would be willing to bet that you would be put in the group on my recommendation. You might not get a chance to say anything, but at least you would be there, and have your foot in the door. Would you be interested?"

"Absolutely," exclaimed Kristie. "Where are you staying on Friday night?"

"The Hilton. Were you planning to go to the game in Atlanta?"

"I don't have a ticket, so I guess I'll fly back to Birmingham on Saturday morning."

"Let me make a couple of phone calls, and see if I can get a ticket for you. You can fly down with me on Saturday, and ride back to Birmingham with Suzanne and me."

"That would be great, Jordan," shrieked a disbelieving Kristie.

After one phone call, Jordan informed Kristie there was a ticket for her at face value. Kristie then checked the airlines, and booked on the same flight as Jordan, and reserved a hotel room at the Hilton where Jordan was also staying. It was all set; Kristie was accompanying Jordan to NYC on Friday. Hopefully, she would get a seat on the star's panel. Then she would be flying to Atlanta on Saturday morning to attend the SEC Championship game on Saturday afternoon. She would ride back to Birmingham with Jordan and Suzanne. Kristie had never met Suzanne, but that was okay. She was not interested in Jordan or seeing anyone who was married. She learned her lesson after Steve Conley.

Jordan and Kristie met at the Birmingham airport on Friday morning, and flew to New York. After checking into their rooms at the Hilton and having lunch, they walked to the news channel's headquarters. Jordan immediately sought out the producer of the Sunday night show and asked her about getting Kristie a seat on the panel. After the producer reviewed Kristie's "tell it like it is" blog, and asked Kristie a few questions, she indicated to Kristie could have a seat in the back. She probably wouldn't get to talk, but she would take up a space.

Before the filming began, the host met the panel in an informal setting. Kristie was introduced to him by the producer, and gave him her card displaying the website addresses for her blogs. He promised to visit the sites. Like the producer, he told Kristie she would not get to speak on this show, but if things developed, she might get a chance to speak during a future show. This was certainly all right with her.

While seated in the back row, and not having an opportunity to speak, Kristie did have the chance to raise her hand a couple of times. Seated next to her was a bespectacled young gentleman whose name tag read: Gunther Frazier, Nashville, Tennessee. When the filming was completed,

Kristie introduced Jordan to Gunther. Because Gunther was by himself in the big city, Jordan invited him to have dinner with him and Kristie that evening.

After having dinner at a French Bistro on Third Avenue, the threesome walked back to the Hilton to the main lounge, and listened to the Jazz band that was playing. Like Kristie, Gunther owned and managed a political blog he hoped would go viral someday. He was also a frequent guest on a local radio show. To get a steady paycheck, he worked in the Nashville office of a Congressman from Tennessee.

Gunther exchanged contact information with Kristie and Jordan, promising to contact them in the next couple of weeks. He then left to walk the short distance to his hotel.

The wheels were already turning in Kristie's head. Southern conservative black male, southern conservative white female. Could they possibly team up and make a splash? Lying in bed in her hotel room, Kristie could hardly get to sleep thinking about the possibilities ahead. All thoughts of Eric Channing and Rita McDonald Fisher were forgotten.

Kristie and Jordan caught an early morning flight out of LaGuardia to Atlanta. Jordan's wife met them at the Atlanta Airport, and the three of them drove to the Georgia Dome for the SEC Championship game against the Georgia Bulldogs.

The game was a tough one for Alabama, and at some point, it looked like they might lose. However, a young Georgia receiver made a huge mistake on the last play of the game, catching the ball in the field of play, short of the goal line. With no timeouts for Georgia remaining, the clock mercifully ran out, and Alabama was once again SEC champions, and headed to the BCS Championship game to play Notre Dame.

On the way back to Birmingham from Atlanta, the three of them were much too wrung out to talk politics and possibilities, but Jordan invited Kristie to his office the following Tuesday to discuss the possibilities that might lie ahead for them.

Much to her surprise, early Monday morning, an assistant to one of the channel's stars called, and informed her the star would like to set up a time for the two of them to talk on the phone. He had visited Kristie's blogs, and was impressed with her insight into political issues. If this conversation had positive results, it would be the first of many steps to Kristie becoming a news analyst. Kristie and the assistant set up the call for Thursday of this week.

On Tuesday, during her meeting with Jordan, the two of them discussed, at length, the possibilities. Even though Kristie's blogs were simplistic, they contained valuable information. During this meeting, they decided to touch base with Gunther Frazier in Nashville and arrange a meeting, if Gunther was interested. When Gunther didn't answer his cell phone, Jordan left him a message, asking Gunther to call him as soon as possible. Before Kristie left Jordan's office, Gunther returned the call and said he was definitely up to working something out with Kristie and Jordan. He had read Kristie's blogs, and liked them. He had also launched a political website himself, and asked Kristie and Jordan to visit his site. It was then decided they would have a conference call on Friday to further discuss possibilities.

Kristie spent most of Wednesday getting ready for her phone conversation with the cable news channel, which was scheduled for the following day. If this conversation went well, it could mean semi-fame for Kristie, plus a steady income stream. If my friends and enemies could see me now, thought Kristie. She envisioned Eric and Rita sitting on the sofa together while watching her on television. She also envisioned the Harpo clan and Anabelle Martin seeing her on

TV. They would probably switch channels, but that was okay. She wanted them to be angry.

Kristie's Thursday conversation with the prominent talking head went extremely well. So well, he wanted her to travel to New York before Christmas to meet with everyone. If things continued to work out, she would begin the New Year as a cable news analyst. It was decided Kristie would fly up to NYC on 12/12, and meet all day on Thursday, 12/13, with various personnel.

After their conversation, Kristie could hardly contain herself. However, she knew actually becoming a news analyst was a long shot. She had never held public office, nor had she ever been a journalist. Instead, she was just an ordinary person with strong political views, and a clear grasp on the issues. She decided not to confide in anyone except Jordan, not wanting to jinx things.

On Friday's conference call with Gunther in Nashville, Kristie and Gunther decided they would serve as guest writers on each other's' blogs. Gunther also agreed to do some appearances on Jordan's radio sow. All of this would begin after the first of the year. In the meantime, they would work on details.

CHAPTER 25

Rita took Maggie to the Birmingham Airport on the Sunday after Thanksgiving for her flight to New York City. Maggie was glad to be going home. You didn't get any more uncivilized than Wentworth and Birmingham. In fact, you couldn't get any more uncivilized than the entire state of Alabama? Who in their right mind would give a rat's ass about a stupid college football game? Her mom was planning to return to New York in the middle of December, and stay through Christmas and New Year's. Hopefully, she would come to her senses. Why didn't her Mom bring Grandmother McDonald up to New York? Any elder care facility in New York had to be better than the one she was in now.

On the plane ride, Maggie found herself sitting next to an older gentleman, possibly in his forties, who was also flying to New York City. When they arrived in Atlanta, Maggie and the gentleman, who said his name was Tim, walked to their gate together. While waiting on the Atlanta to NYC flight, they discovered they both worked for HSBC. Tim was the Senior Vice President of Auditing and Compliance, and Maggie was just a junior accountant. Impressed with Maggie, Tim indicated they had some positions open in his department for which she might qualify. They had their seats changed to where they were sitting next to each other on the plane. When Tim found out Maggie had spent Thanksgiving in Wentworth with her Mom and Grandmother, he indicated he and his wife had a friend who was born and raised in Wentworth, Kristie Tidwell-Channing.

"That name doesn't ring a bell, but my Mom might know her." Channing, thought Maggie. Wasn't that Eric's last name, the guy her Mom was seeing in Wentworth? The guy, who was her Mom's high school boyfriend.

Maggie decided she had better not trash the state of Alabama to this gentleman because he might be able to get her a decent promotion into his department.

When the plane landed, Tim suggested they share a cab to midtown where they both had apartments. When the taxi dropped Maggie off at her luxury apartment, Tim told her to send him her resume first thing tomorrow, and he would review it.

That night, when Maggie talked to Rita, she told her Mom about meeting a Sr. VP of HSBC on the plane, and he was interested in her for a position in his department. She also told Rita he and his wife had a friend who grew up in Wentworth, but Maggie couldn't remember the friend's name. Before saying good-bye, Rita told Maggie she had booked a flight to New York on Wednesday, December 12, and would be staying there until after New Year's.

Rita spent the night of December 11 at Eric's apartment. Eric had agreed to drive her to the Birmingham airport for her flight to New York City. He didn't see how he was possibly going to spend three to four weeks without her, especially with Christmas and New Year's ahead. They exchanged Christmas presents, ate a nice dinner which Eric prepared, made love, and went to sleep in each other's arms.

At 6:00 am on December 12, Eric was pulling into "departing flights" to drop Rita off, so she could catch the 7:00 am flight to Atlanta and then to New York. It was a direct flight. There would be a stop in Atlanta, but no changing planes. Because Rita had clothes and makeup at both houses, all she was taking on the plane was a stylish tote bag. After quickly kissing Eric, Rita got out of his truck, and headed into the terminal.

Eric put the truck in drive and began to move forward when an attractive brunette walked in front of his vehicle, with a rolling suitcase and a large carry-on bag. KRISTIE! Oh my, it's Kristie. Where's she going? She doesn't like to fly, so this must be something business related. Should he acknowledge her, or just let her go to wherever she was going? He decided on the latter. Did Kristie know about Rita? He and Kristie were still Facebook friends. He hadn't unfriended her yet, though he had thought about it. Eric exited the airport, and headed back to Wentworth for what was sure to be a lonely Christmas.

Rita arrived at the gate, and sat down to await boarding. Being in first class, she would be among those boarding first. Just as Rita sat down, an attractive brunette took a seat next to her. The brunette's clothes were stylish, but they screamed they were purchased off the rack. Plus, the large carry-on was middle class. Rita hoped the lady didn't want to talk. During this trip down south, she had her fill of southern accents, southern food, and southern middle class. She longed to return to New York, dine at some classy restaurants, and have conversations about anything but football and national championships.

There was something familiar about the brunette, but Rita could not put her finger on what it was. When the gate agent called first class, Rita got up and so did the brunette, who followed her onto the plane. The flight attendant greeted

Rita, escorted her to her seat, and asked, "Can I get you something to drink before we take off, Ms. Fisher?"

"Some coffee, please."

"Good morning, Ms. Channing, can I get you something to drink before we take off?"

"I'll have some orange juice."

The two women were seated across the aisle from one another; Rita was in row 2, seat B, and Kristie was in row 2, seat C. The flight attendant helped Kristie put her carry-on in the overhead bin after she had retrieved her tablet and a notebook. Then she went off to fetch Rita's coffee and Kristie's juice.

The flight took off from Birmingham on time and pulled up to the gate in Atlanta a few minutes early. Both Rita and Kristie stayed on the airplane. About half way through the flight to New York, the same flight attendant who greeted Rita and Kristie began talking to Kristie, and addressed her as Ms. Channing.

The brunette had a southern accent, lived in Birmingham, and was going to New York on business. Channing? It couldn't be, thought Rita. Never-the-less, she logged into Facebook on her tablet, to Eric's page, to Eric's friends. There was a picture of Kristie Tidwell-Channing. The woman sitting across the aisle was none other than Kristie, herself. She was still beautiful. Since she and Eric had been together, Eric had talked sparingly about Kristie, but did seem to take up for her whenever, Jimmy, Jan, Kathryn, and the others in their little group disparaged her.

She naturally wondered if Eric was still in love with Kristie. But Eric had already said he was falling in love with her all over again. That was going to be a problem. Rita was fond of Eric, and certainly enjoyed being with him and the others in Wentworth. But Eric in her world? It wasn't possible. Eric was as southern middle class as one could get, just a good old boy. She couldn't imagine Eric escorting her to the many balls and socials during "the season." Being a new widow, Rita's social life had taken a downward spiral, but she had been invited to several Christmas parties, and would be attending them with an elderly gentleman, who had lost his wife to cancer several years ago.

The Delta MD-80 set down at LaGuardia Airport precisely at noon. If the limo she had ordered was there, she could get to Maggie's office shortly before 1:00 pm, in time to have lunch with her daughter. Did she overhear that Kristie was going to mid-town Manhattan and staying at the Hilton? Should she offer Kristie a ride downtown in her limo? The two women had not spoken a word to one another, and it would be a little awkward to start up a conversation now, so Rita abandoned the thought. After deplaning, she called Maggie about having lunch. Unfortunately, the answer was no, she had some reports due the next day and had ordered in. However, Maggie indicated she would be up for a nice dinner somewhere, after she left the office. Would her Mom be agreeable to cooling her heels at her apartment for a while? There was plenty of food in the fridge for Rita to have lunch.

Rita agreed to meet Maggie for drinks at the Rose Club in the Plaza at 5:30. They would then decide on a place for dinner.

As Rita was getting into her rented limo, she saw Kristie Channing standing in line waiting for a taxi.

At 4:00, Maggie uploaded her reports to Google Drive for Tim to review. She was sure he would want her to change some things, but felt she had done a good job on her first major assignment since transferring to the department. Maggie could have become a pampered princess after college graduation, but instead, chose to go the career woman route. Her Dad's sisters often commented that she inherited her Mom's southern middle-class genes, and would therefore insist on working for a living. Maggie liked the excitement of mid-town Manhattan, and felt that working in the financial sector was a noble undertaking.

Currently, there were no men in her life, but there would be plenty of time for that once she established her career.

While spending Thanksgiving with her Mom in Wentworth, Maggie noticed her Mom had picked up a slight southern accent. She also thought her Mom had been seeing some of her old high school friends. Wentworth was a picturesque small town, and the people were friendly enough. Never-the-less, during her stay, she counted down the minutes until it was time for her to leave, and was glad her Mom would be in New York for the Christmas season.

CHAPTER 26

Kristie got into the taxi and told the driver to take her to the Hilton via FDR. This trip was going to be all business. If she made it as a political analyst, there would be plenty of time to wine and dine in the Big Apple. Her room at the Hilton was comfortable, and Kristie was planning to spend most of the afternoon studying for her many interviews tomorrow. It appeared she was interviewing with everyone except the janitorial staff. After a light lunch at one of the area's delis, Kristie called Tim to make plans for dinner that evening.

Because Kristie didn't want to make it a late night, Tim suggested they meet at the Rose Club at the Plaza for drinks at 5:00. Then he suggested they have dinner at a little French Bistro he and Natalie discovered called La Bonne Soupe. Kristie had been there many years ago and was agreeable to going there again.

After a couple of hours of studying, Kristie took a short nap and felt rejuvenated for her evening with Tim. She arrived at the Plaza a few minutes after 5:00, and found Tim waiting for her. As soon as she sat down, the waiter took their drink orders, a single malt scotch on the rocks for Tim and a cosmopolitan for Kristie.

Kristie was glad she had someone to hang out with this evening. Tim was a fun guy to be with, and he and Natalie were totally committed to one another, so there were no worries in that area. Tim had made reservations at La Bonne Soupe for 6:30, so they had some time to chill out at the Rose Club.

While Tim and Kristie were giggling about something totally insane, Tim suddenly stopped laughing, and a solemn look appeared on his face. "A young woman who works in my department, who I hired a short time ago, just walked in and sat down."

"So?"

"Even though this is New York City and the second decade of the twenty-first century, some things never change. She shouldn't see me in here drinking and laughing."

"Are you serious, Tim?"

"I am. Her name's Maggie Fisher. She's Long Island crème de la crème. There's a woman with her who looks to be about our age. That must be her Mom."

"Do we need to leave? It's not like this is the only bar in town. We could walk to the restaurant, and wait in the bar until our table is ready."

"Let's do that."

Tim signaled to their waiter for the check, which he paid promptly with cash. Kristie stood up and turned around at the same time Tim stood.

"You see the young girl with the light brown hair pulled back in a ponytail? That's Maggie. We'll have to walk by them to leave."

Kristie stared at the two women while thinking how strange it was that Tim, a senior Vice President, would have to leave a bar just because one of his subordinates was there.

As they were walking past the table, Maggie looked up and said, "Mr. Rolland. Hi."

"Oh, Hi, Maggie," replied Tim as Maggie stood up and shook his hand.

"Mr. Rolland, I'd like for you to meet my mother, Rita Fisher."

"How do you do, Mrs. Fisher."

Maggie seemed much more at ease with the situation than Tim did.

"Maggie, Mrs. Fisher, this is a friend of mine and Natalie's, Kristie Channing."

Kristie shook both Maggie's and Rita's hands, not seeming to remember Rita had sat next to her on the plane from Birmingham this morning.

Suddenly Rita blurted out, "Didn't I sit next to you this morning on the flight up from Birmingham."

"Why, I believe we did. Imagine running into you again, in a place like Manhattan," said Kristie with a thick southern accent.

"We need to be going," said Tim, as he took Kristie's elbow and steered her toward the door. "We have dinner reservations at 6:30. I'll see you tomorrow, Maggie. I plan to meet with Francine about the reports, and she'll get back to you."

"That sounds like a plan, Mr. Rolland. I'll see you tomorrow."

On the short walk to the restaurant, Kristie couldn't get it out of her head that the young woman seemed so together, and Tim seemed so shaken by their encounter.

When Kristie and Tim arrived at the restaurant, the maître de told them he could seat them. Kristie had forgotten about the incredible paintings which hung on the walls, and sat at the table taking it all in. Tim ordered a round of cocktails, while Kristie looked over the menu. Not wanting a heavy meal since she still had some studying to do, Kristie ordered the appetizer onion soup, with smoked salmon and cream cheese crepes. Tim, in the mood for red meat, ordered the Filet Mignon Au Poivre, along with the appetizer onion soup, plus a bottle of wine.

The food was excellent, but Kristie underestimated the serving portions. Of course, that didn't stop her from eating everything on her plate. When it was time for dessert, both declined. Kristie was starting to feel sleepy. It had been a long day for her, and she was expected at the studio at 9:00 tomorrow morning.

After bidding Tim good-night, Kristie went straight to her room, put on her nightgown and crawled into bed with her tablet and study materials. Tomorrow was going to be the most important day of her life, and she needed to bring her A-game. However, Kristie knew if this wasn't meant to be, it wouldn't happen. She said a prayer, asking God to help her do her best.

When staying in a strange place, Kristie, like some people tend to do, would wake up several times during the night; and this night was no exception. However, when her phone alarm went off, and her wake-up call came through, Kristie felt refreshed, and ready to face what was sure to be a challenging day.

"So, that's your new Senior VP?" asked Rita.

"Yes. He appears nice, but folks who work closer to him than I do, say he's hard to please. He'll be reviewing my first reports tomorrow, and I'm a little scared."

"Remember, honey, you don't have to work. You have a trust fund that will allow you to live a good life without working."

"I know, but I do want to contribute something to society, and create a little bit of wealth in my name."

"I guess you get that working-class attitude from me, and you know something; I'm glad. Are you ready to have dinner?"

"Sure, where do you want to go?"

"We don't have reservations anywhere, so how about Tommy Bahama's? The food's good, and on weeknights, you usually don't need a reservation.

On the cab ride to this somewhat famous eatery, located near Grand Central Station, Rita was thinking about Kristie Tidwell. Kristie was someone she knew in high school, who was in NYC for some reason. And she knew Maggie's senior VP.

Upon arriving at the restaurant, Rita and Maggie were seated promptly. To start off the meal, they ordered a bottle of Truchard Chardonnay, and each ordered a cup of the crab bisque. For their entrees, Rita ordered the macadamia nut encrusted snapper, while Maggie ordered the tiger shrimp pasta. For dessert, they split the pineapple crème Brulee.

During dinner, Rita talked incessantly about her trip to Wentworth, and how nice it was to get away from the hustle and bustle of the northeast. She also talked about a few of her high school friends, with whom she had managed to reunite. And she talked about Eric Channing.

Maggie knew her Mom and Eric Channing were inseparable in high school, and everyone thought they would get married after graduation. In the back of one of the dresser drawers, in one of the unused bedrooms, were pictures, and other memorabilia of her Mom's high school years. Eric Channing was handsome and played football. Maggie often wondered if they ever "did it." And if not, just how far did they go. Maggie didn't think her Mom knew that she knew about this stuff. She'd have to see if Eric Channing was on Facebook when she returned to her apartment.

Not wanting to head back to Long Island after dinner, Rita decided to stay at the family's downtown apartment. It was not as big as the one she had purchased for Maggie upon her college graduation, but it was fine when she needed a place to stay when she was in town. She kept clothes, makeup, toiletries, etc. at the apartment. There was also a fully stocked bar, and some non-perishable food in the cupboard and refrigerator. For the upkeep of the two apartments, she and Maggie shared one woman, who lived full time at Maggie's, but would clean and maintain the other apartment also.

When it came time to leave the restaurant, mother and daughter parted ways, with Maggie having a short walk to her Park Avenue apartment, and Rita having a short walk to the family's Forty-Seventh Street apartment. As Rita was entering the building, a gentleman was coming in behind her. The two looked at each other, and the gentleman said to her, "Didn't we just meet a little while ago at The Plaza?"

"We sure did," exclaimed Rita. "Do you live in this building?"

"Yes, on the fifty-fifth floor. What about you?"

"Oh, I live on the sixtieth floor."

When the elevator stopped at the fifty-fifth floor, Tim got out. The door closed, and the elevator sped up to the sixtieth floor. When Rita unlocked the door, and stepped into her city apartment, the lights came on automatically, and the temperature was a comfortable 72 degrees. Rita put her bag down, and retrieved her cell phone. There was a call and a voice mail from Eric, with Eric telling Rita he loved her and missed her.

Later that evening, when Rita was lying alone in the huge bed, she thought of Eric, and thought of Kristie Channing. She rode on the plane with Kristie, and then she had the misfortune of running into her at the Plaza. Whatever Kristie was up to, here in Manhattan, Rita didn't care.

CHAPTER 27

This had to be the longest day of Kristie's career. She began talking to mid-level personnel, then by early afternoon, she was interviewing with the stars. Everyone tried to trick her, and make her say the wrong things. Kristie, though, had studied well, and made it through without a major meltdown. The last meeting for the day was with the producers of the leading programs on the channel. In this session, they reviewed Kristie's interviews and informed her where she had excelled, and where she didn't.

While Kristie thought she had done well during the day, the meeting with the producers was not encouraging. They told her they needed a week to ten days to evaluate her performance before they could talk to her about an offer. In other words, don't call us, we'll call you. At the end, they thanked her for coming.

Well, no dinner tonight, thought Kristie. She had been too busy to call Tim during the day, and didn't feel like going out to celebrate, because there was nothing to celebrate. Even though the door was not shut and locked, the attitudes of the producers toward her, more than likely, meant she didn't make the cut.

Kristie walked the few blocks to her hotel. When she arrived at her room, she lay down on the bed and started crying. She did her best, but her best wasn't good enough. She was scheduled to fly to Birmingham first thing in the morning, and she couldn't wait to get home. But home to what? Jake McPherson had rejected her. Eric was in love with Rita, whatever her last name was now. Christmas was only a couple of weeks away, and she couldn't bear the thought. It was last December 23 that Eric, for no reason, had left her. Then later, he divorced her. Nothing in her life was positive. Maybe if she had just lived a simple life, things wouldn't be so bad.

There were folks in her graduating class who had stayed in Wentworth, took modest jobs there, married, had children, and went to church every Sunday. They were content. In foreseeable future, they could retire, where the remainder of their lives would be spent enjoying life and their grandchildren. Was that so bad? So many people had been mean to her over the years. When she was growing up in Wentworth, she felt, once she left that horrible place, her life would be idyllic forever. Nothing could be worse than living in Wentworth. Everything she did in college, up to when she was well into adulthood, was to keep from having to go back to Wentworth. Now, look at where she was.

As Kristie was rummaging through her makeup bag, she ran upon some Xanax she had forgotten about. How much was in the tiny bottle? Was there enough to "do the trick?" She could buy some booze from one of the many liquor stores in the area. The Xanax should do it. Her life was over, and she was a failure. The hotel staff would find her dead in the room. She didn't care. No one would care. Eric certainly didn't care. Her death, though, would haunt him for the rest of his life. But Kristie didn't care. Eric deserved it for the way he had treated her. Would the Harpo gang be glad to hear of her demise? That was a given. Rita McDonald Fisher could have Eric, but would she be satisfied after Kristie killed herself. She was going to do this to spite Eric, and to get back at so many folks who had treated her like dirt. They wouldn't have Kristie Tidwell-Channing to kick around anymore.

The gift shop at the Hilton sold alcohol, so Kristie went downstairs and purchased a pint of rum. As she was walking through the lobby, her cell phone rang. It was Tim.

"Hey, what's going on with you? You said you would call me if you had the chance."

"Hey, Tim. I was really busy all day. I thought I did well during the process, but the last meeting with the producers didn't go well. So, I guess I'm a failure."

"Do you know for sure they don't want you?"

"They said they would get back to me if they were interested."

"Uh. That's not exactly a rejection."

"I know. But I just have this feeling."

"Have you had dinner?"

"No."

"Well, let's have dinner. What are you in the mood for?"

"Tim, that's awfully sweet of you, but I'm really down tonight."

"Look, Kristie, how many folks even get a chance to audition to be a political analyst on the number one cable news channel? Cheer up. You don't know that they've rejected you. Anyway, it's not the end of the world, you're one of the sharpest individuals I've ever met. Come on, let me take you out to dinner."

"Oh okay."

"I'm in the bar. Come meet me."

"I'll be there in fifteen minutes."

Kristie went up to her room, put the rum away, freshened her makeup, and went down to meet Tim. When he asked her what she was in the mood to eat, she said steak.

"Ever been to Wolfgang's Steakhouse?"

"No, but I've heard it's excellent."

"It is. Want to go there?"

"Sure."

"Okay, but we're going to need reservations. I'll see if they can seat us within the next hour."

"Why don't we see if the concierge can get us in there."

"Good idea."

The young man at the concierge station made a call to the midtown location, and confirmed a reservation for them at 8:00.

Upon arriving at the restaurant, Tim and Kristie were seated at a great table. Tim ordered scotch and water, while Kristie ordered a cosmopolitan. For an appetizer, they split one of Wolfgang's famous crab cakes. Kristie ordered the filet mignon, and Tim ordered the rib eye. They also decided to split a Caprese salad. For sides, they both ordered jumbo baked potatoes, steamed asparagus, and split an order of burgundy mushrooms. Tim also ordered a bottle of Kendall Jackson Cabernet Sauvignon. After finishing their main courses, they were much too stuffed to order dessert, but each had coffee with a shot of Bailey's Irish Cream.

After dinner, Tim walked Kristie back to the Hilton and said to her, "I hope I've been a good host because it doesn't sound like the news executives were."

"Oh, you have."

"I'm sorry you didn't get to go to the theater, but maybe next time."

"If there is a next time," frowned Kristie.

"Natalie's flying up tomorrow, why don't you stay an extra night?"

"Do you know what the rates are here? I really can't justify that."

"Stay with us at the apartment."

"Tim, according to Natalie, your one bedroom with a kitchen, bath, and living room is smaller than my hotel room. Besides, you haven't seen Natalie since Thanksgiving."

"That's okay, it'll be fun."

"I know, but I'd really like to get home. I'm just not up to staying another day."

"Okay, I understand, but if you change your mind, call me in the morning."

"Okay, and thanks for everything. You've done more than you'll ever know."

Upon entering her hotel room, Kristie came face to face with the pint of rum and bottle of Xanax. Was she really going to do it? The state of mind she was in before Tim called her was scary. What had caused her mood to drop so low? Eric's abrupt rejection of her after she fell into bed with him last month? His new relationship with Rita McDonald Fisher?

Rita Fisher, Rita McDonald Fisher!

Kristie immediately called Tim's cell, and when he answered, she asked him the names of the mother and daughter they had seen at the Plaza yesterday evening.

"The daughter is Maggie Fisher, she works in my department, and is several levels under me. I sat with her on a plane from Birmingham after Thanksgiving, and began talking to her. I found out she worked at the bank, and had the qualifications for an opening in my department. I asked her to send me her resume, and I hired her. Her Mom's name, I believe, is Rita, and yes, Rita was born and raised in Wentworth. Do you know her?"

"I do remember her, she was a year behind me in school."

"I don't think I told you, but in addition to a mansion on Long Island, Rita Fisher rents a penthouse apartment in this building. I ran into her last night."

"Is that so?"

"Do I hear some bitterness?"

"Well, I might as well tell you, she was Eric's high school girlfriend, and now that Rita's husband is deceased, she and Eric have started seeing one another again. Her Mom's in assisted living in Wentworth. Rita purchased the family home from her siblings and was staying there in November. Eric is living in an apartment in Wentworth while his lake house is being built."

"Are you okay?"

"I don't know. It just seems weird. I wonder if Rita knows that was me with you last night."

"I think she probably does. Did you just now figure out who she was?"

"Yes. When the daughter introduced her as Rita Fisher, it didn't connect, her maiden name is McDonald. Just before I called you, it did."

"Kristie, please stay over an extra night. Natalie should be in from the airport by 1:00. The two of you can have lunch and shop. Or she can take you ice skating with her. She loves the rink at Bryant Park. We can go to the theater tomorrow night and then have a late supper."

"I don't know about three people in your apartment."

"Natalie's mom stayed with us for a week and so did Patrick."

"But they're family, and Jean said she would never do that again."

"If I took care of the hotel room for tomorrow night, would you stay?"

"Tim, I couldn't let you do that. Picking up the tab for the occasional dinner is great, but I can't ask you to pay for the hotel?"

"If I paid half of it, could you spring for the other half?"

"Are you sure?"

"Positive."

"First, I'll need to see if I can change my flight, and how much it's going to cost. Then I'll see if I can extend the reservation here. I'll do that now and let you know."

Kristie was able to change her flight for a nominal fee, and extend her stay at the Hilton for an extra day. When she called Tim to tell him the good news, she asked him if he and Natalie wanted to spend the night in her hotel room since it was bigger than his apartment. And she could stay at the apartment.

Laughing, Tim told Kristie, "I'll tell Natalie to call or text you as soon as she gets off the plane."

"Sounds like a plan to me. I'll talk to you tomorrow. And Tim, thanks for everything, you've made me feel so much better."

Kristie had just avoided disaster, actually worse than disaster. Earlier that evening she had wanted to kill herself. Kristie believed that killing oneself is a sin and you would certainly go to hell for doing it. At this point, she really wanted to go to sleep, but the thought of Eric with Rita McDonald Fisher was driving her crazy. And the fact the cable news channel was not interested in her as a political analyst, made her feel worse. She'd have fun with Tim and Natalie tomorrow, but what next?

The next morning, Kristie was awakened by the ringing of her cell phone. It was Tim, telling her Natalie's plane had departed on time, and she should be in midtown, and ready for lunch around 1:00. "When she gets off the plane, she'll text you where to meet her. There are several places she likes to go for lunch, and they're all in this area."

"Great, I'll be ready."

After showering and getting dressed, Kristie researched and wrote a blog post for one of her political blogs. She also wrote an article for Gunther Frazier's political blog, per their agreement. With the presidential election having taken place last month, material for articles was plentiful. Kristie also managed to write a post for one of her college football blogs. With Alabama, once again, playing in the BCS national championship game, she easily wrote the post.

Shortly after 12:00, Natalie texted Kristie, and suggested that they meet at a quaint French restaurant for lunch, Le Parisien. When Kristie entered the place, Natalie had not yet arrived, so she got a table and ordered a glass of Chardonnay. Natalie arrived shortly, and the two friends had a great time at lunch. They had salads, entrées, and desserts since the three of them would be attending the theater later this evening and would be eating a late supper afterward. Tim had been able to secure tickets for *Mama Mia*, and made reservations for later at Joe Allen. Kristie loved *Mama Mia*.

After witnessing a spectacular performance of *Mama Mia*, at Joe Allen, the three split the guacamole and steak tartare appetizers. Tim ordered a bacon cheeseburger, Natalie ordered the New England lobster and crab roll, while Kristie, a salmon lover, ordered the smoked salmon and scrambled eggs. To drink, Tim had a Brooklyn Sorachi Ace while Natalie and Kristie split a bottle of Blue Quail Chardonnay. Tim and Natalie walked Kristie to her hotel, and told her they would see her two days before Christmas, when they would be returning to Birmingham for Christmas and New Year's.

CHAPTER 28

The plane ride home was uneventful, and Kristie drove into her garage late Saturday morning. Now that she was home, and back to the real world, the events of the last two days weighed upon her hard. Because she failed to impress the news executives, she would not become a news analyst. Rita and Eric were now a couple, and probably having a great time with their high school friends, most notably Jimmy Harpo and his sister, Jan Franklin.

After moping through Saturday, Kristie, once again, started writing her blog posts for the following week, and posted one Gunther Frazier had written as a guest blogger. Christmas would be here in less than two weeks, and she would have to endure December 23, the anniversary of the day Eric walked out on her. One day, they were a happy couple, the next day, they were separated with Eric having nothing to do with her.

Even though her house was decorated, Kristie didn't feel much like celebrating Christmas in Birmingham with Jennie, Phil, and their large family. Without much thought, she made reservations at a condominium on the Alabama Gulf Coast. She would drive down on December 23, and remain through the January 2. Kristie planned walk on the beach, weather permitting, stare out at the ocean, and continue to do her work. Work was something she couldn't put down. Her Dad had always told her that owning a business meant never getting a day off, and he was right. Kristie did, however, love her freedom, and hoped she would never have to go back to the corporate grind again.

Both Natalie and Tim, along with Jennie and Phil tried to talk Kristie out of spending the holidays away from Birmingham, and the folks who cared about her the most. Kristie, though, felt she needed to get away, but Natalie sensed something wrong and was not inclined to let Kristie go off by herself, especially down to the coast. Tim further indicated that he sensed something wasn't right with Kristie the night they had dinner at Wolfgang's, after her last round of interviews. Kristie sometimes drank a little more than she should, and she was definitely upset about Eric and his new/old girlfriend. She was also upset over the pending rejection by the number one cable news channel in the country.

Natalie and Tim's oldest child, a daughter, would be spending Christmas with her fiancée's family, and Patrick, would be working over the holidays. There would be no visitors over Christmas, so Natalie and Tim decided they would show up at the coast with Jean, Natalie's Mom. They had rented a two-bedroom condo in the same unit where Kristie was staying, and Natalie hoped Kristie wouldn't do anything stupid before the day after Christmas, when they were due to arrive.

Kristie arrived in Orange Beach, Alabama on December 23, a cool, dreary day. After going to the grocery store and stocking the condo for the ten days she would be there, she drove to one of her favorite restaurants for an early Saturday evening dinner. The restaurant was practically deserted, and welcomed Kristie with open arms. Kristie dined on one of her favorite gulf coast entrée's, blackened snapper. After dinner, she went back to the condo, and read for the rest of the evening, trying not to think about what happened one year ago.

CHAPTER 29

Eric had spoken to Rita Fisher only a few times since she left Wentworth, and returned to her home and children in New York. Rita, a New York socialite, was busy attending parties and preparing for Christmas. While Rita planned to spend Christmas with her children, Hamp IV and Maggie, she had no plans for New Year's Eve or New Year's Day. On a whim, Eric decided to invite Rita down for New Year's. They could drive to the Alabama Gulf Coast, and hang out. Eric knew it would sound dorky to someone living on Long Island, but Rita was Alabama born and bred. Besides, they had some great times at Gulf Shores, Alabama when they were in high school.

Eric's thoughts went back to the summer before his senior year in high school. Rita went to Gulf Shores with the Wentworth High School cheerleaders for a cheerleading seminar. While the girls were chaperoned by the faculty cheerleading sponsor, she was lenient, and let the girls do almost anything they wanted to do, except stay out after midnight. The boyfriends drove down separately, and stayed in a hotel a couple of blocks away from the rented house where the girls were staying.

Eric and Rita had been seeing one another about three months, but Rita had never taken all her clothes off when they were together. One night, while the guys were there, he and Rita walked down to the beach, and spread a blanket on the sand. In what seemed like less than five minutes, both were totally out of their clothing. They didn't go all the way, but both enjoyed the delights of young sex. The moon was bright, and Eric could see the outline of Rita's body lying on the blanket. It was the most beautiful sight he had ever seen in his life. Even though she had aged, Rita was still the most beautiful woman he had ever been with. Actually no, Kristie was the most beautiful woman he had ever been with. Even though they were older when they began their relationship, Kristie had no wrinkles, her hair was thick, dark, and luscious, and her body, while on the plump side, was quite sexy. Eric felt he could hold onto Kristie without fear of her breaking.

Why was he thinking about Kristie when it was Rita he loved? He was going to call Rita now, and asked her to come down for New Year's. On Christmas Eve morning, Eric did call Rita, and she answered her phone. She was glad to hear from Eric, but was busy organizing everything for Christmas

Eve dinner at her house, and for Christmas dinner the next day, also at her house. Servants and caterers were to arrive that afternoon, and she was directing the household maintenance staff in some last-minute preparations.

When Eric invited her to come down for New Year's, Rita was caught off guard. She didn't have an escort for the New Year's Eve party at the club, but Harold, the elderly gentleman who had accompanied her to the season's parties, would likely be her escort for New Year's Eve. None of this was confirmed, though. If Harold didn't ask her to New Year's Eve at the club, her social standing would be greatly diminished. Reluctantly, Rita said okay. They would talk the day after Christmas to firm up their plans.

Eric spent Christmas Day with his aunt, his siblings, and his cousins. With New Year's looming and Rita constantly on his mind, Eric couldn't wait until the next day when they would discuss their plans.

When Eric and Rita talked on the day after Christmas, they agreed she would fly into Birmingham on December 28, where they would meet and drive to Orange Beach, a trendy coastal community just east of Gulf Shores. Because Rita needed to be back in New York shortly after the first of the year for a board meeting of one of the many charities she supported, it was decided she would fly out of Mobile on January 2. Eric couldn't wait, and booked a condo in Orange Beach.

Kristie spent Christmas Eve, another cloudy chilly day, walking on the beach, reading, watching TV, and working. Even though the next day was Christmas, and even though she was spending it alone, she wasn't bothered by it as much as she thought she would be.

On Christmas day, the sun was shining, but it was still chilly. Kristie began her day by walking on the beach, after having a light breakfast of toast and yogurt.

For Christmas dinner, she roasted a small turkey breast. To go with the turkey, was cornbread dressing and a sweet potato casserole, both from Lambert's. She also made a green bean casserole and a corn casserole. While Kristie loved cranberry congealed salad, she decided to keep things simple and go with canned whole berry sauce. The wine was a wood-flavored chardonnay. For desert, she had chocolate cake and vanilla ice cream. Of course, there were leftovers, and she made individual plates to eat later.

Dinner was ready about 3:00 pm, and Kristie ate alone at the kitchen table in the condo. This was only the second time Kristie had spent Christmas alone, with last year's disaster being the first. She wasn't depressed, and made it through the day just fine. Would her Mama and Daddy approve of her running off to the beach, and not spending Christmas with Jennie and her family? Probably not, but Kristie didn't think she could have dealt with their huge celebration.

This was good. 2012 was a bad year for Kristie, and she needed to heal. Even though she and Eric had divorced, she was still in love with her ex-husband. Six weeks ago, she spent a steamy night with him after a tornado had flipped her SUV around, with the SUV not even incurring a scratch. She was in the SUV, but didn't have a scratch either. Then Eric lost interest, and dumped her for his high school sweetheart, Rita McDonald Fisher, now a wealthy widow and New York socialite.

Kristie, while attempting to publicize her political blogs, had a day of interviews with the number one cable news channel, for a news analyst position. But at the end of the day, was not given any encouragement. She had blown that, blown her marriage, and blown any attempts of getting back together with Eric. The week between Christmas and New Year's Day would be one for Kristie to pull it together, and decide what she wanted to do for the rest of her life. While she was far from broke, she couldn't spend the rest of her life with little or no income.

Checking her Facebook page while high off Chardonnay, Kristie saw that Anabelle Martin had requested friendship. Why in the world does Anabelle Martin want to be friends with me, thought Kristie? Anabelle had never uttered a kind word to her in her life, and Kristie had never said anything kind to Anabelle, for that matter. Kristie immediately deleted the friendship request, wanting nothing to do with the bitch. Since Anabelle was also dumped by Eric, she might be lonely. But that wasn't Kristie's problem, she didn't care.

The next morning, the day after Christmas, Kristie was awakened by the ringing of her cell phone. It was a New York City area code. The woman on the other end of the line asked Kristie if she would hold for the director of news and politics. Kristie was instantly jolted awake. Her heart was beating rapidly. The director greeted Kristie with a thick New York accent, making small talk with her for about five minutes. Then he told Kristie the channel's political crew and producers were impressed with her, and with her knowledge about politics, especially ideology. They also liked her southern accent and her dark hair. Plus, the channel had never featured a news analyst from Alabama, and the top brass were looking forward to exploring her grasp on the issues. Kristie would do a three-month trial in which they could cut her loose at any time. After the three months were over, they would re-evaluate, and if she was doing well, they would discuss a long-term contract. When the director informed her about the compensation for the first three months, Kristie was blown away. The compensation was based on appearances. For the first three months, about a third of her appearances would be in New York, and the rest would be remote from any network affiliate. Since Kristie lived in Birmingham, most would be from there. When she did travel to New York City, all expenses would be paid.

For orientation, and her first round of appearances, Kristie would have to be in New York on Monday, January 14. Would that work for her? "Absolutely," exclaimed Kristie. The director told her his assistant would be in touch about travel arrangements and other details. He then thanked Kristie for her time, and indicated he was looking forward to working with her.

After hanging up, a jubilant Kristie stood up and twirled around. They did like her, and she had the chance to be on TV. People would know who she was, some might even ask for her autograph. Wow! This was the most exciting thing that had ever taken place in Kristie's somewhat miserable life, and sadly, though, she had no one to share it with.

She had run away from friends and family for Christmas, because she felt sorry for herself, and didn't want to be around folks who were joyously celebrating that most wonderful time of the year. Maybe she would call Natalie. Maybe Natalie could plan her visits to NYC when Kristie was going to be up there. She called Natalie's land line to share the good news, but there was no answer.

To burn some calories, Kristie walked on the beach for a while, then did some research for her blogs. For lunch, she had leftover turkey and dressing. With the sun shining, and the temperature rising, Kristie drove to Fort Morgan, located at the western tip of Baldwin County, where Mobile Bay merged with the Gulf of Mexico, convertible top down, of course. As she headed to the historic landmark, Kristie couldn't help but notice the serenity of Mobile Bay, one of the nation's treasurers. The Alabama Gulf Coast was Kristie's happy place. Maybe she would sell her property in Wentworth, and buy a place down here. There was nothing left for her in Wentworth, and if she continued as a news analyst, she might be able to enjoy life without worrying about money.

While Kristie was staring toward Dauphin Island, her phone beeped, indicating she had a text. It was from Natalie, and said she, Tim, and Jean, Natale's Mom, had just arrived, and settled in their rented condo, in the same building where Kristie was staying. What a surprise! She was no longer alone. Turning the convertible around, Kristie headed back toward Gulf Shores and Orange Beach. She couldn't wait to see Natalie, Tim, and Jean, and tell them her big news.

But why did they all or a sudden appear on the Alabama Coast, thought Kristie? Did they come down here because they were worried about her? There was no need to worry about Kristie. Her life had been riddled with disappointments, but she had always managed to survive.

After learning about Kristie's offer to be a news analyst, Natalie, Tim, and Jean were thrilled, telling her she deserved this break. Then they decided on a restaurant, Cosmo's, one of Kristie's favorites, to have dinner and celebrate.

CHAPTER 30

Rita Fisher stretched and yawned in her huge bed in her huge mansion on Long Island. It was the day after Christmas, and she was planning to spend it reading and relaxing. Because Maggie had to work today, the chauffeur drove her to her apartment in the city last night. Tomorrow she would pack for her trip to Alabama, then she would fly down and meet Eric in Birmingham the following day. While Eric was well past twenty-five, he was a virile man and a great lover. Harold, on the other hand, was much older than Rita, and had never attempted anything but light kisses. Rita did wonder, however, why Harold had not phoned her about New Year's Eve.

As if on cue, Rita's cell phone rang, and it was Harold. He apologized for not having called her before Christmas, but his older sister who was a widow, and lived in Philadelphia, had suffered a stroke on December 23. He had been in Philly with her and her children. Because he was planning to stay in Philadelphia through New Year's, he invited her to come down and spend the evening as a guest of his niece and nephew at one of the Philadelphia's prestigious country clubs. Rita declined, telling Harold she was flying to Alabama day after tomorrow to check on her Mom, who had not been feeling well.

Rita had told Harold a little white lie, justifying it because she would surely check on her Mom while she was in Alabama. Besides, Rita was looking forward to feeling Eric's body next to hers. She had once loved him, but that was so long ago. Her life had changed radically, and while she was physically attracted to Eric and might even still love him a little, there was no way the two of them would ever be a couple.

Snuggling up under the covers with her book, Rita thought about her relationships with Eric, both in high school and earlier this fall. She lost her virginity to him when she was sixteen, and they were one of Wentworth High's most beautiful couples. Now, both had aged, but Rita was still a lovely woman and Eric, even though he had aged, was still a good-looking man.

On the morning of December 28, Rita was at the gate at LaGuardia airport awaiting the call for first class passengers for the direct flight to Birmingham through Atlanta. The last time Rita had flown, it was from Birmingham to New York;

and Kristie Tidwell-Channing, Eric's second wife, had been on her flight. How had Eric managed to get together with Kristie?

Although Kristie was pretty in high school, and still was, she didn't hang out with their crowd, and wasn't in a high school sorority. Eric's friends, Jimmy Harpo, Dean Abercrombie, and Jake Stanley disliked her. So did Jimmy's wife, Ruthie, and his sister, Jan Franklin. They claimed she was snobby, even though Jan and Ruthie were also snobs. Jake Stanley did acknowledge he and Wiley Martin tripped her and caused her to fall on some gravel when they were in the seventh grade. After she fell, he and Wiley laughed at her and ran away, refusing to help her up. Jake then recalled the time they were going to kidnap Kristie and force her to drink whiskey. When she passed out, they were going to tie her up and throw her into some snake-infested woods near a local creek, hoping the snakes would bite her to death. Jake admitted it was Johnny Morton who talked them out of doing that.

Johnny actually liked Kristie, not as a girlfriend, but as a classmate. He and Kristie attended the same church and both were active in the youth organization. Kristie was a faithful member, and a caring person. For many years before his

AIDS-related death, Johnny thought about what he, Wiley, and Jake planned to do to Kristie, and those thoughts haunted him almost every day until he died.

One evening, when Rita and Eric were having drinks with Jake at the restaurant he managed, Jake said, maybe if they had thrown her into the woods and she had died of snake bites, all their lives would be a lot better. Jake's comments infuriated Eric. He threw two twenty dollar bills on the table, grabbed Rita by the arm, and led her out of the restaurant. Several days later, Jake called Eric, and apologized for his comments about Kristie, and Eric accepted.

Rita's phone suddenly began ringing. It was Hamp. Shari, his wife, had been rushed to the hospital because she was hemorrhaging. She had not lost the baby yet, and the hospital staff was doing everything they could to prevent a miscarriage. Rita told Hamp she would get to the hospital as soon as she could cancel her plane reservations and grab a taxi. Rita cancelled her flight, but her luggage couldn't be retrieved. It would travel to Birmingham, then back up to New York, where it would be delivered to her home sometime that night.

Driving to Birmingham to meet Rita three days after Christmas, Eric fantasized about once again being with Rita and holding and stroking her soft body. They would be together tonight at the Embassy Suites in the Birmingham suburb of Hoover. Tomorrow, they would drive to Orange Beach, Alabama to spend a few days of unencumbered bliss. Maybe he would ask Rita to marry him.

Eric pulled into the short-term parking lot at the Birmingham airport. Even though he couldn't be at the gate when she deplaned, he would at least be at the terminal to greet her.

Rita's flight landed, and passengers were making their way up the concourse. Rita was not among them. Upon checking with a gate agent, he was informed that all passengers had deplaned and baggage was being claimed. Could they have possibly missed one another? Eric rode down the escalator to baggage claim, and there was no Rita. He waited until all the bags from her flight were unloaded. What he didn't notice was a set of Louis Vuitton luggage outside the baggage claim office. That luggage belonged to Rita Fisher, who abruptly canceled her flight from NYC to Birmingham. The bags were to be flown back to NYC where they would be delivered to Rita's Long Island home.

Eric was crushed. Had Rita stood him up? He called her cell phone, but received no answer. Should he drive back to

Wentworth? What was going on? He and Rita had a great time when she was down here just a few weeks ago.

As Eric was climbing into his truck, his phone went off. It was Rita. "Sweetie, where are you?"

"I'm at the hospital with my son and daughter-in-law. Shari started hemorrhaging early this morning, and she's currently fighting to save the baby."

"You're in New York?"

"Yes. It doesn't look like I'm going to make it down there. I'm so sorry, but I need to be with Hamp and Shari now. Please pray for us?"

"Oh, absolutely, babe!"

"I really can't make any plans for the New Year holiday. My priority is to be with family."

"I understand."

Eric had a rented condo in Orange Beach, but there was no one to share it with. Should he cancel and lose some of his deposit, or go on down and enjoy the beach? He had friends in Gulf Shores, maybe he could hang out with them.

Eric stayed by himself at the hotel in Hoover. The next day he drove down I-65 to Gulf Shores Parkway and onto Orange Beach, where he checked into the one-bedroom condo he and Rita were to share. A guy he went to

Wentworth High with was living down here. Perhaps he could hang out with him and his wife during the evenings.

Eric parked his truck in one of the parking places, got out, retrieved his bag and his ice chest from the back, and went to find his unit, not noticing the black convertible also parked in the lot. After looking the place over, he placed a call to Rita to see how things were going in New York. Shari had not lost the baby, but things were not so great. If the baby remained alive, Shari would probably be on bedrest for the remainder of the pregnancy. As a result, Rita would remain in New York.

Shit, thought Eric. He might not get to see Rita until summer. Maybe he would go up there for a visit.

After getting settled into the condo, Eric went to a liquor store and stocked up on booze for the next few days. He then stopped at one of the area supermarkets, and bought breakfast and lunch food. He anticipated having dinner out at the great seafood restaurants on the Alabama Gulf Coast, but breakfast and lunch would be at the condo.

CHAPTER *31*

December 29 was a mostly cloudy day in Orange Beach, Alabama.

After awakening, showering, and having yogurt, toast, and orange juice for breakfast, Kristie took a quilt with a book and her tablet down to the beach. After walking on the beach for a while, she stretched out on her quilt to enjoy the slightly cool to mild weather. In a few minutes, her eyelids became heavy, and she fell asleep on the white sands of the beaches of the Alabama Gulf Coast, thinking about the Bob Dylan lyrics, "How many seas must a white dove sail, before she can sleep in the sand?"

What seemed like minutes later, Kristie woke up to see Natalie and Tim staring down at her. "We're going to drive to Pensacola and have lunch at the Margaritaville Hotel, want to go with us?" asked Natalie.

"Thanks, but I think I'll hang out here. I've been there before. The food's good, though."

"Is there someplace else you would rather go, we're not stuck on going there?"

"No. I just have a lot on my mind right now."

"Kristie, you have to eat, and you've been moping around since we got here. In a couple of weeks, you're going to the Big Apple to begin a new career, what's with you?"

"I don't know."

"Is it Eric?"

"Well, sort of."

It was Tim's turn to chime in. "That son of a bitch doesn't deserve you. You're going to be a star, I just know it. Enjoy this time in your life. Quit moping around and drinking yourself to sleep at night. Eric Channing was never good enough for you. He's small potatoes, Kristie. Get up. If you don't want to go to Pensacola for lunch, what about Bahama Bob's, we haven't been there yet?"

"Bahama Bob's does sound good, and it's closer, okay."

Kristie gathered up her stuff, took it to the condo, and met Natalie and Tim in the parking lot. As the three of them were turning left onto Perdido Beach Boulevard, a silver Chevrolet pickup truck was turning into the condo parking lot.

CHAPTER 32

Two years ago, Eric and Kristie were seeing each other, and went to a party at Jan Harpo Franklin's house. The party was a disaster. To avoid having to drive any distance after the party, Eric reserved a room at the Wentworth Holiday Inn Express. When he and Kristie returned to their room after the party, Kristie, angry about some of the things happening at the party, started to leave. Then something got into him. After grabbing Kristie and trying to push her down on the bed, she stumbled and fell to the floor. In seconds, a manager was knocking on the door. Kristie left and drove to her home in Helena, but the manager called the Sheriff's Department, and a deputy escorted Eric to his home in the John's Landing area of West Wentworth County. That had to be one of the worst evenings of Eric's life.

Last year, he and Kristie were still married, but he had left her on December 23, after having words with his gay brother Roger and Roger's partner before dinner at Kristie's house. He drove straight to Orlando and spent both Christmas Eve and Christmas Day there. The day after Christmas, he drove to Key Largo, spending New Year's Eve in a Key Largo beer joint.

Maybe he would spend this New Year's Eve at the Flora-Bama. While the famous roadhouse on the Alabama/Florida state line carried both good and bad memories for Eric, most were good. If Shari remained in the hospital, Rita would probably spend New Year's Eve with her and Hamp. If Shari was released, he wasn't sure how she would spend the evening.

His thoughts turned to Kristie, who still turned him on. He wondered what she was doing for New Year's Eve. Uh-oh, before they began seeing one another, Kristie spent many New Year's Eves right here on the Alabama Gulf Coast. Could she possibly be down here now? Even if she was, the chances of him running into her were negligible. She always stayed at Island House Hotel, but Island House was next door. Shit. He knew where Kristie's her favorite restaurants were, so he wouldn't go to those places, but he also liked those places.

Why was he worrying? Kristie's probably not here, and if she is, the chances of him running into her were slim to none. Eric put Kristie out of his mind, and grabbed a beer from the refrigerator, and turned the television on to the news.

His phone rang, and it was Jimmy Harpo. "What's up Jimmy?"

"Nothing much. Are you and Rita in Orange Beach yet?

"I am, but Rita's not here, her daughter-in-law is pregnant and having complications, so she's not coming."

"I'm sorry about her daughter-in-law, but maybe it's for the best. Anabelle is at her beach house on West Beach. She sold her place in Navarre and bought something there."

"Oh shit."

"Yeah, since you dumped her and started seeing Rita, she's been drinking heavily. The whole town knows it. She's also put her Wentworth house up for sale. She says she hates Wentworth, and once she leaves, her goal in life is to never set foot here again."

"Well, I'm in Orange Beach, so I probably won't run into her, but guess who else has been known to spend the New Year's holiday on the Alabama Gulf Coast?"

"You gotta be kidding, Kristie?"

"Yeah."

"Do you know if she's there?"

"No, but she usually stays at Island House Hotel, and Island House is next door to the condo where I'm staying."

"You may run into her on the beach."

"I know, but I'm not going to let Kristie interfere with this trip. Besides, I'm planning to go to NYC to visit Rita as soon as things settle down with her daughter-in-law."

"Okay buddy, stay safe and keep away from the women."

"Sure thing."

It was pleasant outside, and Eric decided to sit on the deck, and surf the net with his tablet. On Facebook, he asked that his friends pray for Rita's daughter-in-law. The sun, which had come out after a mostly cloudy day, was setting, and the sky was beautiful with various shades of crimson, coral, turquoise, and gun metal gray. This is what Kristie would call a fire and ice sunset. It was December, and the sun would be setting on the water. So, Eric decided to walk down to the beach and watch it.

As he was standing up, he noticed what appeared to be two ladies sitting on a blanket on the beach, watching the sunset also. He couldn't tell if they were young or old, large or small, but one was definitely a brunette.

The elevator, going down, opened, and there stood Tim Rolland.

"Tim."

"Eric."

The two guys shook hands.

"How are you," asked Tim.

"Fine."

"Where are you headed?"

"Out to the beach to watch the sunset."

"Kristie's out there with Natalie, and you're the last person she needs to see. She's been depressed lately, and I don't want you upsetting her."

When they got to the ground floor, Eric told Tim he wouldn't go out to the beach. And Tim told Eric he wouldn't tell Kristie that he was, not only in Orange Beach, but staying in the same condominium complex where they were staying.

Instead of heading out to the beach to watch the sunset amid streaks of coral and gun metal gray, Eric got in his truck and headed west toward Gulf Shores. He called his friend, Jeff, to see what he and his wife were doing this evening.

When Jeff answered his phone, he assumed Eric was with Rita. "Well, when did y'all get in?"

"Y'all? It's just me. Rita had a family emergency. Her pregnant daughter-in-law is in the hospital trying to keep from losing her baby."

"I'm sorry to hear that. I hope mother and baby are okay. I always thought a lot of Rita, and I'm so glad the two of y'all are back together."

"I decided to drive down here by myself for New Year's, and I'm staying at Tidewater."

"You know you can stay for free with Alice and me."

"I know, but I've already paid the deposit, and it's non-refundable."

"Suit yourself, what are you doing for dinner?"

"I guess I'll go somewhere, maybe pick up something at the Flora-Bama."

"Not by yourself, buddy. Alice hasn't started supper yet. Let's go somewhere, and catch up on things. Where are you now?"

"I'm headed west toward Gulf Shores."

"One of our favorite places is Tacky Jacks. Would you like to meet us at the Orange Beach location?"

"Sure. I'm at the turnoff to go there."

"Okay, we'll be there in twenty minutes."

"I'll be there in less than five. I'll get us a table overlooking the bay."

Alice, Jeff, and Eric had a great time at Tacky Jacks, talking about the old days and the old gang. Both Alice and Jeff encouraged him to keep pursuing Rita, because she was a great girl, and they felt she and Eric were destined to be together.

When Eric reminded them that Gina Hanover and Kristie Tidwell were both Wentworth girls, Jeff said, that while he barely remembered Kristie, she wasn't a part of their crowd. Gina Hanover was younger than they were, so they didn't remember anything about her.

After spending a few hours at Tacky Jacks, the threesome left. It was too early to call it a night, so they decided to hit the Flora-Bama. It was a beautiful evening, and the Flora-Bama would be a nice place to hang out for a while. This being the week between Christmas and New Year's, it wouldn't be too crowded.

CHAPTER 33

On the evening of December 29, Kristie decided to eat at the condo. She had gone out for seafood every night since she had been there and wanted something different. Natalie, Tim, and Jean wanted her to join them at a restaurant they liked in Foley. Because this restaurant wasn't one of Kristie's favorites, she told them to go without her, and she would catch up with them in the morning.

Different turned out to be steak. Kristie drove to the Orange Beach Publix, and picked out a good-looking ribeye. Then she picked up a baking potato, salad, and a nice merlot. Her condo was equipped with a George Foreman grill and a microwave, so dinner was prepared in less than ten minutes.

After eating, Kristie decided she needed something sweet, maybe a frozen bushwhacker from the Flora-Bama. Driving the short distance to the Flora-Bama, Kristie parked the convertible, paid the cover charge and went inside. Because the place wasn't crowded, she was able to get a drink quickly and sat down at one of the tables close to the tent. A band was playing, so she decided to listen to the music for a while.

After fifteen minutes or so, a couple who looked to be about Kristie's age, sat down at the same long table where Kristie was seated. They introduced themselves as Jeff and Alice. When they asked her if she was alone, Kristie said yes. Her friends had gone to a restaurant for dinner she didn't like. She had cooked a steak at her condo, and decided to come here for the remainder of the evening.

After a few minutes, the guy, who said his name was Jeff, told Kristie they had a friend who was sitting on the beach. The friend was missing his girlfriend, who couldn't be with him. Could she possibly keep their friend company tonight?

"What! You can't be serious! You expect me to snuggle up to your friend tonight because he's lonely? I'll have you know, I'm not some bimbo waiting to get picked up. I'm a well-respected political blogger and analyst. How dare you suggest such a thing! If I knew where management was, I'd report the two of you and have your sorry asses thrown out of here."

"Okay, okay," said Jeff. We're sorry."

"Low-down too," replied Kristie. "I was here before you, I think you need to get up and go somewhere far, far away from me."

Jeff and Alice stood up and walked out to the beach to find Eric.

When they found Eric, Jeff said to him, "We found a pretty lady sitting under the tent. We thought she might at least talk to you and keep you company tonight. But when we asked her about it, the uppity bitch start screaming at us that she was some prominent something or other, and threatened to have us thrown out. She seemed like the type that just might do it, so I think we had better get out of here."

"If you asked her to keep me company tonight, I don't blame her for screaming at you. Let's leave. I'll go back to the condo and think about Rita as I'm falling asleep."

When they were walking by the long tables, Jeff pointed out the woman to Eric, and he froze. "That's Kristie, my second wife."

"You're kidding," said Jeff.

"Nope. I knew she was down here before I called you. And to make matters worse, she's staying at the same condominiums as I'm staying. I found that out shortly after I arrived. I was hoping to be able to avoid her while I was here, but I guess that's going to be impossible."

"If we leave quickly, maybe she won't notice us," said Alice.

"No, Kristie was my wife, it would be classless if I didn't acknowledge her."

Jeff, Alice, and Eric walked over to where Kristie was seated. Kristie noticed Jeff and Alice first, and yelled, "I thought I told the two of y'all to stay away from me. I guess I'll have to call the police and tell them you're harassing me."

"Hello, Kristie."

"Eric?"

"In the flesh."

"What the hell are you doing here with these two pieces of white trash?"

"Kristie, this is Jeff Nichols and his wife, Alice. Jeff was in high school with us, and hung out with Wiley, Jimmy, and some of the others in our gang. Do you remember him?"

"No, nor do I want to. Do you know what these two low-class dirt bags said to me?"

"Yes, but, can we start over?"

"Why?"

"This is a big misunderstanding, and we need to straighten it out. Jeff and Alice meant no harm."

"Meant no harm? They approached me as though I was some hooker."

"No, we really didn't think that at all, Kristie," said Jeff. We were just hoping you would have a couple of drinks with Eric and talk to him for a little while."

"Just where is your girlfriend tonight, Eric?" seethed Kristie.

"She's in New York with her son and daughter-in-law. Her daughter-in-law is pregnant, and having difficulties. She was supposed to be with me down here for New Year's, but that's not going to happen."

"I'm so sorry," said Kristie sarcastically. "Now if you will excuse me, I really do have to go."

Kristie stumbled as she stood up at the table, which was really a picnic table.

"Kristie, how much have you had to drink?" asked Eric.

"What's it to you?"

"I'm not sure you should be driving. Cops are all over this place. As nasty as you've been to my friends and me, I still don't want you to get in trouble."

"Oh, aren't you noble."

"I found out you were here earlier this afternoon. I ran into Tim at the condos. I'm staying where you're staying. Ride back with me, and we'll come back and get your car in the morning."

"Why are you being so nice to me? You've never been nice to me before. When we were seeing one another, and then after we married, you were always running off to see your friends, the old gang, as you called them, that I was never a part of."

At this point, Eric asked Jeff and Alice to leave them alone. He felt it best if he took care of this situation without them listening. When they were out of earshot, Eric, once again, asked Kristie to ride back with him in his truck.

"I'm really fine, Eric. Besides, I don't want anything to happen to my car. I'm scared to leave it here overnight."

"I'm sure you're not the first person to leave their vehicle at the Flora-Bama parking lot overnight. But if you don't want to leave it here, let me drive it back, then tomorrow you can drive me over here to get the truck, or Tim can drive me, or maybe even Jeff."

"Won't Rita be jealous?"

"Don't bring Rita into this."

Kristie caved and allowed Eric to drive her back to the condos in her car. When they arrived, Eric gave Kristie the keys. When they got into the elevator, Kristie pushed seven, the floor where she was staying. Eric didn't push a button, but instead, got out with Kristie.

"So, you're on the seventh floor, also?"

"No, I just want to make sure you got to your unit."

"Eric, I'm hardly drunk, I think I can make it."

When Kristie was at her door, she inserted the key card and opened the door.

"Thanks, Eric. I'm really all right, but I do thank you for your concern."

"Are you going to ask me to come in?"

"No, why?"

"I thought we could talk for a little while."

"Talk for a little while," said Kristie in an incredulous tone.

"What do we have to talk about? You've made it clear you now have a girlfriend you're serious about."

"She's not here."

"So."

"I just thought maybe we might be able to get together. It's going to get awful lonely here without someone to snuggle up with."

"ERIC, ERIC CHANNING! GO BACK TO YOUR UNIT RIGHT NOW! What kind of person do you think I am? Do you think you can just love the one you're with, since you're not with the one you love?"

"It's not like I've never seen you naked. In fact, I'm conjuring up some visions even as we speak."

"ERIC, LEAVE RIGHT NOW," shouted Kristie.

Kristie slipped inside the door of her condo, locked it and chained it.

Despite being furious, she fell asleep, and woke up early the next morning to a thunderstorm. It was going to be a humid day on the Alabama gulf coast, and severe weather was a possibility.

CHAPTER 34

Eric was here. Eric was staying in the same building as she was. Could she possibly have the relaxing, energy renewing time she hoped for, if Eric was here? Today was December 30, and rain along with severe weather, made it an ideal day to stay inside. However, Kristie was antsy. She wanted to get out of the condo, go somewhere, and get away from Eric. Where should she go, and what should she do?

What about Biloxi? The drive was a little over two hours. Once she arrived, she could go to Biloxi's famous casino, the Beau Rivage, where she could lose herself inside the massive complex, putting all thoughts of Eric Channing and his new squeeze, Rita McDonald Fisher, completely out of her head. But inclement weather was predicted on the Gulf Coast today, and they were saying the "T" word. Kristie had recently been up close and personal with a tornado, and wanted no part of them. Because of that experience, she was still frightened of severe storms, and probably would be for quite a while.

Sadly, she was even more frightened of Eric, and her feelings for him. Eric didn't want her, and had rejected her. There was no way she could stay at the condo today, even if Natalie and Tim were there, and on her side.

Kristie showered, dressed, and headed off to Biloxi, arriving at lunch time. She didn't tell Natalie and Tim where she was going, much less Eric, who didn't care whether she lived or died. They could all just wonder where she was today.

After having lunch at one of Biloxi's seafood restaurants, Kristie headed to Beau Rivage where she played the slots for a couple of hours then took up blackjack. Kristie set aside $250.00 she was fully prepared to lose, but much to her surprise, she won close to $500.00.

It was almost 4:00 pm, and severe weather alerts had been coming into her phone. An active system with a history of rotating thunderstorms was off-shore and could be in Mobile by 5:30 or 6:00. Kristie either needed to get out of there and head east, or remain there for a while. She decided to head east, and get ahead of any severe weather that might hit the Mobile area.

Kristie drove toward Mobile, and was in the tunnel going under the Mobile River at 5:00. Driving under an ominous sky, and still being freaked out by storms, she decided to stop at Felix's Fish Camp, a popular restaurant, just off Battleship Parkway in Spanish Fort, Alabama to have a glass of wine to calm her nerves. Maybe she would have some of their famous boiled shrimp or crab soup. Even though it was nearly dark, Kristie couldn't help but notice the black clouds to the southwest. She had heard earlier that the area was under a tornado watch. It was decision making time. If there were a tornado embedded in that cloud formation, it would travel either northeast and miss Kristie, or if it was a large tornado, it could make a right turn and head due east. How fast was it moving? Could she outrun it? Kristie was trapped. The restaurant was not the sturdiest of buildings, having been built on stilts to protect it from Mobile Bay flooding.

It was starting to rain hard, and the wind was picking up. Kristie ran up the ramp and into the restaurant, where the hostess indicated a funnel cloud had been sited over the central part of Mobile. She directed Kristie to one of the bars with huge picture windows, allowing one to see over into the city of Mobile. Restaurant patrons were gathered around the windows staring outside. While it was dark outside, continuous flashes of lightning allowed the customers and staff to witness a wedge tornado spinning through the city of

Mobile. Transformers were exploding, and the city suddenly became dark from extensive power outages.

Even though the rain was coming down in torrents, lightning was flashing, and thunder was booming, Felix's never lost power. The restaurant patrons went back to their tables, and the staff continued their duties. Felix's and Spanish Fort had been spared. Kristie decided to sit at the bar and watch the continuous coverage on TV. She ordered a glass of wine with a cup of crab soup, and the jumbo steamed shrimp.

When Kristie was about halfway through the soup and shrimp, she began to feel bone-weary. To return to Orange Beach, she had about an hour and a half drive, make that two hours since the weather was bad.

Because she hadn't checked her phone since lunchtime, Kristie retrieved her cell from her purse and saw several text messages and a couple of voice mail notices from Natalie wanting to know where she was. In one of the voice mails, Natalie said Eric appeared to be upset by her disappearance, but would never admit it. Well, if Eric was so damned worried about her, why hadn't he sent her a text or called her?

Kristie texted Natalie telling her she was at Felix's Fish Camp having dinner, and would soon head back to Orange Beach. "Don't tell Eric that you've talked to me." If Eric was worried about her, let him to be miserable.

Even though Kristie was not a coffee drinker and avoided all caffeinated drinks after 3:00, she ordered a cup of coffee, the first real coffee she had consumed in more than ten years. After drinking half the cup, Kristie still felt terrible, but jittery. Maybe she could stay awake to get back to Orange Beach.

When Kristie left the restaurant, it was pouring down rain. As she walked to her car, sloshing through puddles in the dirt/gravel parking lot, she hoped the pet alligator that lived in the saw grass on the other side of the restaurant hadn't decided to migrate to the parking lot side.

It was a short drive on I-10 East to Gulf Shores Parkway. Then after exiting onto Gulf Shores Parkway, she had about an hour's drive, maybe longer with the wet weather. Also, this area was prone to flooding, and Kristie hoped she would not encounter areas where water covered the roadways.

Kristie made it over the causeway, and even though the rain had picked up to the point of being torrential, she didn't miss the Gulf Shores Parkway exit. However, a few minutes after exiting, as she was headed toward Foley, and eventually

Gulf Shores and Orange Beach, she started feeling sick. It felt like a large knot had formed in her stomach or esophagus just below her breasts. Then she began having chills, followed by sweats.

What's happening? Am I having a heart attack, thought Kristie? She wasn't having chest pains, shortness of breath, or numbness in her left arm, but knew the heart attack symptoms were different for women than they were for men.

She would be in Foley soon, the location of the South Baldwin Hospital. Should she stop there? Maybe it was just indigestion, exacerbated by stress. She'd had enough of that lately. Eric had shown up on what was supposed to be her time. Even if he didn't have the petite perky Rita in tow, they were a couple now, and Eric was pining away for his first love. Then she witnessed the Mobile tornado, which she missed being right in the middle of, by about twenty minutes. She was driving through torrential rains, high winds, and vivid cloud to ground lightning in an area where flooding was common.

As Kristie approached Foley, the knot in her stomach wasn't getting any better, and she was feeling weird. Because she had never quite experienced these feelings before, she decided to stop at South Baldwin Hospital, just a couple of blocks from Gulf Shores Parkway.

She found the emergency room entrance and parked in the adjacent lot, opening her umbrella as she stepped out of the car. But with the high winds, her umbrella turned inside out, and by the time Kristie entered the emergency room, she was soaked. Being a quiet night, Kristie, after completing the required paperwork, was quickly admitted.

CHAPTER 35

Eric awoke around 8:00 am on December 30, recalled the events of the evening before, and realized he needed to retrieve his truck from the Flora-Bama parking lot. Because Kristie was a late sleeper, he doubted she would be up at this hour. However, Tim and Natalie were early risers, and should be up by now. When he called Tim's cell phone, Tim told him they were leaving in a few minutes to go to breakfast at Café Beignet. Would he like to go? Afterward, they would be glad to drive him to the Flora-Bama to get his truck.

"Sure, if you can give me fifteen minutes to shower and dress?

"Okay, we'll meet you in the lobby in fifteen minutes.

As the three of them were walking to Tim's vehicle, Eric saw Kristie's convertible, but didn't say anything about Kristie.

"I don't like the way it looks and feels out here," said Eric. "They're predicting severe weather today, and they're also saying the T-word."

"Before we moved to Alabama, I never thought of Alabama as having tornadoes," said Natalie.

"Guess you know different now," said Eric. I think statistically Alabama is the deadliest state in the nation for tornadoes."

After having café au lait and beignets, Tim and Natalie drove Eric to the Flora-Bama where he picked up his truck, and drove back to the condo. It was the day before New Year's Eve, the weather was bad, his girl wasn't with him, what was he going to do? There were a couple of bowl games being played, but these games didn't excite him. Alabama would be playing in the BCS Championship game against Notre Dame on January 7, and it was the only game that really mattered to him. He wondered if Kristie had tickets and was going.

When Eric returned from the Flora-Bama, he didn't recall seeing Kristie's car, so he walked outside the unit and stared over the railing. Kristie's car wasn't there. Guess she had gone somewhere, leaving while he was out with Tim and Natalie.

Faced with a day of nothing to do, Eric decided to call Rita and find out how things were going in New York. He got her voice mail immediately and left her a message that he missed her and hoped they would be able to see each other soon. After the attempted the phone call, Eric, for some reason, walked out of the door to check the parking lot side of the building to see if Kristie had returned. Why was he concerned about Kristie? Well, the weather was supposed to be rough, and even though he didn't want her in his life, he didn't want anything to happen to her.

Could Kristie possibly have returned to Birmingham? She looked so crestfallen after finding out he was in Orange Beach and staying at the same condominium complex where she was staying. Kristie was also upset with Jeff and Alice for what they had said to her last night at the Flora-Bama. Even though he really wanted to know where she was, Eric couldn't bring himself to call her.

His thoughts went back to a time when they were still dating, before they got engaged, and Wiley Martin was still alive, but had recently been diagnosed with lung cancer. One autumn weekend when Alabama didn't have a football game, Eric, Wiley, and some of Wiley's friends planned a fishing trip to Gulf Shores, and Eric told Kristie about it. Natalie, Natalie's mom, and one of Natalie's aunts were spending that week in Panama City Beach, Florida. At the last minute,

Kristie decided to go to Panama City and hang out with them for the weekend.

The guys' plans for Gulf Shores changed at the last minute when they found they could get a better deal on a fishing excursion in Panama City. Eric and the guys ran into Kristie at Panama City's famous eatery, Captain Anderson's. Instead of being glad to see Kristie, Eric accused her of stalking him, trying to ruin his fishing trip with Wiley and some of the other guys she didn't care for. The following day, a devastated Kristie returned home to Birmingham. Eric sincerely hoped Kristie would stay this time.

While this was supposed to be a vacation, and if Rita were with him, they would be spending this stormy day in bed, Eric decided to open his laptop and do some work. He had four articles to submit by the middle of January, and he should probably take this time to get started.

Before he knew it, it was lunch time. Even though Eric had stocked up on breakfast and lunch food, he wanted to go out somewhere. So, he picked up his phone to call Tim to see what he and Natalie were doing for lunch. Eric didn't complete the call. Tim and Natalie were Kristie's friends, and he didn't want to put them in the middle of this. So, he fixed himself a ham and turkey sandwich, opened a bag of chips, and poured himself a Diet Coke.

Still curious about Kristie's whereabouts, he peeked into the parking lot, and noted that Kristie's car still wasn't there. If indeed she left and went home, she should be there by now. Maybe he would call her landline, and hang up if she answered. But the caller ID would display his phone number, and she would most likely recognize it. Maybe he would ask Jeff to call her on his cell. But that would be a south Alabama area code. Sandy, he'd get his sister Sandy who lived in Trussville to call Kristie's landline on her cell phone. The number would be a 205 area code, and Kristie would not recognize the number. If Kristie answered, she could say she had a wrong number. But wait, Kristie might recognize Sandy's voice. Maybe Sandy's husband, Walter, would do it. Kristie wouldn't recognize Walter's voice.

Eric called Walter's cell phone, and Walter immediately picked up. When Eric asked him to call Kristie, Walter said to him, "Why don't you just bite the bullet and call her?"

"I don't want her to think I'm concerned about her."

"Well, aren't you?"

"Yes, but I don't want her to think I am."

"Okay, I'll call her and call you right back, but I think the only thing you're concerned about is your crotch."

Within less than two minutes, Walter was calling Eric, telling him that Kristie didn't answer her phone.

CHAPTER 36

After Tim and Natalie had returned from dropping Eric off at the Flora-Bama, Tim decided to work for a couple of hours while Natalie watched a movie. At lunchtime, they drove into Gulf Shores with Jean, and had lunch at the Oyster House. Because the weather was deteriorating, they stopped at the grocery store, and purchased the ingredients for Tim's special thin crust pizzas, and his famous mostaccioli. Also included in their purchases were several bottles of red wine, ingredients for a salad, and two flavors of gelato. This would be a good night to eat in.

When Kristie returned from wherever she went today, they were going to ask her to have dinner with them. Tim and Natalie chose, however, not to ask Eric to join them. Even though they considered Eric a friend when he and Kristie were married, they didn't like the way he had treated her. In fact, they were furious at the way he had treated her. Their allegiance was to Kristie.

When they arrived at the condo, a light rain was falling, and a steady wind was blowing. The sky and clouds had a green hue, and the humidity made Natalie's usually stick straight hair, frizz. Kristie's car wasn't in the parking lot.

After unloading the groceries and putting them away, Tim started the mostaccioli. He could put it together, then put it in the oven to bake later.

Natalie tried to call Kristie several times in the afternoon, and sent her several texts wanting to know where she was and when she would be returning. Kristie hadn't answered any of them. Just as soon as Tim was about ready to put the mostaccioli in the oven and start preparing the pizza dough, Natalie got a text from Kristie saying she was at Felix's, and would be having dinner there, and then would be on her way back to Orange Beach.

Natalie decided to get on her tablet while Tim finished dinner. Even though they were counting on Kristie having dinner with them, they decided to cook up everything anyway.

"Oh shit," exclaimed Natalie.

"What?"

"A tornado just touched down in Mobile, like about ten minutes ago."

Tim flipped the TV on to one of the Mobile stations, and they both viewed footage of the tornado as it ripped through the central part of Mobile.

Eric's phone rang as he was putting the finishing touches on one of his articles. Picking up the phone and looking at the screen, he was disappointed the caller was Jeff and not Rita. He wondered why Rita had not called him back.

"Did you see the tornado that hit Mobile just a few minutes ago," asked Jeff.

"No. A tornado hit Mobile?"

"I don't know a lot, but according to the news reports, it plowed right through the heart of the downtown area."

Eric flipped on the TV and viewed the videos that were being shown. "Holy shit!"

"Yeah, and we're under a tornado watch here. It's going to be a stormy night, but would you like to come over to the house anyway? Alice is making shrimp and grits."

"Sure, what else do I have going on? Can I bring anything?"

"No, we have shrimp and grits, salad, bread, plenty of wine, and leftover pecan pie and coconut cake."

"Sounds great. I'll be over there in fifteen to twenty minutes."

It was dark, but the sky was lighting up with streaks of lightning as Eric walked through the parking lot to his truck. At first glance, he didn't see Kristie's car. Before turning onto the highway, he cruised the parking looking for her car, but it wasn't there. Not really caring whether she recognized his number or not, he called her landline, but got the voice mail. He then called Tim's phone.

Tim answered, and when Eric asked about Kristie, he handed the phone to Natalie, who informed Eric that Kristie had texted her about thirty minutes ago, saying she was going to have dinner at Felix's, and would be back at the condo shortly. Eric was relieved that Kristie was okay, but really wished she had gone back to Birmingham. That way, he might have a decent New Year's Eve and New Year's Day.

"Where are you?" Natalie asked.

"I'm heading over to Jeff and Alice's, friends from Wentworth who now live here, for dinner."

"Okay."

Even though he missed Rita, Eric had a great time with Jeff and Alice. They were such cool people, but then most folks from Wentworth were cool; except for maybe his ex-wives. How had he managed to hook up with those two losers? It was getting close to 11:00 pm. Alice had decided to go to bed, but Eric and Jeff decided to play some pool.

Eric's phone rang. Thinking it had to be Rita this time, he snatched the phone out of his pocket and saw it was Natalie. What in the world does she want, thought Eric?"

"Yes."

"Eric?"

"Yes."

"I'm sorry to bother you at this hour, but by any chance is Kristie with you?"

"Of course not!"

"Well, I got a text from her right about the time the tornado hit Mobile, after 5:00. She said she was going to have dinner at Felix's, then she would be driving back here. There's torrential rain and high winds in the Mobile/Spanish Fort area. She should have been back here way before now."

"Well, call her and ask her where she is."

"Duh! I've been calling her, she doesn't answer her phone. Felix's is on Battleship Parkway. To get here from there, she would have to drive over a stretch of the causeway. I hope she didn't somehow end up in the bay."

"There's high guardrails and concrete barriers on I-10. Even if she slid and hit one, I don't think she would have gone into the bay."

"I hear water has spilled from the bay over Highway 98."

"I don't think Kristie would have been taking 98. She would have taken I-10."

"Well, she should have been here a long time ago, and she's not here."

"Where Kristie is, is not my problem, or my concern. She took off early this morning, and didn't tell anyone where she was going. Not my fault if she's at the bottom of Mobile Bay."

With that, Eric hung up the phone.

Jeff overheard the conversation, but stayed quiet. He remembered Kristie as being overweight and not well-liked by a lot of students, including Wiley Martin and his bunch. He did remember, though, that she lost weight while they were in high school. Jeff had attended college at St. Randolph, married his high school sweetheart Alice, and raised their two children in Wentworth. When the children left for college, he and Alice moved to the Alabama Gulf Coast. Jeff had worked on an oil rig for a while, then in construction. He now owned his own construction company and was doing quite well.

Did Eric not care that his second wife might be at the bottom of Mobile Bay? Kristie was certainly nasty to him and Alice last night at the Flora-Bama, rushing to judgment, but that didn't make him hate her, and wish her dead. Maybe his old friend, who was a nice guy in high school, had changed.

The two of them shot pool for another fifteen minutes, or so, then Eric left to drive back to his condo. It was raining with thunder and lightning, and the wind was still blowing. Not a good night to be out, and he was glad to be pulling into the condo parking lot safe and sound. When he stepped out, he looked around and didn't see Kristie's car.

When inside, he flipped on the TV and discovered there were several tornado warnings for Baldwin County. There was evidence of circulation over Bay Minette, and waterspouts had been sighted in the Gulf, one just off the shore close to where Highway 61 ended at Perdido Beach Boulevard.

Uh oh! That was close to where he was staying. Eric stood up and went out on the balcony, and saw a waterspout when lightning lit up the sky, which was about every ten seconds. He watched it move eastward, then dissipate. When

Eric went back to the TV, he learned that while the Highway 98 causeway had been closed for hours, Highway Patrol had just closed the I-10 causeway, both directions. Water from Mobile Bay was flooding the interstate. No accidents on the causeway were mentioned. But what if one of the barriers or guardrails had broken away, and Kristie had driven into the bay. No one would know it.

Again, that wasn't his problem. He was not responsible for Kristie. Yes, she was upset when she discovered he was here and staying in the same complex. Then she had rushed to judgment at the Flora-Bama last night when Jeff and Alice, not knowing who she was, had asked her to have a couple of drinks and talk to him. She hardly thanked him for driving her to the condo last night. Kristie Tidwell-Channing, who might be dinner for the fishes, was of no concern to him.

In an hour or so, the storm slackened, and there were no more tornado warnings for the area. Eric decided it was time to go to bed, but not before he walked out to the parking to see if Kristie's car was there. It wasn't.

CHAPTER 37

After being taken back to one of the holding rooms, Kristie slipped into a hospital gown. A nurse then hooked her up to the EKG machine. As Kristie lay back on the narrow hospital bed, she became weary and fell asleep. The next thing she remembered was being taken to X-ray. After they had taken the X-rays, they wheeled her back into the small room. Looking up at the clock, she saw several hours had passed, and it was well after midnight. She was suddenly wide awake and feeling much better.

In a few minutes, a doctor came into the room and told Kristie that what she experienced wasn't a heart attack. Instead, it appeared to be a bad case of indigestion. What she had eaten earlier had passed through her stomach. She was ready to be released. What a relief!

Kristie got dressed, left the hospital and drove to the condo. What a long day, possibly the longest day of her life. She had left her phone in the car while she was in the ER, and had several calls and text messages from Natalie wanting to know where she was. Natalie asked her to call when she got the messages and texts, no matter what time of day or night it was.

What a miserable life she was having. Thinking she might be having a heart attack, she had to drive herself to the emergency room, where she was all alone. Not one single person on earth cared whether she lived or died. Then after being released, she had to drive herself back to her condo. Eric, her ex-husband, who cared nothing about her, was pining away for his high school sweetheart.

Even though it was after 1:00 am, and Tim and Natalie generally went to bed before 10:00, she thought she had better call them. When she did, Natalie sounded angry, yet so relieved when she heard Kristie's voice.

"I thought you might have driven into the bay."

"No, but I was scared. I could feel the wind moving the car and water was splashing over the concrete barriers."

"Why did you decide to go all the way over to Biloxi?"

"I just wanted to get away from here. And get away from Eric. Is he still here?"

"Yes."

Natalie didn't want to tell Kristie that Eric was not the least bit concerned about her. "Are you feeling better? Do you want me to come over there and spend the night?"

"I don't think that'll be necessary. I feel fine, it was just indigestion, not a heart attack."

"Okay, I'll see you tomorrow, I love you, and I'm glad you're safe."

"Thanks. I love you too."

Kristie went to bed, and immediately went to sleep after what had been one of the longest and worst days of her life.

However, Kristie didn't sleep well. She kept waking up, tossing and turning. She also had some strange dreams, and in one of them, she was driving along the causeway, and her car went into Mobile Bay.

Still exhausted, she got out of bed about 8:00 am, took a shower and washed her hair. After drying her hair, she crawled back in the bed and dozed for a while. About 11:00 am, her phone rang. It was Natalie, wanting to know how she was.

"I didn't sleep well last night, and I feel awful."

"Do you need to see a doctor?"

"I don't think so. I'm just tired and can't seem to get any decent sleep. Guess when my body's tired enough, I'll sleep."

"Tim and I are going to drive over to Pensacola, and have dinner at the Margaritaville Hotel? We don't plan to spend

New Year's Eve there. We'll probably be back here by 9:30, our bedtime, you know. Want to go?"

"Thanks, but I don't really feel like going anywhere. Even though it's New Year's Eve, I think I'll just stay here. I've had so many disastrous New Year's Eves in my lifetime, the ceiling will probably cave in on me, though."

"We had Italian night last night. Tim fixed pizza and mostaccioli. There's plenty left over. Would you like some, perhaps to eat this evening?"

"Sure."

In a few minutes, Natalie brought the food to Kristie. They talked a while, but she did not dare mention Eric. What Eric had said about Kristie last night, that if Kristie had driven her car into Mobile Bay, it wasn't his problem, shocked Natalie. Eric had been a jerk more than he had been decent since she had known him, but his comments last night were off the chart. Even Tim said he didn't care if he never saw Eric again. They were both glad Kristie had landed the position at the number one cable news channel in North America. She would be traveling more, and perhaps become semi-famous.

After Natalie left, Kristie got back into bed and dozed. A little after 2:00, she woke up, finally feeling refreshed. In contrast to yesterday, it was sunny and cool. Putting on some light makeup, a sweatshirt, and sweat pants, Kristie went down to the beach with her phone, a blanket, and a book to read. Maybe the sea and the salty air would lift her spirits. She wondered what Eric was doing. Was he pining over Rita? Was she still in love with Eric, or was she just depressed that her only hope for marriage and happiness was gone?

Eric awoke about 8:00 am, and fixed himself a cup of coffee. Maybe he would go out someplace for breakfast. It was New Year's Eve, and he had no plans. Jeff didn't say anything about what he and Alice were doing. Tim and Natalie would probably never speak to him again after his outburst last night about Kristie not being his problem. KRISTIE! Did she ever return? He ran out the door, peered over the railing, and saw that Kristie's car was, at long last, in the parking lot. Whew! What if Kristie had ended up at the bottom of Mobile Bay? He wouldn't have been able to live with himself had that happened.

He still had not heard from Rita, so he picked up his cell and called her. It would be after 9:00 am up there. Her phone went to voice mail and he left her another message asking her to call him, and telling her he loved her. After showering and dressing, he left the condo in search of some breakfast, and ended up at Kitty's Kafe on the other side of the Intercoastal waterway. He ordered the tenderloin Benedict with cheese grits and a bloody Mary. This would probably be his big meal for the day since he had no plans for the evening. Eric returned to the condo just before noon, and decided to watch football for the rest of the day. As he entered the parking lot, he noticed Kristie's car was still in the parking lot in the same spot it had been a little while ago, and so was Tim and Natalie's SUV. He wondered what the four of them were doing this evening. Why hadn't Rita returned his calls?

After a hideous day yesterday, the sun was out. In December and January, the sun rose and set on the water on the northern gulf coast. The way the clouds looked, the sunset later today should be beautiful. Maybe he would go out to the beach about 4:00. It was winter in Alabama and darkness would fall around 5:00.

At 4:00, Eric tore himself away from the ballgame, grabbed an afghan off the sofa, and started down to the beach. As he was walking toward the beach on the boardwalk, he saw a lone figure sitting on the beach about ten yards from where the waves were breaking. As he got closer, he saw it was a lady with long dark hair dressed in a dark red sweatshirt. Of course, it was Kristie. Her hair was blowing in the ocean breeze.

Stopping in his tracks, Eric couldn't decide whether to turn around and go back inside, or continue out to the beach. He was a paying customer, and had just as much right to the beach as Kristie did. He started walking again, and walked right up to where Kristie was sitting on a quilt. Sensing someone's presence, she turned around and look startled.

"Do you mind if I join you, the sunset's going to be beautiful tonight."

"Your choice. Maybe you can call Rita. If the sunset is pretty on Long Island, perhaps the two of you can watch it together while you're on the phone with each other."

"I haven't talked to Rita since I've been down here."

"Sorry."

Eric noticed Kristie's eyes looked weak, and the dark circles under her eyes were ever so prominent. She looked like he remembered her looking after she had migraine headaches.

"Are you feeling all right?"

"I'm just weak after last night."

"Huh?"

"Oh, I don't guess you know, unless you've spoken to Tim or Natalie."

"I don't think they'll ever speak to me again. Now what?"

Eric's mouth gaped open as Kristie reiterated last night's events, and the two of them sat silent for a few moments. Eric's heart went out to Kristie as he thought of her driving through a torrential thunderstorm, on the causeway, with tornadoes dropping. On top of that, she was having heart attack symptoms. Before they married, she had been diagnosed with heart failure. While she was controlling it with medication, her cardiologist had indicated that at some point in time, she would require open heart surgery. Driving to a small-town hospital to go to the emergency room all alone, must have been beyond traumatic.

But again, Kristie, for no other reason than wanting to get away from him, left that morning, and drove to Biloxi for a little adventure. The fact that severe weather, including tornadoes, was in the forecast, didn't matter to her. Eric could understand her wanting to get away from him, and not telling him she was leaving, and where she was going. But what about Tim, Natalie, and Jean? Jean, especially worried about Kristie. Since Kristie's mother had died, Jean considered her as a daughter. The three of them were worried sick at her disappearance.

Finally, Eric broke the silence. "The last time we watched a sunset on the beach was in February, before the divorce was final."

"I remember," said Kristie, as tears began rolling down her cheeks. Tears she couldn't stop.

"Now, now, let's watch the sunset."

Eric took her hand in his and she didn't pull it back.

It was one of the most beautiful sunsets the two of them had ever seen. The clouds were gunmetal gray, and the sun was a deep coral.

After the sun had slipped into the water, Eric put his arm around Kristie, drawing her closer to him, and began kissing her. She kissed back. Both sort of laid down on the blanket and held each other.

"I'm sorry you had to go through all of that yesterday, but what made you take off to Biloxi knowing the weather was going to be bad, and not telling anyone where you were going?

"I just wanted to get away from here."

"Away from me."

"Yes."

"I really feel responsible for all of that. If I hadn't shown up, you would be doing your thing with Natalie and Tim."

"I've never been in the right place at the right time doing the right thing. You know that."

"Me neither. How about letting me take you out to dinner tonight. It's still early. Maybe we can get a table somewhere. What about Cosmos or Big Fish? Those are your two favorite places."

"Thanks, I'm not bedridden by any means, but I do feel tired and weak. Last night Tim fixed pizza and that Italian dish that's popular in the St. Louis area. Natalie brought me their leftovers this morning, and there's plenty for both of us. I have wine and champagne, so why don't we stay here."

"That sounds great to me, thanks."

CHAPTER *38*

As Kristie and Eric were walking back to the building, Kristie had mixed emotions. She would be spending New Year's Eve with Eric, and how was it going to end? Eric had a girlfriend who was supposed to be here with him. Since Rita wasn't here, he was coming on to her, and she was letting him. Maybe they would have dinner. Then she would send him back to his condo. He and Rita could have phone sex at midnight.

As they were walking down the hall to Kristie's unit, Eric's phone rang. He looked at it, then looked at Kristie and said, "I'll be down there in just a minute."

Guess that was Rita, thought Kristie, as she opened the door and entered her condo. Did she really want to go through this? Then she remembered New Year's Eve two years ago at Jan Harpo Franklin's house, and the scene afterward at the Wentworth Holiday Inn Express.

When his phone rang, while he was in the hallway, Eric was sure it was Rita, but was relieved when it wasn't. Instead, it was Jimmy Harpo.

"Hey."

"Guess what?"

"What?"

"Ruthie and I drove down today, and we're staying at the Island House Hotel, next door to where you and Rita are staying. Unless the two of you have romantic plans, we thought we could go out, maybe to the Flora-Bama or the Hangout."

"Jimmy, Rita's not here. Her daughter-in-law is pregnant and having complications. She said she needed to be up there with her and her son."

"Oh, I'm sorry. But if you're down here all alone, there's nothing wrong with the three of us going out. We're an old married couple, you won't be interfering with our plans."

"I already have plans. I'm sorry you drove all the way down here for nothing."

"Hey, hey, hey big guy, that's great. I promise I won't tell Rita."

"Look Jimmy, I really do have to go. Catch you later."

"Okay, maybe we can watch ballgames together tomorrow."

"We'll see."

With that, Eric hung up. Spending New Year's Eve with Jimmy and Ruthie would be a lot more fun than spending the evening with Kristie. She was all mopey and teary, plus she didn't feel well. He would much rather be at the Flora-Bama, and was starting to feel guilty about kissing Kristie, and coming on to her when he had a girlfriend he loved, and planned to marry. Should he call Jimmy back and say he would love to go out with them? Then tell Kristie that Ruthie and Jimmy were down here, and he was going to spend the evening with them? That's what he really wanted to do. Was he a jerk or what?

When he knocked on Kristie's door, he was prepared to say thanks for her offer, but he had been offered something better. What was Kristie to him? He didn't care if he hurt her. She was strong and would get over it. Poor Kristie. People tended to treat her shabbily, but she managed to carry on, always landing on her feet. She did carry grudges, though. She hated Jimmy and Ruthie, Jan, and Kathryn. They had treated her shabbily, and even though she would bounce back, she would hold a grudge against them forever.

When Kristie opened the door, Eric saw that she had put some extra make-up on. Her cheek color was a dark rose, and she had applied some concealer, because there were no more circles under her eyes. Her lips were the color of red wine, and she was wearing a velour turquoise tunic top with black leggings. On her feet were black slippers. Kristie had gotten all prettied up for him, and now he couldn't bear to tell her he would be doing something else for New Year's Eve.

"You didn't have to get all gussied up just for me."

"I didn't do it for you, I did it for me. I've yukked around here all day and needed to get back to the world of the living."

When he saw Kristie had put out some cashews, along with her signature cream cheese and red pepper jelly with wheat thins, he said he had some steamed shrimp he could add to the spread.

Eric sat his phone down and left to get the shrimp. As soon as the door closed, Kristie wasted no time in checking his phone to see who had called him, expecting it to be Rita. However, it was Jimmy Harpo. What in the hell could he possibly want? Even though Kristie knew Rita and Eric were a couple, and would more than likely marry, she was relieved the call wasn't from Rita.

CHAPTER 39

Rita McDonald Fisher was putting the finishing touches on her hair and makeup. Her royal blue sequined gown was hanging on a hook on the backside of her closet door. The elderly gentleman, Harold DePalmer, who had been serving as her escort, was due to pick her up in thirty minutes, and take her to the New Year's Eve dance at the country club. Harold was almost thirty-five years older than Rita, but he had proven himself to be a fantastic dancer, and had lots of energy for someone of his age. She had seen pictures of him when he was young, and he was indeed handsome. In fact, he wasn't all that bad now. The two of them had kissed a few times, but nothing heavy. Kissing someone old enough to be your father was loathsome to Rita. Because Harold had shown no signs of wanting anything else except companionship and the occasional kiss, Rita enjoyed his company.

Being assisted by her housekeeper, Rita slipped into the dress, and into her black satin pumps with two-inch heels. No way was she going to wear the stiletto heels that were popular with the younger women. The housekeeper retrieved her white mink jacket from another closet, brought it into the bedroom, and laid it on the bed. The housekeeper would let Harold in when he arrived, and then go upstairs to fetch Rita.

As Rita was sitting at her dressing table, awaiting Harold's arrival, she thought about Eric Channing. He had called her several times since she told him she would be unable to fly to Alabama for the New Year. She hadn't returned the calls, and was avoiding talking to him.

Rita was physically attracted to Eric and enjoyed the sex, but he would never fit into her lifestyle. She knew he wanted her to move back to Alabama and bring the children with her, but that was impossible. Their lives were in New York. Even if she moved to Birmingham or Huntsville, the children would still suffer culture shock. Since the last time they were together, Rita had fantasized about Eric many times. She loved the way he kissed her, the way he held her, the way he touched her, and the way he made love to her. Nonetheless, she and Eric would not happen.

Rita had been the one to break up with him when he was a freshman at Georgia Southern University, and she was still a senior in high school, and had started seeing someone else. But her Mom practically had to stand over her and make her do it. No one was here to make her break up with him now, but she would have to do it sooner or later. Not wanting to let Eric down after Christmas and before New Year's, she decided to wait until after the first of the year. She didn't want to do it before January 7, when Alabama was to play for the national championship. Maybe she would wait until the middle of January. The housekeeper knocked quietly on her bedroom door. Mr. DePalmer was downstairs.

CHAPTER 40

Eric arrived with the shrimp and the cocktail sauce. When they were ready for the main courses, Kristie would heat the pizza in the oven, and the mostaccioli in the microwave. The salad was already in bowls in the refrigerator.

"What do you want to drink?" asked Kristie. "We have two bottles of champagne, want to start on one now, and save the other for later?"

"Sure."

Kristie retrieved two champagne flutes from the refrigerator where they were chilling. Then Eric opened and poured the champagne. They picked up their glasses and stared at one another. It was an awkward moment with neither one knowing what to say.

Kristie broke the silence and said, "Here's to what we hope will be a celebratory New Year's Eve. Roll Tide!" They clinked their glasses, and drank their first champagne toast of the evening.

The couple sat on barstools drinking champagne and eating the appetizers. Then Kristie put the pizza in the oven to heat. She took out the bowls of salad, and put them on the kitchen table, along with the salad dressing Natalie said was a St. Louis favorite. Just before the pizza was to come out of the oven, Kristie put the mostaccioli in the microwave. Dinner was served, and Eric opened one of the bottles of red wine for them to have with dinner. The conversation was stilted, but both managed to get through the main meal and dessert of eggnog gelato and shortbread cookies.

Eric helped Kristie clean up. When the dirty dishes were in the dishwasher, and the leftovers were stored in the refrigerator, Kristie and Eric stood in the kitchen looking at one another. Eric took her by the shoulders and drew her to him. The two began kissing. When they pulled apart, Kristie asked Eric, "Do you need more wine?"

"Sure. I'll get it. Are you ready for another glass?"

Kristie looked at her almost empty glass and said, "Sure."

After pouring the wine, Eric followed Kristie into the living room area of the condo where they sat down beside each other on the sofa. Eric picked up the remote and flipped on the TV to the Chick-Fil-A Peach Bowl, being played in Atlanta, where LSU was battling Clemson. The two watched the game in silence until Kristie couldn't stand it any longer.

"I'm about to utter four words no one wants to hear, we need to talk."

Eric replied, "I was hoping to get through New Year's Eve without having to talk seriously, but it's obviously not going to happen. So, let's talk."

"What's your status with Rita? The two of you were supposed to be down here together for a romantic beach get-a-way. She's not here. Were you planning on sleeping with me, then dumping me for her after the holiday weekend?"

Eric gazed up at the ceiling and contemplated his response. After what was probably several minutes of silence, Eric replied, "I've called Rita several times since we've been here. She has not seen fit to return any of my calls. I'm not the love-struck schoolboy I was when we were in high school. Her failure to return my calls, more than likely, means she doesn't want to talk to me. She's a wealthy Long Island socialite, and we all know I'm nothing but a southern red-neck. We're worlds apart, and I don't think the worlds could ever fuse."

"Does that mean you are not planning to see her anymore?"

"I don't think we'll be seeing each other anymore."

"Do you want me?"

"Yes."

"And I don't mean just for tonight. Will you want me a week from now? Will you tell Rita it's over between the two of you, if she were to come crawling back?"

"Look, Kristie, I can't possibly answer these questions now. I'm confused, and I hope you can understand that. Rita and I were getting along just great, but like I said, our worlds are different, and now she won't return my calls, I've prepared for the end of our relationship. If you want a commitment, a relationship at this point, I can't say yes or no."

"You want to go to bed with me tonight, but you're not sure how you will feel tomorrow. And if Rita does call you, you're not sure if you would toss me aside and go back to her?"

"Damn it, Kristie! Yes, I was hoping we could spend the night together. Do we have to sort all this out right now? It's New Year's Eve, there are plenty of couples out there who will be making love tonight with no thoughts about tomorrow. Can't we be one of those couples? If you're expecting me to say I'll completely give up Rita and start up again with you, it's not going to happen, or it's not going to happen tonight. You know, I'm not even sure we should spend the night together. After this conversation, how could it be good? I think I had better go back to my place."

Eric stood up and walked out the door, leaving Kristie sitting there in silence for several minutes before she burst into tears. Damn it, would she ever have a happy New Year's Eve, one without drama? By backing Eric into a corner, and insisting he make the decision to drop Rita, and start a relationship with her, Kristie had driven him away. But what if they had spent the night together, and she gave herself to him, then he dropped her and went back to Rita? She had given herself to him on that stormy night in November. The next day he asked her if he could move in with her while his lake house was being built, after deciding to leave Anabelle Martin. Kristie, at first said no, but contacted him later to tell him it would be okay, only to discover he had rekindled his high school relationship with Rita McDonald Fisher. Oh well, another tragic New Year's Eve. What else is new?

Kristie decided to sit for a while on the balcony, listening to the ocean waves. The stars were out, and the moon was bright. She could see the lights on the buoy off in the distance, and further out, she saw what she thought might be a fishing boat. She could also hear fireworks warming up for the big celebration coming shortly, as 2012 came to an end. It was still a couple of hours until midnight, but Kristie decided to go inside, put on her nightgown, get into bed, and read for a while. She wanted to sleep through the festivities, but knew that probably wouldn't happen.

After slipping her nightgown over her head, she heard a knock on the door. Hoping it would be Eric, she ran to the door and opened it with the chain still in place. It was Eric. She let him in, and he wasted no time in grabbing her and kissing her passionately.

"Kristie, when I said I couldn't make a decision about you and Rita, I was overwhelmed and couldn't make it right there, on the spot. But once my head cleared, I was able to make a decision. I want you, I want to be with you. Yes, I'm attracted to Rita, but she and I aren't suited for one another. I want us to start over. I can't predict how things will end, but let's start the New Year together, and see what life's going to hold, down the road."

Kristie turned out the kitchen and living room lights. As she and Eric headed to the bedroom, Eric was taking his clothes off. When he was finished, he removed Kristie's nightgown and panties.

The sound of Eric's phone awakened him and Kristie. The bright sun was streaming in the room, and the clock on the nightstand said 9:30. As Eric looked his phone, he said, "Shit." Kristie didn't say anything. It was Jeff, reminding Eric he and Alice were having a New Year's Day gathering at their house. Eric took his phone into the bathroom and closed the door. Jeff told him to be there around 1:30. When he asked if he could bring anything, Jeff said no, just bring yourself, we have plenty of food and plenty of liquid refreshment, alcoholic and non-alcoholic. On an impulse, Eric asked Jeff if he remembered Jimmy Harpo, Jan Harpo Franklin's younger brother.

"Sure."

"Would I be overstepping if I invited Jimmy and his wife, Ruthie, to come with me?"

"Of course not, Alice and I would love to see them. Anyone from Wentworth is welcome, well almost anyone from Wentworth, if you get my drift."

"Okay, sure, we'll see you about 1:30.

Was Kristie at the door listening to his conversation? He wouldn't put it past her to do so, but when he opened the bathroom door, he saw Kristie was lying in bed, still unclothed, staring at her phone. It was like they were husband and wife again. He went over and kissed Kristie good morning, and told her he was going to run over to his unit, grab a cup of coffee, and come right back.

Kristie's condo was on the seventh floor, and his condo was on the ninth floor. In the corridor, he ran into Natalie, Tim, and Jean. He said good morning to the two of them, but that was all.

When he arrived at his place, he called Jimmy, who answered his phone immediately. Eric told Jimmy about the party at Jeff and Alice's and asked if he and Ruthie would like to go. Jimmy remembered Jeff, who was a senior when he was a freshman, and said he would like to go, and thought Ruthie would like to go also. He told Eric that he would drive, and pick him up at his place at 1:15.

As his coffee brewed, Eric wondered how he was going to break it to Kristie that he would be attending a party she specifically wasn't invited to. Since they had spent the night together, was she thinking he was going to spend all day with her? Well, he did tell her last night he wanted to start a relationship and see where it went. It seemed like a good idea at the time, but was the instant fun worth the lie; or was it a lie?

If Eric told Kristie he was going to a party given by Jeff and Alice, and she wasn't invited because they didn't like her,

Kristie was sure to throw a hissy fit. Maybe he should call Jeff and tell him the truth, that he and Kristie were planning to start all over with their relationship, and would they care if he brought her to the party. Then there was Jimmy and Ruthie. Kristie didn't like them, and they didn't like her. He couldn't see Kristie going with him to the party, knowing Jeff and Alice, plus Jimmy and Ruthie were going to be there. When things get this complicated, the truth will set you free, or that's what he was told as a child. Ultimately, Eric decided to tell the truth for once in his life, and see where he ended up.

First, he called Jeff and Alice, told them he and Kristie were getting back together, and would they mind if she came to the party. They thought Kristie had rushed to judgment the other night, but after hesitating, they said it would be all right. Then Eric called Jimmy and told him he and Kristie had sort of gotten back together. Jimmy was incredulous, telling Eric he was crazy. He and Ruthie would find something else to do rather than be with Kristie.

Was Eric going to lose four of his best friends because of Kristie, a woman he had once loved, and may be falling in love with again? Guess it was time to face Kristie with the news that Jeff and Alice hesitantly said it would be okay if she came to their party, and Jimmy and Ruthie refused to be anywhere near her.

When he got to Kristie's floor and got off the elevator, Kristie, Natalie, and Tim were standing in the hallway talking. Natalie and Tim said they had plenty of food and libations and wanted Kristie and Eric to spend the day with them.

"Kristie, I need to talk to you alone for a few minutes."

When they got to Kristie's unit, Eric told her the truth about what Jeff and Alice had said about her, and what Jimmy Harpo had said about her. "I don't guess I should be surprised. Jimmy and Ruthie Harpo have always hated me, and now Jeff and Alice Nichols hate me. These are your friends, and I'm not sure we can have a relationship with your friends hating me like they do. Why don't you go to the party with Jimmy and Ruthie? I really need to think things out today. I'll party with Jean, Natalie and Tim."

"Kristie, are you sure?"

"Yes. We've been through this time and time again. The failure of your friends to accept me, plus my attitude toward them, caused major problems during round one. And while I hate to say it, it's not going to get any better for round two."

"Are you telling me you don't want to try to mend our relationship?"

"Eric, I want you more than anything on the face of this earth, but we hung out in separate crowds in high school. The crowd you hung out with didn't care for me because of my weight problems. They made fun of everyone who wasn't physically perfect. Those folks stayed in Wentworth, and they still have their clique in Wentworth. You were a part of them. They're your friends. Even if we get back together, I'll never be a part of that group, and you will continue to resent me for it."

"Maybe if you went with me to Jeff and Alice's, we could talk some things out. They're good people. Everyone's changed. I know there's still the Wentworth clique, formerly headed up by Wiley Martin, now headed up by Jan and Jimmy."

"You go on to Jeff and Alice's, take Jimmy and Ruthie with you. Have a great time talking about the wild times you had in high school, the times you scored in the backseats of your cars, the times you purchased alcohol even though you were under age, the times you smoked in the bathrooms and didn't get caught, etc. I didn't drink or smoke in high school. I didn't lose my virginity until I was a junior in college. I can't talk about all those wild parties you and your crowd had, because I was either fat or formerly fat Kristie Tidwell,

National Honor Society, church choir, yearbook staff, etc., and wasn't invited to your parties."

With tears in his eyes, Eric replied, "That was so long ago. Why can't we put things aside and go forward?"

"Eric, I really don't want to go to that party. I'd just end up being a bitch."

"Jeff and Alice have been living down here for a while, it's not like they're part of the Wentworth clique. While they remember Jan well, they barely remember Jimmy. Besides, what are you going to do today?"

"I might party with Natalie and Tim, or I might catch up on my reading and prepare for my new position. Or I might spend the day watching football. I've spent New Year's Day alone before. This won't be the first time."

"New position?"

"Yes, I'm going to be a political analyst for the top-rated cable news channel in the country."

"Are you serious?"

"Yes, I thought you knew."

"I had no idea. When did this happen?"

Kristie told Eric about her trips to New York and the offer. "I'm flying up there on the fourteenth for two weeks. I may be so bad they send me home, but it's a chance for me to finally be somebody and maybe earn some respect, respect in certain circles, that is."

Tears were streaming down Eric's face. "Kristie, you are somebody, you were my wife, you were Mary and Bobby's daughter, you're a special person, you're beautiful, both inside and out. You're smart, you're a hard worker, you're an over-achiever. How can you say this might be the chance for you to finally be somebody?"

"I never got the corner office with a view. Nothing I've ever done has been right or good enough. Maybe this time, I'll do something right, for once in my life."

"So, you consider yourself a failure because you've never had a corner office with a view?"

"That's pretty much it, plus I was beyond child bearing years when we married, so I've never had children?"

"Did you want children?"

"Well, if I had married when I was younger, like most people, I would have wanted children."

"You have Tanya, you know. She loves you, I know she does."

At this point, Kristie started to cry. Eric drew her to him, and held her while she sobbed. Then he pushed her back to where they were looking into each other's eyes. "Kristie, please don't cry. I don't want you to be sad, your Mama and Daddy don't want you to be sad."

"Eric, shouldn't you be getting ready to go to your party?"

"I'm not about to go the party, and leave you here crying and alone."

"You won't be the first to leave me alone and crying, and probably won't be the last. Everything I've ever done in life, I've done alone. I can certainly spend this New Year's Day alone. It's okay. I'll study, and I'll watch football. And Eric, I do need some time to think about things. I want you in my life, I really do, but we have to talk, seriously talk."

"Are you sure you're okay with me going to the party, Jeff did say I could bring you."

"Yes, go on."

Eric reluctantly left Kristie. Was she allowing him to go to the party, but arranging it so he couldn't possibly enjoy himself? He called Jimmy, and found he and Ruthie were watching football, but were about to go out and get lunch.

"Kristie's not going to the party, so if you would like to go, let's go."

"You mean it?"

"Sure."

"Okay, great. Ruthie and I will pick you up."

"I'll be in the parking lot."

CHAPTER *41*

Kristie was watching New Year's Day bowl games, while looking over some of the material she had to be familiar with before traveling to New York in a couple of weeks. She didn't care if she and Eric got back together. Yes, she slept with him last night and enjoyed it, but the thought of being a semi-celebrity trumped all feelings, physical and emotional. What if her name became a household name? What if people recognized her, and started asking for her autograph? She had a chance to really be somebody, but she had to work hard. Kristie wanted this, and was willing to put everything else on the back burner to achieve it, including Eric. She wanted everyone who had been mean to her, to be pea green with envy.

Her phone went off, bringing Kristie out of her trance. It was Natalie wanting to know if she and Eric were still coming over. She informed Natalie that Eric had gone to a party over at someone's house who was from Wentworth, and she didn't want to go, but she was hungry, and would come over and get something to eat.

"Are you all right?" Natalie asked Kristie when she arrived.

"Yes."

"Why didn't you go to the party with Eric?"

"The people hosting it are his friends. Both the husband and wife are originally from Wentworth, but I barely remember them, and they barely remember me. There was some drama this morning. I don't know if I want Eric back or not. I thought I did, but now I'm not sure. He's so attached to the old gang he hung out with in high school. I didn't hang out with that bunch, and didn't like them. I don't know if we'll be able to work things out. Eric's in the middle. I kind of feel sorry for him."

"Would you like a mimosa?"

"Sure."

"I'll let you make it since you like your drinks rather strong. Fix a plate of food. I guess you want to watch football."

"I'm good with whatever y'all want to watch."

"We'll watch football with you."

Kristie had a couple of mimosas and a couple of plates of sausage balls, miniature quiches, stuffed mushrooms, and cheese and crackers.

"Lambert's is serving ham, black-eyed peas, and turnip greens today. We thought we'd go there for supper. Want to go with us?

"I suppose I should. I don't have any of those things."

"I bet Hazel's Buffett will be serving today," said Tim. "I'll call and ask. If so, we can go there. It's closer."

Sure enough, Hazel's was serving ham, turnip, greens, black-eyed peas, fried green tomatoes, macaroni and cheese, and cornbread until 9:00 pm.

Natalie and Kristie thought Hazel's was a better idea. They would go there later in the day.

After drinking another Mimosa, Kristie decided to go to her place to chill out for a while. It was evident she was depressed because Eric went to the party without her, even though she encouraged him to do so.

Just as the Rose Bowl was about to kick off, Kristie's phone rang, and it was Natalie. She went to Publix to pick up some things and ran into Cheri Noble and three friends of hers from the Mobile area. They were headed to a New Year's Day party. The hosts were roasting a couple of pigs and were providing the sides, desserts, appetizers, and all the booze. Cheri had just talked to the hostess, and she indicated they had way too much food and to bring people to the party.

A local entertainer they all liked was performing later. Cheri gave Natalie the address and said bring Kristie and Tim, and Jean, if she wanted to go.

"I might as well go. If Eric can go out partying, so can I," replied Kristie.

Kristie thought it would be cool if Eric came home from his party before she returned from her party. She decided to drive separately from Natalie and Tim. That way they wouldn't have to leave at the same time since Natalie and Tim were early to bed, early to rise folks.

It was almost dark when the three of them arrived. There were many cars parked outside the rambling one-story brick house, and they immediately went around to the back where two large roasted pigs were lying on picnic tables. Other tables were loaded with all kinds of appetizers and sides, including a black-eyed pea and cornbread casserole and a large pot of turnip greens. A tiki bar was set up with a bartender serving drinks to the guests.

Kristie grabbed a beer, and went off to explore the premises. Of course, the kitchen was packed with folks spilling over into the dining room and living room. Kristie then ventured down the hall, and entered a large room that was a combination game room/den/man cave. As she entered the large room, among the folks in there laughing and socializing, she saw two couples standing together, Ruthie and Jimmy Harpo, with Eric and some woman, who was quite attractive.

Oh my, gasped Kristie. This is Jeff and Alice's party. I'm at Jeff and Alice's. Eric's here, and he's with another woman. Kristie immediately did an about face and left the game room. She was going back to the condo. She didn't belong here.

As she was heading out the back through the patio and the back yard, she saw Brian Burch, a local entertainer, warming up in preparation to entertain the crowd. When he saw Kristie, he smiled and hugged her, wished her a happy New Year, and said he was delighted to see her.

I can't very well leave now, thought Kristie. She needed to stay and listen to Brian for a little while, at least. She found Natalie and Tim, an extra chair, and sat with them during Brian's first set. At the end of the set, Brian said he was thrilled to be here, and was even more thrilled to see friends from Birmingham, Natalie and Tim Rolland, and Kristie Channing. No sooner than Brian had put down his guitar to take a break, Eric walked up behind Kristie and grabbed her shoulder.

"What are you doing here, you followed me here, didn't you?"

"No. Natalie ran into a friend of ours, Cheri Noble, at the grocery store. Cheri invited us. She had talked to the hosts, and they told her to bring friends because they had plenty of food and beverages."

"They do, don't they? All this food will never get eaten."

Tim told Eric what Kristie was saying was the truth. Cheri had asked Natalie, Tim, and Jean to come to the party, and when she found out Kristie was here, she told them to bring Kristie, as well. Jean opted to stay at the condo. It was kind of a spur of the moment thing.

"Jimmy and Ruthie are here with me. And, as I guess you know by now, Jeff and Alice are hosting this."

"I've already determined that. I'll leave before I get close to Jimmy, Ruthie, Jeff, and Alice. I wouldn't want my germs to rub off on them. Even though Jeff told Cheri to bring her friends to the party, I'm sure they never thought, in their wildest imaginations, I would be considered a friend of anyone's."

Even though Kristie was finishing her first beer, and hadn't eaten anything, she stood up, tossed the beer can in one of the trash receptacles, and headed toward her car, telling Natalie and Tim she would catch up with them later. They wanted to leave with her, but Kristie told them to please stay. She needed to be alone.

As she walked to her car, which was parked down the street, she heard a voice yelling her name. It was Eric.

"Don't go, please don't go."

Kristie stopped and let Eric catch up to her.

"Don't go."

"Why? You obviously don't want me to be here and embarrass you in front of your friends."

"Do you know that guy, Brian Burch?"

"Yes, I've known him for several years."

"I didn't realize you were so popular down here."

"I don't know that I'm popular down here, but I do know some people who live in this area."

"I'm sorry I kind of yelled at you. I was surprised to see you here. Have you had anything to eat or drink?"

"Just a beer."

"Well, the food is great. Jeff and Alice really put a lot into this. They're not really that bad. The other night at the Flora-Bama, they saw you, a single lady, and they just wanted you to sit with us and talk for a while. They knew I was depressed, and they wanted to cheer me up. They weren't trying to get you to go to bed with me on the fly. Let's get some food."

With that, Eric put his arm around Kristie, kissed her, and steered her back toward the house. When they entered the back area, there were two seats at one of the picnic tables. "You sit down and save me a seat, I'll fix our plates."

When Eric returned with their plates, utensils, and beers, he and Kristie ate in silence, but it was a good silence. Eric's right leg was interlocked with Kristie's left leg, and they sat as close together as possible, like a couple of teenagers or early twenty-somethings.

"By the way Eric, did I tell you I got a friendship request on Facebook from Anabelle Martin?"

"No."

"Well, I did, along with a private message from her asking if we could be real friends. I deleted the request. I have no desire to have any sort of contact with her. Besides, she has millions. I wouldn't be able to keep with her lifestyle."

"She just might be willing to pay your way for things like cruises and trips abroad," said Eric.

"In addition to being a snobby bitch, there's just something a little strange about her."

"You mean you think she might like women."

"I don't know, but I wouldn't be surprised to find out she gets her kicks anyway she can. By the way, you never told me what happened to Anabelle's family."

Eric told Kristie the story about Anabelle's Dad losing his business, and their palatial home in Huntsville. And about Anabelle's father killing her Mom and then turning his own cold hand.

"At the time, Anabelle was pregnant and miscarried."

"Wow, that's pretty overwhelming. Even though I don't care for her, I wouldn't wish than on anyone. It must have been terrible for her. But at least she was able to get hold of Wiley's millions."

"Kristie!"

"Oops, sorry."

"Oh, here he is," said Jimmy Harpo, as he, Ruthie, and the woman with whom they were talking earlier approached the table. Jimmy's and Ruthie's mouths fell open when they saw Kristie. The three of them turned and walked away.

"Was it something I said?" laughed Kristie.

"I don't think you said anything."

In a few moments, Jeff and Alice appeared at the table. "I see you decided to join us, Kristie," said Jeff.

"I know Cheri Noble. She invited a couple of friends and me to come. I had no idea the party was the same as your party."

"I also see you know Brian."

"Yes, I've known Brian for years."

"Kristie knows a lot of people, and she's also been hired as a news analyst for the number one cable news channel in America. Pretty soon, her name may be a household name in certain circles," said Eric.

"Oh, is that so," said Alice.

"Well, good luck," replied Jeff as he and Alice walked away.

"I guess I'm the belle of the ball," said Kristie.

"They were expecting me to be here with Rita. They're just surprised I'm with you, that's all."

"Yeah, right."

When Eric and Kristie finished eating, Eric suggested they go back to the condos. Since he rode with Jimmy and Ruthie, he could now ride back with Kristie.

"You came by yourself, didn't you?"

"Yes, Natalie and Tim drove their car separately."

"Let's find Jeff and Alice, and tell them we're leaving, and we had a good time. You did have a good time, didn't you?"

"I did. There's a lot of people here I know and enjoyed seeing, and I always love to hear Brian sing."

Eric and Kristie went inside the house, finding Jeff and Alice in a tight circle with Jimmy and Ruthie.

"Guess they're discussing me and how much they hate me."

Eric, not wanting to make Kristie mad, said nothing. He shook hands with Jeff and Jimmy, then hugged Alice and Ruthie, telling Jeff and Alice he had a great time, and Jimmy and Ruthie he would see them back in Wentworth.

As they were making their way through the crowded patio area, they spotted Natalie and Tim who were talking to someone Kristie didn't know. When they approached them to say they were leaving, Tim introduced them to a gentleman from Daphne. The gentleman was trying to unload two spaces on a charter flight from Mobile to Miami for the BCS Championship game on Monday, January 7. The flight was to leave about mid-morning of the seventh, and take them to Miami. Then after the game, the plane would fly back to Mobile. Tickets for the game were included in the package.

CHAPTER *42*

Kristie and Eric looked at one another.

"Want to go?" asked Eric.

"Ugh, yeah."

Kristie, Eric, and the gentleman negotiated a price and agreed to meet him in Daphne the next day to transfer the paperwork. They were going to the BCS Championship game to see Alabama play Notre Dame for the National Championship.

Because Kristie's condo was booked through January 3 and Eric's condo was booked through January 2, they would need to extend their stay for one of the units or try to find another place to stay. The next day, Kristie extended her stay at her unit until January 9, so Eric moved his stuff into her unit early on January 2, and turned in the entry card. That afternoon, they drove to Daphne to pay for the game tickets and the charter flight from Mobile to Miami and back on January 7.

The early days of 2013 were idyllic for Eric and Kristie. Both worked on their writing jobs, and Kristie studied for her new position as a news analyst. At night, they made love like they did on their honeymoon.

On January 7, the charter flight from Mobile took them to Miami and the BCS championship game, which Alabama won easily, and was once again number one. As the game ended, Kristie had her arms around Eric, and her eyes were filled with tears. This was the last time A.J., Barrett, Eddie, and many other Alabama players would put on the crimson jersey. She was going to miss these guys so much, but as always, with the Crimson Tide, others would step up to fill the shoes of the great players who were leaving.

As they left the stadium heading toward the chartered bus that would take them to the airport and their chartered plane, Kristie had never been so happy in her entire life. She was in love, embarking on an exciting new career, and Alabama was number one.

Not being twenty-five anymore, Kristie and Eric were exhausted as they deplaned in Mobile, to the point that both were concerned about falling asleep on the drive to Orange Beach. They thought about getting a room in Mobile or Daphne, but decided to try to drive the distance. Kristie took her turn first, and made it to Foley. Eric slept while Kristie drove. Then he drove from Foley to Orange Beach. They arrived at the condo, crawled into bed, and immediately went to sleep. Celebrating being crowned number one, would have to wait.

The next morning, the two love birds spent time on the phone talking to friends about the game. Then they prepared the condo for their departure the next day. That evening, they went to Kristie's favorite restaurant on the Alabama gulf coast for dinner. The next day, they left in separate cars. Eric was headed to his Wentworth apartment, and Kristie was headed to Birmingham. On January 14, she was due in New York, for two weeks, to begin her contract with the news channel.

Eric kissed Kristie as they departed in their separate vehicles, but didn't say anything about what would happen when they got back to Wentworth and Birmingham. Was this just a fling for Eric? Would Rita McDonald soon be back in his life, and Kristie forgotten about? These thoughts made Kristie's stomach lurch. After the few days spent together, Eric should have said something about the coming days and months, but he didn't. Kristie had put up with this kind of treatment all her life. Was she going to have to endure it again? It looked that way.

CHAPTER *43*

On the morning of December 14, Anabelle Martin was sitting in her attorney's office signing papers for the sale of her upscale home in Wentworth. As soon as she was finished, she would be heading south to her luxurious vacation home on West Beach in Gulf Shores, Alabama. She and Wiley had purchased a vacation home in Navarre Beach, Florida a few years after they married, but Anabelle had sold that house, opting instead for the Alabama Gulf Coast. Now, heading to Gulf Shores, Alabama, she would ponder what she was going to do for the rest of her life.

As she drove down I-65, which would take her to her destination, she couldn't help but remember the time when she, Wiley, Eric and Gina Channing, Jimmy and Ruthie Harpo, and Jan and Jeremy Franklin spent a week together at the Navarre beach house. The couples were in their thirties, good looking, and into having a blast, lying on the beach during the day and partying at night. One evening after everyone else had gone to bed, she, Wiley, Gina, and Eric were smoking pot by the pool. Everyone got high, disrobed, and jumped into the water. While Wiley took her perfect body for granted, Eric Channing couldn't stop gazing at her. Eric's wife, Gina, had small breasts and a big derriere, while Anabelle had perfect breasts, a tiny waist, and rounded hips.

When they had enough of the water, the foursome went inside and smoked some more pot. Anabelle got up to go to the bathroom. When she came out, Eric was standing there awaiting his turn. As the two passed each other, they touched.

Wiley had been dead for a year and a half now. After his divorce from that loser, Kristie Tidwell, she and Eric had an extremely brief, but tantalizing, physical relationship. Then Eric unloaded her for his newly widowed high school sweetheart, Rita McDonald Fisher. Because her friends in Wentworth were also friends with Rita, and were jubilant that Rita and Eric had resumed their relationship after all these years, Anabelle was out of the loop; alone with no friends.

Her plans were to move into the Alabama Gulf Coast house and begin a new life. Money was not a worry for her, but she was lonely. All her life, she had been breathtakingly beautiful, getting attention from dozens of guys. When she was in her early twenties, she caught the eye of Wentworth's most eligible bachelor, Wiley Martin. They married and had an idyllic life until cancer claimed Wiley when he was too young to die. Now, her beauty had faded, and she no longer had any friends.

Was there anyone she could call and talk to? Someone who didn't despise her because she was once beautiful, and had guys falling at her feet? She thought of Eric. What had she done wrong? She did ridicule his ex-wife, Kristie. Even though they were divorced, Eric still had feelings for her. The few times she had been around Kristie, she seemed arrogant and confident. Kristie was a beautiful woman, and age didn't mask her beauty. Anabelle knew Wiley was a bad boy in high school, and had given Kristie a hard time about her weight. For that reason, Kristie despised Wiley, and despised her also.

Kristie had been dumped by Eric, and so had she. The two women had that in common. Would Kristie Tidwell-Channing possibly consider being her friend? There was only one way to find out; contact Kristie and see what she was doing these days.

After three weeks in Orange Beach, Alabama, Kristie arrived at her Helena, Alabama home. Everything was as she had left it. The kitty cat was glad to see her after three weeks of having a pet sitter come in two times a week to put out food and water and change out the litter box.

Always the geek, Kristie unpacked her laptop, and set it up on her desk in her office. When checking her personal email, she saw something from one of the "point persons" in her high school graduating class. Her class, along with the two classes behind her class, would be getting together for a summer social in April. Jimmy Harpo, Jan Franklin, and Rita Fisher would all be included in the gathering, along with Eric and Kathryn Campbell Harpo, who graduated with Kristie. The "reunion" would be held at the Jones Lake home of James and Hannah Winston, both in Kristie's class. This gathering was months away, so Kristie chose not to dwell on it.

Eric had not called her during the drive from Orange Beach, nor had he called to see if she had arrived home safely. He played me for a fool, Kristie concluded. He'll surely be back in Rita's arms soon.

Alabama was number one, and Kristie was about to embark on a new career as a news analyst in less than a week. Never-the-less, she started crying. Why couldn't things work out for a change? Why wasn't Eric with her, sharing the Alabama Football Team's good fortunes, and her good fortunes? She wanted someone to share her life with, and she wanted that someone to be Eric.

The days following Kristie's return, she spent every waking moment preparing to go to New York for her initial stint as a news analyst. She poured over documents, and spent hours doing research on foreign policy and domestic issues. If she performed satisfactorily during her first six weeks when her one on one interviews would be taped for later broadcasts, she would go to the next level where she would do one on one live interviews. If she still performed satisfactorily, she would be placed beside someone whose views were diametrically opposite to hers, but these segments would be taped. If she continued to perform optimally, she would get opportunities at doing live segments against an adversary.

Instead of pulling her down, being ignored by Eric seemed to give her extra energy. This was Kristie's one big chance to become somebody, to be a semi-celebrity, to possibly laugh all the way to the bank. With potential new-found fame, she might write a book or several books. She might even develop a following. Would this anger Jimmy Harpo, Ruthie Harpo, and Kathryn Campbell Harpo or what?

When the big day arrived, Kristie boarded the plane in Birmingham, that would take her directly to New York, and hopefully a new life. The last time she was in New York, she contemplated taking her own life. Her guardian Angel, directed by her Lord and Savior, Jesus Christ, had intervened. He had plans for Kristie here on earth.

CHAPTER 44

After quite a start to the new year, Eric was headed north on Gulf Shores Parkway, when he received a call from his daughter, Tanya. She was crying, and Eric could hardly understand what she was saying. "Slow down honey, what's wrong?"

"Mama has a malignant brain tumor, it's the kind that breaks up and spreads. It's inoperable and fatal."

"Where's your Mom now?"

"She's asleep. She's on heavy medication to ease her pain. She doesn't want you to know, but I can't deal with it."

"Where's her boyfriend, Luke?"

"Oh, he took off several months ago."

"What stage is the cancer in? Is she able to do anything at all? How long does she have left?" Eric hated asking Tanya these questions, but they had to be answered. "Why aren't you in school?"

"Mama's been swallowing pills to ease the pain, and has been going to work, but today, she wasn't able to. I decided to stay home and take care of her."

"I'm about four hours from you. I'll drive directly there."

Eric pulled over at the next convenient place because he was much too shaken to make phone calls and drive at the same time. He immediately called Tanya's school, and talked to the assistant principal, telling her Tanya was not in school because she was taking care of Gina. He had just been informed Gina was suffering from a malignant brain tumor. The assistant principal was surprised, saying she had no idea. Tanya's grades were top notch, and her attendance record was perfect until today.

"I've been in Orange Beach, but I'm on my way back today. I will be stopping at the house to see what's going on. I'll have Tanya back at school tomorrow."

Damn, thought Eric. What the hell is happening? The thought of Gina being terminally ill, and in excruciating pain hit him like a load of bricks. He turned the motor of the truck off, and laid his head on the steering wheel. Tanya says Gina's tumor is inoperable and fatal. What if she's over-reacting? Still! It can't be. Is Gina, his first wife and the mother of his only child dying? Eric burst into tears and sobbed.

The next thing he knew, someone was tapping on the left window of the truck. Eric looked up and saw a policeman. He let the window down. When the policeman asked if he was okay, he replied, "I'm okay, officer; well I'm not okay. I just got off the phone with my daughter. Her Mom, also my ex-wife, has been diagnosed with a malignant brain tumor, and it's one of the bad kinds. According to my daughter, it's the kind which breaks up and spreads throughout the brain. I'm trying to get my arms wrapped around this. My ex-wife and my daughter live in Birmingham, and I'm headed there now."

"Okay, buddy, you be careful. I'll be praying for you."

"Thanks, officer."

CHAPTER 45

On January 14, 2013, Kristie deplaned at LaGuardia airport, retrieved her bags from baggage claim, and took a cab into midtown Manhattan. She checked into her hotel, and called her boss at the channel.

He was glad Kristie had an uneventful trip up, and was anxious to see her and get things moving. She had been studying hard, and considered herself up to date on current events, both domestic and foreign. She also felt she could win any argument someone from the other side of the political spectrum might possibly throw at her. Because Kristie had not eaten lunch, her boss told her to grab some lunch and meet him at the studio at 2:30 pm.

When Kristie met up with her boss, he gave her a tentative schedule of her initial interviews, which would be "one on one" and taped.

If Kristie performed satisfactorily, she would stay in New York for three weeks. Then she would return to Birmingham, where she would continue the one on one interviews, but from the affiliate in Birmingham.

While Kristie never thought of herself as a lucky person, her three weeks in New York were spectacular. Everyone was pleased with her work, and the hits on her blog had tripled, resulting in substantially more income for her. Kristie returned to Birmingham on February 7 to do interviews from the network affiliate in Birmingham. She did not have a schedule, but was told they would email the interview details to her, and try to do it at least twenty-four hours in advance.

During her first week in Birmingham, Kristie had three interviews, and all went well. In fact, her boss at the channel indicated she was doing so well, he wanted to see how she operated in a venue other than Birmingham. He asked her to drive to Nashville, and check into a hotel close to the affiliate up there, so she could do some segments. It was anticipated, if Kristie were successful, she would be expected to appear at different network affiliates, depending upon where she was at the time.

After three days in Nashville, Kristie was southbound on I-65, and had to pass by her hometown of Wentworth. She had not been in Wentworth since driving back from Nashville last November, when Jake Stanley almost threw her out of his restaurant, her car was spun around by a tornado, and she spent the night with Eric. But she was hungry and decided to have an early dinner at The Coach, Wentworth's finest eatery.

Even though she was a lone diner, the hostess smiled and escorted her to a good table. However, in a private room close by, employees were arranging tables and chairs in preparation for what appeared to be a large party. Oh great, thought Kristie. I wanted a quiet dinner, and it looks like there's going to be a large group, which will probably be loud and disruptive, in here shortly.

CHAPTER 46

A crowd of twenty-five to thirty gathered close to the funeral tent on a cold February day. Gunmetal colored clouds were forming in the western sky around a fiery sun. In a couple of hours, the folks of Wentworth, Alabama would be able to witness what some called a sunset of fire and ice.

Most of the graveside attendees were huddled close to the tent, to catch a glimpse of the family, and listen to the minister read scripture, while weaving into his message, accolades of the deceased. But about twenty yards from the crowd stood two lone figures. One was a tall gentleman, and standing about ten feet to his side was an attractive woman.

The tall man had wavy blond hair and a beard. As the minister was talking about the deceased's dedication to the Lord Jesus Christ, to family, to work, and to Alabama football, the man, handsome in his own way, appeared to be somewhat nervous, shifting his weight from one leg to another. He also had his cell phone in hand and was checking the screen every two or three seconds.

The lady had chestnut colored hair mixed with strands of gray. It would be obvious to anyone she had once been a beautiful woman. In fact, she still was. Also straining to get a glimpse of the folks seated in the tent, she appeared as nervous as the gentleman standing a short distance from her.

While the woman was not able to see the folks seated in the front row, she spied someone in the second row who looked familiar. This woman had gray hair woven in with her dark hair. But not being able to see her face, she couldn't be sure if this woman was indeed Anabelle Martin.

The chestnut-haired woman and the blonde gentleman nodded to one another as the message continued. Neither had any idea who the other was.

When the graveside service concluded, both lone figures slowly made their way to the tent. The woman saw Barry Tidwell staring at the casket, and then she saw him look toward one of the people still sitting in a chair in front. Barry didn't look happy, but was anyone supposed to look happy at a funeral. The chestnut-haired woman and the blond stranger arrived at the front row at the same time, both with tears in their eyes.

Eric and Tanya stood up, and both hugged Rita McDonald Fisher. "It was kind of you to come, Rita," said Eric in a subdued tone.

"I'm so sorry, Eric. If there's anything I can do, please let me know."

"Thanks. I will."

With that, Rita turned around, walked to her rented car, and left the cemetery.

Next, the blonde stranger sidled up to Eric and Tanya.

"I'm Luke Turley. I was a friend of Gina's for a while. I'm so sorry."

Eric shook his hand and thanked him for coming. Tanya didn't acknowledge him.

Attendees of the graveside service departed, leaving only family and close friends of Gina Hanover Channing. Darkness was approaching, and the stately gates of the Wentworth City Cemetery would be closed and locked soon. Jan Harpo Franklin grabbed Eric's arm and indicated she had touched base with The Coach and they would have the tables set up for their group by the time they arrived. The Wentworth Civitan Club was meeting in the main private dining room, but their table would be set up in another private room.

Barry Tidwell, a cousin of Kristie's, whose wife Jessica was a close friend of Gina's, paid his respects to Eric, who he didn't particularly care for, and Gina's aging mother. Then he steered Jessica toward their car, and they drove out of the cemetery.

While Kristie was eating her salad, a crowd of folks entered the restaurant and headed toward the private room close to Kristie's table. To her surprise, the group seemed rather subdued. Kristie caught a glimpse of an older woman being led by a younger couple. What she saw next caused her to gasp. There was Jan Harpo Franklin, with husband Jeremy. Kristie immediately picked up her phone and began to fiddle with it, hoping Jan and Jeremy would not see her.

"KRISTIE!" The shout came from someone who sounded like a young teenager. It was from the group.

Kristie looked up to see Tanya Channing racing toward her. Seeing her stepdaughter, Kristie stood up, and Tanya ran into her outstretched arms.

"Mama died, and we just buried her."

Kristie, taken aback, almost stumbled with Tanya in her arms. "Oh honey, I'm so sorry, so very sorry. What happened?"

Before Tanya could speak, a somber looking Eric appeared at the table. Because his life had been so hectic since finding out about Gina's terminal illness, he had not bothered to get in touch with Kristie to inform her of what was taking place. "Kristie, what can I say? I've been so consumed with Gina and Tanya, that everything else in my life had to be put on hold."

"Eric, I did wonder why you didn't call me after we returned from Orange Beach." A group, including Jan Franklin and Rita Fisher, had gathered around Kristie's table.

"Kristie, can we talk later? Come on Tanya."

"I think we probably need to."

"Can I stay with Kristie, Daddy?"

"No, honey, we need to be with our friends and family who are here with us this evening."

"Please, Daddy?"

It was apparent Tanya needed to be hugged and comforted, and what better person was there to do it, but Kristie, her stepmother.

"Can Kristie come sit with us?"

"I'm afraid not, dear. The room is set up for only so many guests."

Reluctantly, Tanya let go of Kristie and started toward the private room, steered by Eric.

Kristie's server appeared and asked her if she was finished with her salad.

"Yes. And I hate to do this, but can I get my entrée to go, along with a half dozen orange rolls?"

"Of course, is something wrong?"

"Yes, but it's not the restaurant's fault. Some drama has arisen, and I think it best I walk away."

"Of course."

While Kristie was waiting on her order, one of the managers appeared at her table and asked what had made her change her mind about dining at the restaurant? He was several years younger than Kristie and had sung in the church choir with her Dad, Bobby Tidwell.

"You're Bobby Tidwell's daughter, aren't you?"

"Yes."

"I sang in the choir with your Dad. He was a fine man."

"Thank you."

"I'm sorry you feel the need to leave. I hope we haven't done anything to offend you, and that you'll come and dine with us again."

"You did nothing. My ex-husband is with the party over there, along with my stepdaughter. I just found out that Tanya's Mom passed away. It's complicated and dramatic, and I just want to leave, plus I've been out of town, and I'm anxious to get back to Birmingham. I live there now."

"You were married to Eric Channing, you're his second wife?"

"That's me."

"I understand."

The server came back with Kristie's order, indicating he had put another salad with her order.

"Let's take 50% off Ms. Tidwell's order," directed the manager.

Kristie gave the server her card, and he left.

"Ms. Tidwell, please come again soon." With that, the manager left.

Kristie signed the credit card slip, grabbed her order and started to depart. She really should say good night to Tanya, though. As awkward as it would be to enter the private area, Kristie couldn't leave without seeing Tanya. As she entered the room, Kristie heard several gasps. She saw Tanya, sitting between Eric and Rita, and walked over to her. Tanya got up and hugged her stepmom with Kristie telling Tanya she loved her and would see her soon.

As Kristie walked toward the door, Eric stood up and followed her out.

Thinking Eric would surely scold her for coming in and interrupting the intimate gathering, Kristie said, "I'm sorry to interrupt, but I couldn't leave without saying goodbye to Tanya."

"Kristie, don't go."

"What?"

"Don't go, stay here with us. There's plenty of room for you."

"That's not what you said earlier."

"I didn't know how many the room was set up for, but there's plenty of room. Kristie, I'm not exactly the devil."

"I already have my "to go" order, and I'm shook up enough as it is. Besides, I don't know most of these people. They're all friends and family of Gina, except for Jan Franklin, and didn't I see Jimmy and Ruthie among the crowd, and there's Rita McDonald Fisher?"

"They came out of respect for Tanya and me. Jan helped arrange this dinner."

"You seem to have had time to inform Rita and the others about Gina, but you didn't have thirty seconds to call me."

"I didn't talk to any of them. Somehow Rita and the others found out. By the way, what brings you to Wentworth tonight?"

"I've been in Nashville, and as I was passing through, I thought I would have dinner at the Coach. It's been a while since I've been here. I'm headed back to Birmingham."

"Stay with Tanya and me at my apartment tonight."

"WHAT? You, Rita, Tanya, and me. That'll be cozy."

"I'm not with Rita. Again, she just showed up out of respect for Tanya and me."

"And you just happened to invite her to go out with the group, and she just happens to be sitting with you and Tanya?"

"Actually, yes."

"I see Jimmy, Ruthie, Jan, and Jeremy are here also."

"Kristie, please stay with us tonight. Nothing's changed between you and me since we were in Orange Beach, I hope."

"Here's the key to the apartment, if you don't want to stay here with us. There's a fully stocked bar along with beer and wine. You can finish your dinner there. Tanya and I will be in shortly. I know it would mean a lot to Tanya. So, please."

"Eric, I don't even know where your apartment is."

"It's just off Graham Street close to Ancestry Park. In fact, the complex is named Ancestry Park Apartments. My unit number is 121. It's on the first floor. Here's the key. Please stay with us."

Eric had tears in his eyes, so Kristie said yes. As she turned to leave, Eric grabbed her by the arm, leaned forward, and kissed her on her forehead.

Kristie found Eric's apartment with no difficulty, and let herself in. Her food from the Coach was still warm, and she was hungry. As if Eric knew she would be at the apartment this evening, a bottle of chardonnay was in the refrigerator. She ate half of her entree and two orange rolls. She could have eaten another one, but didn't.

So, this was Eric's crib until his lake house was completed. It wasn't all that bad. The furniture was quality and so were the other furnishings. Someone had to have helped him choose these things. Kristie guessed it was Rita. Jealousy stabbed her.

Kristie set her bags in the living room, not knowing where to take them. The bedroom that was obviously Eric's had a king-sized bed, two nightstands, a dresser, and a chest of drawers. The second bedroom contained a double bed, a nightstand, and a dresser. There were also some boxes piled against the wall.

She decided to suggest that she and Tanya sleep together in Eric's room. Tanya needed to be close to someone and that someone should be a woman.

Kristie undressed in the second bathroom and put on a sweatshirt and yoga pants. Then she took out her tablet, and started to read one of the downloaded novels. Finding herself falling asleep, she wondered where Eric and Tanya were. Because of her insecurities, Kristie was scared Eric may have had second thoughts about spending the night with her, and taken Tanya over to Rita Fisher's house.

Then she heard a key in the door, and in walked Eric and Tanya. Immediately running to Kristie who was sitting on the sofa in the living room, Tanya sat down beside her and hugged her. It was evident Tanya needed someone who could serve as a substitute for her mom.

"Eric, is it okay if Tanya and I sleep in your bedroom and you sleep in the second bedroom?"

"Ugh, yeah. Actually, that's perfect. Thanks."

Eric was upset with himself for not thinking of that. But leave it to Kristie to always have the perfect solution. Making love that night was out of the question, but he was looking forward to having Kristie sleep beside him. Eric was now the parent of custody and Tanya's well-being would always come first for the rest of his life.

"Okay, Tanya, move your stuff out of the second bedroom and into your Dad's room."

Because it was only 8:30, a little early for bed, Eric suggested they watch some TV for a while.

After moving her things into Eric's room, Tanya closed the door, apparently wanting to put on something comfortable. She was still dressed in the clothes she wore to the funeral. When she opened the door a few minutes later, she was dressed in a long granny-styled gown, and fuzzy house slippers were on her feet. Eric was sitting in his recliner and Kristie was sitting on the sofa. Tanya joined Kristie on the sofa, but was sound to sleep within minutes.

Eric and Kristie jostled Tanya. When she awoke, Eric gently took her arm and led her to his bedroom and to the king-sized bed. After Tanya crawled into the huge bed and slid under the covers, Eric closed the bedroom door, sat down on the bed beside her, and took her into his arms. She started crying, and so did Eric. "Sweetheart, you mean more to me than anything in this world. I love you so much, and I'm going to take care of you always. I don't want you to ever have to hurt again."

Tanya began to sob even louder, making Eric hug her even tighter. "It's okay sweetie, it's okay to cry. I'm here for you forever." Tanya continued to sob, and Eric continued to hold her tight.

In the living room, Kristie heard Tanya's sobbing. To lose your mother at that age had to be devastating, even though her Dad would always be there for her. Kristie then teared up thinking about her Mom and Dad, and how much they had loved her and had been there to comfort her. She wished she could hug her Mom and Dad, and cry while in their arms just like Tanya was doing now. It would surely be nice to have someone's shoulder to cry on. But she was an adult, an adult who had no one who cared for her. Yes, Eric was being decent tonight, but what about tomorrow? His first love was Rita McDonald, now Fisher, and he still cared deeply for her. Kristie knew she would never be Eric's one true love, that one true love was Rita.

Kristie was so deep in her own thoughts, she failed to notice that Eric was back in the living room and standing over her. "Are you okay?"

"Is anyone really okay tonight?"

"Look, I'm sorry you had to find out about this by chance. I know you weren't planning on spending the night in Wentworth with Tanya and me, but I'm so glad you're staying. Tanya loves you and needs you, and so do I. I know we need to talk about some things. New Year's was a whirlwind of emotions. Then came the news about Gina. Now, I have a daughter to finish raising, and I know nothing about raising children, teenagers, whatever. I was there when she was born, but the time I got to spend with her since then was sterile. I'm scared."

"And I'm supposed to step right in and forget all the pain you have put me through? Then I'm to assist you in every way I can in continuing to raise Tanya? Is that what you want?

"I'm ashamed to say it, but yes, that's what I want. I know I'm a horrible person, and I wouldn't blame you if you walked out of this apartment tonight. But I need you, and don't know if I can manage without you."

"Oh, you'll manage. You always do. There are lots of women who would run to you if you only winked at them. I'm sure Anabelle Martin would be happy to accommodate your needs if Rita turns you down. She bought a house on West Beach with her millions, you know."

"Kristie, if you want to leave, and drive back to Birmingham, and continue your life, go right ahead. Tanya was counting on you to be with her tonight, but that's okay. I'll explain it to her somehow."

"I'll stay for Tanya's sake only. Tomorrow morning, I'm heading back to Birmingham. Tanya, though, deserves as much love as she can possibly get right now. I love her, and I don't want her to feel rejected and unloved as a child. It's bad enough when you are an adult and are lonely and unloved."

With that, Kristie arose from the sofa, and headed toward the master bedroom. A night light was on, and Kristie saw that Tanya was lying on her stomach, and appeared to be asleep. After slipping on her nightgown, Kristie crawled in the bed on the other side of Tanya. As she was settling under the covers, she heard a sob come from Tanya. She sat up, touching Tanya lightly on the shoulder. Tanya immediately sat up and started crying.

"It's all right, honey. It's all right. I'm here for you, and your Daddy's here for you. If there were any way we could keep you from hurting, we would."

There was nothing Kristie could say to comfort Tanya. She was well into adulthood when her parents died, and Bobby and Mary were together.

Tanya was conceived during a trial separation. After finding out about the pregnancy, Eric remained with Gina throughout the pregnancy and delivery. But soon after that, Gina and Eric divorced. Often quarreling about Tanya's upbringing, Eric thought Gina was too lenient, and he didn't get to spend as much time with Tanya as he would have liked.

According to Eric, Gina had a string of live-in boyfriends, and never took Tanya to church. Gina must have done something right, though, because Tanya was a beautiful teenager. She was respectful, well groomed, made good grades in school, and was headed to college at the University of Alabama. Hopefully, she would qualify for some scholarship money.

As the older long-haired brunette hugged the younger long-haired brunette, the bedroom door opened. Eric had heard Tanya's sobbing. He sat on the bed, and somehow the three of them managed a group hug. Kristie then pulled back and let Eric hold Tanya.

Tanya eventually stopped crying. And when she did, Eric got up, turned on a lamp, went to the closet, and retrieved an inflatable bed. "Do you ladies mind?"

"Daddy, stay in here with Kristie and me tonight, please!"

Eric looked at Kristie, and she nodded. He then plugged in the bed. When it was fully inflated, he put a fitted sheet on over it. Eric then retrieved a pillow and a blanket, turned the lamp off, and laid down.

Kristie couldn't go to sleep, and thought about what Eric said to her earlier, that he wanted her back with him so she could help him finish raising Tanya. What was going to happen when Tanya went off to the University in the fall? Did Eric really want her, or did he want Rita McDonald? She knew if Eric had his choice, he would pick Rita. Rita was his first love, and she was thinner than Kristie.

Kristie finally fell asleep, into what seemed to be a very deep sleep. When she awoke, Eric and Tanya weren't there. She heard some noise that sounded like it was coming from the kitchen. Things seemed surreal. Twenty-four hours ago, she was waking up in a Nashville hotel, getting ready to go to the network affiliate and film three segments. Now, she was at Eric's apartment, comforting her stepdaughter following the death of her mother.

Tanya would need to get back into school, and would need someone to live with her in Gina's house until graduation this spring. All of that would have to be worked out. Eric was her Dad, but he had never been a real Dad before, but he was going to have to start. Kristie would do what she could to be there for Tanya, but she was embarking on a new career which was going quite well. Eric had given her no encouragement other than he wanted her help in raising his daughter. If Eric truly loved her and wanted to be with her as they guided Tanya from a teenager into adulthood, she would gladly give up her budding career. But he wanted nothing more than help in raising his teenage daughter. Furthermore, if Rita chose to be with him, he would drop her like a hot potato.

Suddenly, Tanya bounded into the master bedroom and announced she was going to take a shower and get dressed. Then she and her Dad were going to Birmingham. Her Dad was going to stay at Gina's house for the time being while they adjusted to their new life.

Kristie got up and went to the second bathroom. Then she walked into the living room where she found Eric talking intensely to someone on the phone. Kristie retrieved her suitcase and her makeup bag, and went back to the second bathroom to shower and dress. Forty-five minutes later, she emerged dressed and ready to go somewhere, anywhere. When she walked into the living room, Tanya and Eric were sitting on the sofa. Eric had his arm around Tanya.

"Sweetie, I need to have a few minutes alone with Kristie," said Eric, as he stood up, took Kristie by the arm and steered her toward the master bedroom. He closed the door and motioned for her to sit down on the unmade bed.

"After I shower and dress, and throw a few things in a suitcase, Tanya and I are going to Birmingham to Gina's house. Gina knew in advance she was going to die, and she did take care of things. The house will be paid for, and Tanya will have enough money to attend college without student loans. I'll also be helping her. I want some time alone with Tanya so we can get used to each other. I'm her next of kin. Gina's folks aren't getting any younger, but they will be available to help. They're nice people, and I'm grateful for them. That's who I was talking to when you walked into the living room."

"Okay, I'll head back to Birmingham, also."

"Tanya will be going back to school on Monday. We'll talk then."

"Okay. I'll straighten up this room while you're in the shower. Then I'll be off."

It didn't take long for Kristie to straighten up the master bedroom, and put away the inflatable bed and the bed linens. She retrieved her bags, tearfully hugged Tanya, telling her she would see her in Birmingham. And off she went without saying goodbye to Eric.

CHAPTER 47

Traveling down I-65, Kristie realized just how little sleep she had gotten the night before, and was scared she might fall asleep at the wheel. She also realized she was hungry. What did she have at the house to eat for breakfast? Nothing. Fighting sleep, she made it to the house after stopping at McDonald's for a sausage and biscuit.

When she drove into the driveway, she noticed a package, about the size of a shoebox, on her front step. Before going to Nashville, Kristie had ordered a bracelet from jewelry.com, but it shouldn't be in a box that big. The box was light, and Kristie went inside to open it. What was inside made her gasp. Oh shit! That looks like marijuana and lots of it. She looked at the return address, and it said the package was from a small town in California. Kristie had been to this town on business many years ago. The packaged was addressed to someone else, but the address was Kristie's.

She immediately called the Helena police, and told them what she had discovered. In five minutes, a squad car was in front of her house. Kristie informed the officers she had been up all night with the daughter of her ex-husband, because the daughter had just lost her mother. She was sleep-deprived and shook up. Kristie wrote her statement while the officers called for a drug-sniffing dog. When another officer arrived with the dog, he took the alleged marijuana and let the dog sniff it. Sure enough, the dog sat, a sign the green weed was indeed an illegal substance. Kristie laughed and said she had always thought of drug-sniffing dogs as big German shepherds or Doberman Pinschers. This dog was a cute little white mutt.

The officers took the suspicious package and said they might send someone from DEA over to talk to her later today, and advised her to get some rest.

Get some rest, thought Kristie? There's no way I'm going to sleep now. But at least I can crawl into my own bed and pull the covers over my head.

CHAPTER 48

Eric and Tanya headed down I-65, and arrived at Gina's house about 11:00 am. They had eaten a late breakfast, so neither was hungry. Tanya took her bags to her room, and Eric took his bags to what appeared to have been Gina's bedroom. The bed was unmade, and some of Gina's clothes were thrown over a chair.

I can't do this, thought Eric. He, instead, moved his bags to a third bedroom that appeared to have served as Gina's office. In the room was a day bed, a computer desk, and a small dresser. This would have to do for one night, at least.

Eric suggested to Tanya they both try to get some sleep since neither had gotten much sleep the night before. Eric crawled into the day bed and was asleep immediately. When he awoke, it was almost dark and he was hungry. He found Tanya in the living room watching TV. "Want to order a pizza, honey?"

"That'll be fine, Daddy."

After ordering the pizza, Eric found some soft drinks in the pantry and poured a Coke for Tanya and a caffeine-free Diet Coke for himself.

"Can we invite Kristie over?"

"Not tonight. Kristie feels, and so do I, that you and I need some time alone together. She'll be a part of our lives, but not tonight, you and I need this time."

As they were finishing dinner, Eric's phone rang. It was Gina's mother. She and Eric talked for a while. It was agreed that Gina's mom and dad would drive down from Wentworth tomorrow. They would gather up Gina's clothes and take them to the Salvation Army.

Shortly after 10:00, Eric and Tanya went to their respective rooms with Eric telling Tanya if she needed him, to knock on the door and come right in.

CHAPTER 49

Despite being exhausted, Kristie slept fitfully, and woke up with a pounding headache on this Friday morning. What a nightmare the last two days had been. Two days ago, on Wednesday, she had been in a good mood, returning from Nashville where her opinion segment went well. Then she had the bright idea of stopping at the Coach, Wentworth's famous steak house, for dinner. From there, everything had gone downhill.

After taking some Advil, Kristie padded off to her home office and checked a couple of her blogs and social media sites. As she was checking her personal email account, she noticed an email from a recruiter. There was a software engineer position in the Birmingham area, and the recruiter thought Kristie would be a good fit. The job required certain computer skills, management experience, and business analyst experience. Kristie met the requirements.

Should she pursue this job? She was doing well as a news analyst, and the thought of going back into IT made her nauseous. Kristie told the headhunter she wasn't interested at the moment, but that could change in a heartbeat, so she asked the recruiter not to forget about her.

Then Kristie remembered the marijuana she found on her doorstep yesterday. What was going to become of that? She had done the only thing she could do, and that was call the police and turn it over to them. But what if the person the package was meant for came after her?

The Advil wasn't working on her headache which appeared to be turning into one of her "killer migraines." Not having anything planned for the day, Kristie went back to bed and was soon asleep. She awoke to the sound of a text coming in on her phone. It was Natalie, inviting her to out to dinner. Kristie texted her back that she wasn't feeling well and would have to pass.

While checking her email on her phone, Kristie noticed an email from a jfranklin. In the subject line, it said: "Classes Getting Together." The email was from Jan Harpo Franklin reminding the recipients that her class and the class above hers and the class below hers would be having a joint social in April at Jim and Hannah Winston's house on Jones Lake. Kristie was in the class one year ahead of Jan's class, and Rita was in Jan's class, and Jimmy Harpo was in the class one year behind Jan's. Well, that should be a lot of fun, thought Kristie sarcastically, having forgotten about the first notice.

For the next few weeks, Kristie immersed herself in her career as a news analyst, spending half of her time in New York City. Her ability to get her points across plus her glossy sounding southern accent quickly made her a favorite of everyone at the channel. Frequently, while in Alabama, she would be asked for her autograph and to pose for pictures. She was a celebrity of sorts and loved it.

While Kristie was in NYC, the channel paid for her to stay in a hotel suite not far from Tim's apartment, and they would occasionally go out for dinner and drinks.

One evening, the food was great, the drinks were flowing freely, and the band played eighties music. Kristie didn't have to be at the studio until mid-afternoon, so she could stay out a little later than usual, and she did, staggering out of the trendy club after midnight, and giggling with Tim. In fact, Kristie was sort of having to hold onto Tim as he held onto her. When they got to her hotel, Kristie asked him if he would be okay for the two-block walk to his apartment.

"Well, I don't know."

"Come on up to my room, you can sleep on the sofa-bed, if necessary."

Kristie led a wobbly Tim through the lobby, into the elevator, and into her hotel suite.

"Ya know, I've always liked you, Kristie," said Tim as he fell backward onto the sofa-bed.

"Yeah, I like you too Tim," yelled Kristie from the bedroom as she removed her coat, sat down on the bed, and began to remove her boots.

"Come over here and sit down. Let's raid the mini-bar."

"I think you've had enough to drink."

"Well, just come over here and sit down a minute."

Uh-oh, what had Kristie gotten herself into? While Tim could be a flirt, he would never think of cheating on Natalie. Even though he was physically attractive enough, Kristie had never thought of Tim in that way.

Grabbing some sheets and a blanket from the closet in the bedroom, Kristie went into the living room prepared to help Tim fix the sofa-bed on which he was to sleep. What she found was a passed-out Tim sitting on the sofa. Not about to disturb him, she quietly put the sheets and blanket beside him, turned out the light and made her way to the bedroom where she quickly put on a long flannel nightgown and crawled into bed.

Kristie had just fallen asleep when her cell phone went off. It was Tim from the living room.

"Hey, was I obnoxious?"

"Not really."

"I don't feel so hot, but I'm going back to my apartment. Thanks for taking care of me."

"No problem."

"You're a real lady and a good friend, Kristie. Natalie and I are blessed to have you in our lives."

"Thank you, Tim, I'm blessed to have the two of you in my life also." And Kristie meant every word of it.

After hearing Tim walk out, and the door close, Kristie got up and made sure the door into the suite was chained and bolted. Then she went back to bed where she fell asleep immediately.

The next morning, Kristie decided to order room service for breakfast, and do some work before she had to be at the studio that afternoon. She wrote two blog articles and prepared for her segments at the channel later that afternoon and evening.

As she was checking her personal email, she came upon the message from Jan Harpo Franklin about the class social. She wondered if Eric would attend. He and Jim Winston did ang out some in High School, and Jim's wife, Hannah, and Rita were cheerleaders together at Wentworth. While Jim didn't play football, he was on the track team with Eric. Kristie and Hannah were in the National Honor Society together, but Kristie didn't think she ever uttered a word to Jim while they were in school.

Since the morning she, Eric, and Tanya left Eric's apartment, the morning after Gina's funeral, she had not heard from Eric. It did bother her because she had, much to her dismay, fallen back in love with him. Kristie had encouraged him to spend time with Tanya and get to know her before resuming their relationship, but Eric never contacted her, not even to ask how she was doing. Did he ever watch her on TV? Did any of the Harpo's ever see her on TV? When they did, did they laugh at her? Well, maybe the Harpos laughed at her, and maybe others laughed at her, but Kristie didn't care. She was somewhat of a star.

Kristie finished her work at the studio after recording a session with one of the prime-time hosts and a politically opposite contributor for the channel. It was getting late, and Kristie was famished, not having eaten anything since breakfast in her suite. Jonathan, the opposition party consultant, was single, somewhat attractive, and maybe ten years to fifteen years Kristie's senior. He was a nice person, and Kristie really did enjoy being around him.

As both rode down the elevator together, Jonathan asked Kristie if she would like to get something to eat, and Kristie answered in the affirmative.

Jonathan took Kristie to a cozy little Italian bistro across the street from the studio. Both being pasta lovers, they ordered two kinds of pasta and split them. Johnathan was a wine connoisseur and ordered the best cabernet sauvignon Kristie had ever tasted. The salads were a perfect mix of arugula and baby spinach garnished with walnuts, strawberries, and a tangy vinaigrette dressing. For dessert, they split a piece of chocolate cake garnished with whipped cream and mint sprigs.

After dinner, Jonathan walked Kristie to her hotel. At the entrance, he took both of her hands, squeezed them, and told her he had a good time. Even though he was leaving for Chicago the next day, he told her he would call her in the next few days. Because she was flying to D.C. tomorrow to record two segments there, and then would fly to Birmingham that night, Kristie made sure Jonathan had her cell number.

Kristie's plane arrived in Birmingham after midnight during a cold rain. As always, she stood by the baggage carousel alone, with no one to meet her and hug her. When her bags arrived, she retrieved them from the moving conveyor belt, and made her way to the dismal airport parking deck. Heading toward the area where she thought she parked, she saw that her car wasn't there. She always had good recall about where she parked in the Birmingham airport, and tried to park as close to the elevator as possible. For this trip, she distinctly remembered parking in first row about 5 spaces to the left of the elevator. Her SUV wasn't there, and was nowhere to be seen.

A panicked Kristie, with her bags in tow, headed toward security to report that her car had been stolen. But wait! She then realized she had flown out on one airline and had returned on another airline which unloaded on a different concourse. Her car should be near the concourse C elevator, and she was at the concourse B elevator. Kristie hurried toward the concourse C elevator, and there was her SUV. Relief set in! After throwing her bags into the cargo bay and paying the parking charge, she headed west on I-59 and south on I-65 to her Helena, Alabama home.

Kristie was exhausted. The rain and the headlights from other vehicles weren't helping her vision. Suddenly, the tears came. She was alone. No one cared. What if she collided with one of the huge tractor-trailers passing her? Who would care? Not Eric. Jonathan, maybe? Who am I kidding, thought Kristie? Jonathan had women hanging all over him. Besides, the two of them were political opposites. James Carvel and Mary Matalin managed it, but that was an anomaly. She would never get that lucky.

Tears were still rolling down Kristie's cheeks when she pulled into her driveway and into the garage. As always, the kitty-cat was glad to see her.

CHAPTER 50

Eric decided to give up his apartment in Wentworth, and move in with Tanya in the house Gina had left to her. His house on Jones Lake was nearing completion, but Tanya came first. He would stay with her in Birmingham until she graduated from high school and went off to college. Then maybe the Birmingham house could be rented out.

Eric and Tanya settled into a routine where Eric was the man of the house, and Gina's Mom and Dad would come and stay every other week. Eric didn't think it was necessary, but it did give him some time to himself.

He thought about Kristie, but that was about it. Tanya was his first priority, and she was all that mattered. Besides, he often saw Kristie on TV, and she appeared to be doing well. She had lost some additional weight and looked good on the tube, even beside the younger, blonde, stick-figured ladies of the channel. Kristie's full figure, dark hair and ruby lips were quite a contrast to the blondes.

He remembered promising Kristie the three of them would become a family, but somehow that hadn't happened.

Having received the same email Kristie did about the classes at Wentworth High getting together at Jim and Hannah Winston's house on Jones Lake, he wondered if Rita would attend and, of course, wondered if Kristie would go.

Kristie was not scheduled to visit NYC or Washington D.C. for several weeks, so she decided to spend the last week in February in Orange Beach. The last time she was in Orange Beach was late December/early January. She booked a hotel room, and was putting the finishing touches on her packing, on Saturday afternoon before the Sunday she was planning to leave.

A loud knock on her front door startled Kristie. Opening the door, she saw a rather emaciated looking young man with piercings. He was wearing sloppy jeans and a plaid shirt. The young man said to her he wanted his package which had been delivered to her by mistake.

"A package? I haven't received a package."

"Yes, you have, you know all about it. It was supposed to be delivered to me at 519, but it was delivered here to you at 511."

"Again, I haven't received any package."

"If you don't give me that package, I'm going to call the Helena Police," the young punk said, holding up his cell phone. "I'm going to call them right now."

"Please quit harassing me, and get off my property," muttered an agitated Kristie.

"I'm calling the police. I'm calling them now."

Out of nowhere, another young man appeared behind the punk. This young man was clean-cut, in contrast to the other young man. The second young man grabbed the punk by the shoulder and said, "Let's go." He then nodded to Kristie, and again said to the other guy, "Let's go."

Kristie shut the front door, and made sure both locks were secure. Frightened, she got her cell phone, went to the kitchen in the back of the house and called the Helena Police.

When they answered, she could hardly get the words out of her mouth. The dispatcher was aware of the case, and said she was going to send a patrol car to Kristie's street, and asked Kristie to describe the young man who came to her door and requested his package. Kristie described the young man as best as she could, and made sure the dispatcher documented the street number where the package was supposed to be delivered.

The dispatcher then instructed Kristie to stay in her house, and make sure all doors were locked. The policeman she was sending over was going to try to locate the young man, and then he would come by her house.

In what seemed like only a minute or two, Kristie saw a patrol car go past her house heading toward the cul-de-sac, toward 519. In a few moments, the patrol car parked in front of her house. The officer got out of the car and walked to her door. Kristie invited the him into her living room and asked him to have a seat. He told Kristie he had talked to the two young men, and told them it was no guarantee the tracer he put on the package would correctly identify where the package ultimately ended up. He also confirmed to Kristie he told the guys, "You leave that lady alone." He then said to Kristie to call the police if either one of them stepped on her property.

When Kristie told the officer she was going on vacation for a week, starting tomorrow, he made a note and said he would have extra patrol cars drive through for the following week. The officer recognized Kristie as being on one of the cable news channels, asked for her autograph, and left.

The next day, Kristie drove the 4-1/2 hours to Orange Beach, Alabama, her favorite place in the whole wide world.

Her house and her cat were on her mind, and she was scared the guys who showed up at her door might break into her home and do some damage. But if this happened, the guys would be the first suspects, and so maybe common sense would dictate to them that breaking into her house was not such a good idea. But again, criminals don't have common sense, or a sense of practicality.

Kristie's week in Orange Beach was idyllic. While it was still too cold for bathing suits, Kristie would walk on the beach in the mornings and evenings. During the day, she would work on her websites, which were now bringing in some decent money. At night, she would go out to eat at some of her favorite restaurants. While Eric and Tanya were often in her thoughts, she was not obsessed. Guess Eric had decided he didn't want her in his life, and for some reason, she didn't care. There was the guy in New York. However, Kristie could never see herself moving to New York, and she knew Jonathan would never consider a move to a place like Alabama. He was a dyed in the wool northerner, and thought indoor plumbing was a luxury in the south.

After checking out of her hotel, a rejuvenated Kristie drove north on I-65 to Birmingham. She had some scheduled appearances on the news, which she could do from the affiliate in Birmingham. Plus, she had scheduled two speaking engagements at local political organizations. While she didn't care that Eric had not called her, she did want to see Tanya, but didn't have her cell phone number. She'd just have to call Eric and ask about Tanya. Maybe she could take Tanya out for lunch or dinner on one of the upcoming weekends.

Late one afternoon, Kristie called Eric's cell phone. It was really no surprise when he didn't answer. Kristie really wanted to see Tanya and left a message asking Eric to give her Tanya's cell phone number. A couple of hours later, she was surprised when her phone rang, and it was Eric.

"How are you?" He asked when Kristie said hello.

"Okay and you?"

"I've never been happier in my life, being a real father to Tanya."

"That's wonderful, Eric. I would really like to see Tanya, and take her out to lunch or dinner soon. Is that okay with you?

"Tanya's a busy young lady. Her teachers and I are working desperately to keep her on track with her studies, so she can graduate and start college at the University this fall."

"I see."

"With her grandparents and me involved in her life, she really doesn't need anyone else."

"I understand. Take care."

With that Kristie hit the end button. While it was a good thing Tanya's teachers were taking such an interest in her, so she didn't get behind, would graduate, and then attend college, Kristie felt a tinge of jealousy. Her teachers at Wentworth High, while they were good teachers, seemed only to care about the top three or four in their classes. Even though she was in the college prep program, Kristie was maybe sixth or seventh in her classes, thus not getting much attention from her teachers. They thought of Kristie as a good student who would go to college, get a good job, and do fine in the world. But as far as taking a special interest in her or the other students, they didn't.

Through some investigation, Kristie discovered the punk, who accused her of stealing his drugs, was renting the house from a man who was living in Greenville, Alabama. She contacted this gentleman and told him what had transpired. In a matter of weeks, the punk and his girlfriend were evicted.

CHAPTER 51

Kristie sounded so disappointed, thought Eric. Was she using Tanya as an excuse to get to him? Eric had promised Kristie they would be together after the Alabama Gulf Coast trip and national championship game. Tanya was his one and only priority. He loved that young girl so much. In fact, he never knew he was capable of so much love as he now had for her. Eric had left Kristie before, and she got over it, she could do it again. In fact, Kristie could go on doing her thing as a news analyst and as administrator of her websites. She would be all right without him. Besides, the three-class social was coming up soon, and he had learned through social media that Rita was flying down for it. He, Rita, Jim Winston and his wife, the Harpo clan…it was going to be great being together with those folks again. Kristie didn't like those people, and they didn't like her.

But what about Kristie? He had promised her so much, and had let her down so many times. He was a jerk, he knew it, and he hoped Kristie would realize it soon, so he could get on with his life with Rita and his Wentworth friends. Was he still carrying a torch for Rita? Yes, Eric admitted to himself. Perhaps at the reunion, he and Rita could talk. All the gang would be there. Rita should surely realize that, while they were separated for years, they were all meant to be together in the end. Rita's children could stay in New York, and Rita could visit them regularly. Sometimes he would accompany her and sometimes he would stay in Wentworth. It just had to work out for them, didn't it?

Would Kristie show up at the reunion knowing the Harpos would be there? He doubted it. Kristie was a celebrity of sorts now. Even though she was friends with some of her high school classmates, he doubted she would show up at this social.

What attracted so many people to Jones Lake, Kristie would never know. Jones Dam was constructed in the late 1950s on the Sipsey Fork of the Warrior River. The water backed up, creating an incredibly deep, dangerous reservoir. The backwater filled in the valleys and covered the trees and brush. Bobcats, mountain lions, and snakes, poisonous and non-poisonous, were native to the area. Even though it was a great place to fish and the area was beautiful, Kristie, as an adult, never had much of a desire to spend time there.

One could walk into the lake, still touching bottom for about six feet from the shore, then there was a drop-off, and no one could dive to the bottom because it was hundreds of feet deep. Kristie's parents, Mary and Bobby, had forbidden her to swim or boat on Jones Lake when she was growing up. Of course, that didn't stop Kristie in her younger years. Now, she had no desire to stick a toe in Jones Lake.

CHAPTER 52

On the day of the reunion, Kristie was making her way down a narrow dirt road in her convertible with the top down. Branches from the trees lining both sides of the road were low hanging, and she hoped nothing would fall out of the tree branches into her car. Driving with the top down was a stupid thing to do. Suddenly, the trees stopped, and Kristie came to a clearing seeing Jim and Hannah Winston's estate-like lake home. Beyond the house was a large expanse of Jones Lake.

Jim and Hannah had spent a fortune clearing off the lot to make it one of the nicest places on the lake. Instead of sitting on top of a bluff where one had to walk down a bunch of steps to get to the lake, the Winston home sat close to the lake. Below the house, stood a large dock and boathouse. As Kristie drove up, she saw several cars already parked in the yard.

Now that she was finally here, Kristie wondered what she was doing here. This was a class gathering for her high school graduating class and the two classes behind her class. Kristie never hung out with Jim and Hannah, plus all the Harpo clan were sure to be in attendance. Kathryn Campbell Harpo, a member of Kristie's class would surely be in attendance with hubby, Sam. Then there was Jan Harpo Franklin who was a year behind Kristie. And last, but not least, was one of Eric's best friends, Jimmy Harpo, who was in the class two years behind Kristie's. Would Eric be here? Would he be with someone, maybe Rita, who was a year behind her and Eric?

For a split second, Kristie thought about turning around and leaving. Instead, she got out of her convertible and walked toward the house with her head held high. No one was required to bring anything. Hannah Winston was a partner in a rather large catering outfit in Wentworth, and all the food and beverages were being provided. The attendees just had to contribute $25 to help with the cost.

As Kristie approached the house, she heard voices coming from inside. Finding the front door of the house unlocked, Kristie entered the upscale vacation home. Upon entering, she saw several folks standing or sitting in what appeared to be the living room. Most of them had drinks in their hands, and were making small talk. Kristie didn't recognize any of them.

A short, petite woman walked up to Kristie, stuck out her hand and said, "Annie Jenkins."

Kristie took the woman's hand and said, "Kristie Channing."

The woman pointed to a guest book, and asked Kristie to sign it, and make herself a name tag. She told Kristie that others were mingling in the den, on the porch, and out back. Several tables of appetizers were set up throughout the house, and there were two bars.

Kristie thanked the woman, and set off to other areas of the house in search of food, drink, and hopefully someone nice to talk to.

The house was impressive, and Kristie especially loved the large screened-in back porch where most of the attendees had gathered. However, she still recognized no one, and no one seemed to recognize her.

One of the bars was set up on the porch with a young guy tending it. Could he be one of Jim and Hannah's sons? In addition to the bar, an extensive buffet was set up with boiled shrimp, several types of cheeses and several types of crackers, stuffed mushrooms, cocktail wieners, a veggie dip, tortilla chips with several types of salsa, and plain old potato chips and French onion dip. Outside, a huge grill was set up. Two people were manning the grill, basting chickens and ribs, obviously for the main course.

Still not recognizing anyone, Kristie went to the bar to get a drink. Then after getting some food, she looked around to find a place to sit. Kristie was surprised she didn't see one person she knew or remembered. After finding a chair and sitting down, a rather homely couple sauntered up to Kristie and introduced themselves as David and Sharon Simmons. Both had attended Wentworth. When Kristie introduced herself as Kristie Channing, the guy asked her if she was Eric Channing's sister.

"No, I'm his ex-wife," replied Kristie.

"Oh, you're the political blogger, and sometimes you appear on cable news?"

"Yes," replied Kristie.

"Did you attend Wentworth," asked the woman?

"Yes, I was Kristie Tidwell."

"Oh, I remember you. You were one of the smart people."

"Well, I don't know about that," laughed Kristie.

"Can we get your autograph and a picture with you," asked David."

Kristie awkwardly signed a cocktail napkin while David got up to find someone to take their picture. He came back with none other than Rita McDonald. Rita, not immediately recognizing Kristie, stuck her hand out and said, "Rita McDonald Fisher."

Kristie stuck her hand out and replied, "Kristie Tidwell Channing."

"Oh, Kristie, I wasn't expecting to see you here," said Rita.

"Remember, I'm a classmate."

"Of course, you are."

Sensing the awkwardness between the two women, David handed his phone to Rita and said, "Let's take the picture."

After taking the picture, Rita handed the phone to David, and Kristie, excused herself saying she was going to take a walk outside.

The Winston's lake home was sprawled over two lots that faced west over a broad expanse of the finger lake. The house was built on the north lot. It was a five-bedroom three bath luxury home with a large wrap-around screened-in back porch. From the porch, a set of steps led to the shore of the lake. At the end of the steps there was a dock which extended out over the water, and at the end of the dock, the Winstons had constructed a large gazebo.

The lot to the left was a grassy knoll where the attendees parked their cars. There were also numerous grills set up, where college-aged young men were grilling everything from hot dogs and hamburgers, barbecue ribs and chicken, seafood kabobs, grouper, and red snapper. From the grass, stepping stones led down to another dock. On the left side of the dock, there was a boathouse with spaces for four boats. On the right side of the dock, there was a small tiki bar. At the end of the dock, there was a ladder to aid swimmers when they entered and exited the water. Between the gazebo dock, and the boathouse dock, there were more stepping stones along the lake shore to make it easier to walk between the two docks.

This is such a fabulous place, thought Kristie. *Jim and Hannah had obviously sunk a fortune into it. But if I had the kind of money to afford something like this, I wouldn't be affording it on Jones Lake. I'd have something on the beach, even if it were just a condo.* Maybe one of these days she would be able to swing it.

Was Eric here? Did he come with Rita? Kristie was sure he would attend, even though she didn't see his truck when she drove up. Maybe he rode with Rita. Eric's buds, the Winstons, and the Harpos, were running this event, plus Rita was here. Eric had not fully gotten over Rita McDonald, now Fisher. It was evident during their time together.

Kristie decided to walk down to the gazebo where ten or so folks were gathered, plus food and beverages were available. A buffet table was set up with various snacks including chips and dip, cheese and crackers, mixed nuts, chips and salsa, fruit, hummus, etc. To keep the various dips chilled, the bowls were placed in a shallow tray of ice. Two ice chests contained beer, and two more chests were full of soft drinks. A guy who looked to be in his late teens or early twenties was overseeing the food and beverages. Kristie guessed he was also one of Jim and Hannah's sons, or maybe a nephew.

Several guys were floating on large truck inner tubes on the lake. While this was a balmy April day, Kristie could only imagine how cold the deep lake was, much too cold for her to swim in.

As Kristie stepped from the bottom stair onto the dock, movement to the left caught her eye, and she gasped. About two feet from the shore, a triangular shaped brownish black head was sticking up out of the water. Kristie could see its slithery body undulating just below the water's surface. No doubt, the snake was a cottonmouth, a highly venomous snake found in or near fresh or brackish water. The snake seemed to be swimming parallel to the shore and heading toward the dock where Kristie was standing. Could it possibly climb upon the dock where she was? Or could it crawl out of the water and onto dry land, possibly crashing the festivities? Or could it swim out in the lake toward the guys on inner tubes? No matter where that snake chose to go, things wouldn't end well.

Suddenly, Kristie heard heavy footsteps approaching from the gazebo area. Then she heard a loud noise that startled her as she collapsed on the dock. Gun shots! Several more rang out before Kristie felt herself being helped up by a couple of guys.

"It's Kristie Tidwell, isn't it? Are you okay?"

Kristie nodded and stared blankly at one of the guys who still had hold of her by her arm. "I'm Zeke Chastain, I was in the class right below yours, and I follow you faithfully on the news channel, and read your blogs daily."

"Zeke, we either killed that bad boy or stunned him, he seems to be just floating in the water. Kristie cover your ears, I'm going to take a few more shots."

The other guy took a few more shots with his revolver at the floating snake. One of the shots appeared to partially dislodge the head from the body. While Kristie, Zeke, and the other guy watched, the gentle lake waves carried the snake to the shore where it lay motionless.

The second guy said, "Kristie Tidwell, I'm Charlie Billingsley, we were in the same class. I also read your blogs and follow you on the news, and I have to say you're tops at what you do."

"Thanks guys for your kind words, and thanks for killing that snake."

"I wouldn't recommend anyone picking him up, he might still be able to bite. I'm going up to the house and fetch a hoe or shovel and chop off its head," said Charlie.

As Charlie headed up the steps to the house to find a sharp tool. Some of the women had gathered at the top of the steps. Jim Winston came running down the steps meeting Charlie, asking what had just happened.

"I'll show you where we keep the gardening tools," said Jim.

"Are you all right, Kristie," asked Zeke?

"I am," replied Kristie.

"Well, let's get you something to eat and drink," said Zeke, as he took her arm and steered her toward the gazebo.

As always, snakes were out in droves during the early spring in Alabama, and Jim Winston had already killed three copperheads on the property. He had also seen some cottonmouths in the lake while taking the boat out. He had sprayed some sort of concoction around the property which would supposedly keep snakes away, but he wasn't sure how effective it might be. Also, Jim realized that some snakes were "good" snakes and would kill insects and rodents. The speckled and black king snakes are common in Alabama and will kill poisonous snakes.

Kristie chose a Bud Light from one of the coolers and grabbed a small paper plate to get some snacks.

Charlie Billingsley retrieved a hoe from the basement of the lake house. As he and Jim Winston headed back toward the lake, Eric Channing and Jimmy Harpo joined them. After Charlie had chopped the head completely off the snake's body, Jimmy said, "That snake's larger than average for a cottonmouth. Let's take it out on the gazebo and show everyone up close and personal."

Kristie saw the four guys, Eric, Jimmy, Jim, and Charlie heading toward the gazebo with Jimmy using the hoe to hold up the headless dead snake.

Seeing Eric made Kristie's stomach lurch. Why did the guys she really cared about make promises, then not follow through on those promises? Eric indicated last winter, after his first wife died, he loved her and wanted his daughter, along with her, to be his family. Then nothing! He never called her or attempted any other contact with her.

Was he back together with Rita? Rita was his first love, and Kristie knew Eric was not completely over her, even after all these years. Rita's back in town, probably to visit family and attend the reunion. How convenient?

Eric hadn't seen her yet, and Kristie, deciding to be as inconspicuous as she could, took her beer and snacks and sat down on a bench underneath the gazebo. Because Eric had just arrived, some of the guys were slapping him on the back saying how happy they were to see him, and that they were sorry to hear about Gina's death.

As the four men entered the gazebo, Eric started talking to several folks, but Jimmy, who had spotted Kristie, walked over to where she was sitting, and threw the dead snake body at her. It hit her legs and landed at her feet. "Hey Kristie, you're not scared of snakes, are you? I hear there's lots of them out and about."

Even though the snake, without a head, was harmless, its nervous system was somehow triggered, and it began to writhe at Kristie's feet. She screamed, dropping her beer and her snacks. In her rush to get away, she ran into several people underneath the gazebo, and thought she heard some laughter. This gathering is just another extension of high school, she thought. Will some people ever grow up?

Eric, seeing Kristie, and realizing what had just happened to her, followed her onto the dock, with Jim Winston not far behind. Eric and Jim caught up with Kristie as she stepped off the dock and onto the grass.

"Kristie, I'm so sorry. Let's go in the house and get you something else to drink and eat," said Jim Winston.

"Jim, I've really had it with you people. Can't you just grow up and quit acting like savages?"

"Kristie, I didn't think you would be here. What with your new-found celebrity, I thought you would be too good to hob-nob with us Wentworth low lives," said Eric.

"Low lives, you got that right. In fact, I'm in the process of selling my Wentworth property, and after the sale is final, I don't plan to set foot in this area ever again. I think I'll go over to the boathouse and watch the sun set."

"I didn't know you were selling your property," exclaimed Eric.

"Well, maybe if you had called me after we left Orange Beach, and if we had pursued a relationship like you promised me we would do, you would know some things about me."

Feeling awkward, Jim Winston excused himself, telling Kristie and Eric dinner would soon be ready. Then he headed out to the gazebo where Jimmy Harpo was still showing off the dead snake.

"Jimmy, why did you throw that snake at Kristie? This is my home, and she's a guest of ours. I won't have my guests mistreated."

"Lighten up Jim! You didn't like Kristie either when we were in high school. Most of our crowd didn't."

"That was then, and this is now. I would have hoped we had grown up. Kristie's beautiful, smart, and nice. In the early years after graduation, when Kristie ignored reunion notices, Hannah and I were worried about her. A lot of folks didn't treat her right. We were both glad when she responded to the reunion notice a couple of years ago. I'm glad she's back in the fold, and I don't want her hurt anymore."

"Well, if you like her so much, maybe you should start a Kristie Tidwell fan club."

"Look, Jimmy, I don't want to have to ask you to leave, but I will if you don't settle down and quit acting like a sophomore."

After the drama, some of the guys standing by the gazebo kicked the dead snake into the water.

The dock where the boathouse was located opened to a larger expanse of the lake. Anticipating that folks might wander onto this dock, a cooler filled with ice, soft drinks, and beer had been placed there. There was also a cardboard box filled with single-serving bags of potato chips and other snacks. After helping herself to a beer and a bag of chips, she sat on one of the tiki bar stools, planning to watch the sun set. Then she would head back to Wentworth and down to Helena. She didn't want to see Jimmy Harpo ever again, nor did she want to see any of his family ever again. Did she want to see Eric again? That, Kristie didn't know.

As Kristie watched the sun slowly setting in the west on the water, she asked herself why she even came to this gathering. She was okay with the folks in her graduating class, but she did have some problems with the two classes behind her class.

It was peaceful out here on the dock, and Kristie was enjoying the calm after what had been a harrowing few hours. Even though the sun was still a little while from completely setting, dark clouds were rolling in. This would be what Kristie liked to call a sunset of fire and ice. Today's sunset was unusual because sunsets of this type generally took place in the fall and winter months.

Suddenly, Kristie heard splashing and a guy muttering a string of curse words. She emerged from the tiki bar to see Jake Stanley climb onto the dock. Around one leg was coiled, what appeared to be a cottonmouth. Jake was reaching down, grabbing the deadly creature by its middle. He was able to get the snake uncoiled from his leg, but because the deadly reptile had been picked up by its mid-section, the snake curled around and bit Jake on the forearm. Jake then threw the snake down, and it landed about six feet from where Kristie was standing. Being the aggressive creatures they are, the snake started slithering toward Kristie.

Noticing boat paddles in the tiki bar, Kristie quickly grabbed one and attempted to push the snake back into the water. The snake bit the oar, and while the fangs were locked into the wood, Kristie threw the oar, snake included, into the water.

Meanwhile, Jake Stanley was lying on the dock screaming, one leg was beginning to swell, and the arm that was bit was swelling also. Jake Stanley had never said a kind word to Kristie in his life, but now, he was begging her to get help. She could leave and drive to her home in Helena without saying a word to anyone. Jake had been bitten multiple times. Was this enough to kill him? Back in high school, Jake, Johnny Morton, and Wiley Martin were planning to kidnap Kristie, tie her up, and throw her into the snaky woods around one of Wentworth's many creeks. Wiley and Johnny were both dead. Wiley had died from cancer and Johnny had died from AIDS. If Jake died, this would surely be poetic justice for all the trauma the three of them had put Kristie through when they were teenagers.

What was Kristie thinking? She couldn't leave him to die on the dock. She had to go get help. She took off running toward the house. As she got closer to the house, she observed there was a crowd of folks on the huge back porch. Perhaps they were in line for the dinner buffet. Kristie started screaming. "Help, help! Eric, Jim, Charlie, Zeke, help!

About the time Kristie reached the steps leading up to the house, several of the guys were running down the steps, including Eric and Jim Winston.

"Jake, Jake." Kristie was hyperventilating.

"What about Jake," questioned Eric?

"He's been snake bit by a cottonmouth. Maybe several times. He's lying on the dock."

"Anyone who's a medical doctor, get out here," yelled Jim.

A woman who Kristie didn't recognize rushed down the stairs, along with a couple of other guys, one of them was Jimmy Harpo who failed to acknowledge Kristie as he brushed past her.

When the men and the doctor reached Jake, he was lying motionless. The doctor, who identified herself as Pam Weldon, asked if there was a flashlight she could use. The sun was setting, and darkness was creeping in. Jim Winston quickly retrieved a flashlight from the boathouse. Dr. Weldon examined Jake and indicated there were four places on Jake's extremities where he could have been bitten. "The only chance he has of surviving this would be if some of the bites are dry bites or if the snake only injected a limited amount venom into him. By the looks of this leg, that doesn't appear to be the case. We have to get him to a hospital immediately."

Jim Winston took his cell phone from his pants pocket and called 911. Because the lake house was in an isolated rural spot in Wentworth County, Jim indicated he and friends would take Jake to Tracy's Barbecue, and the paramedics could meet them there for the ride to Wentworth Regional Medical Center.

"You don't happen to have any blankets or quilts down here?" asked Pamela.

God was on their side, because Jim retrieved two quilts from the boathouse.

"Wrap him up and let's get moving," said Pamela.

"We'll take him in my Expedition," replied Jim.

Kristie was still hyperventilating as she was climbing the set of stairs to the back porch of the house. As soon as she stepped onto the porch, Kathryn Campbell Harpo rushed up to her with an irritated look on her face, and asked Kristie what had happened.

As Kristie was recounting the tragic incident, several other folks stepped up and joined her and Kathryn.

"Well, Jake hated you, and from what I understand, you had nothing out for him. How long did you let him lay there before you ran back here and got help? You disappeared from the crowd, and could have left him there to die. Or did you?"

Marie Nicole Harper

What was going on here? Was Kathryn Campbell Harpo accusing Kristie of trying to kill Jake? This was surreal. By now everyone on the porch was silent, listening to them, including Rita McDonald Fisher, Jan Harpo Franklin, and Ruthie Harpo.

"Look, Kathryn, I've had enough of you. And enough of Jan and Ruthie as well. Ever since I reunited with some of the Wentworth folks and began my relationship with Eric, the three of you have been nothing but hateful to me. At your stupid New Year's Eve party, you practically threw me out, letting me know I wasn't welcome. You tried to fix Eric up with that homely friend of yours. I forgot her name. Then after Wiley Martin died, you sought to fix Eric up with Anabelle Martin. Again, you've been awful to me, and for no apparent reason. Kathryn, we were good friends in high school. What happened?"

Kathryn stared at Kristie for several seconds seeming not to know what to say. Kristie had become emboldened since their high school days when folks could say just about anything to her, and she would accept it and move on.

"I think I know. Jan's crowd treated me like dirt because I was chubby as a freshman. But after the weight came off, along with the braces, I was quite a looker. However, Jan, you and your crowd never saw the new me, and kept treating me the same as you always treated me. Kathryn, while you were once decent to me, you married into Jan's family and became a Harpo woman."

By this time, Kathryn had gained her composure and replied, "Why Kristie, we just didn't think you were right for Eric, and apparently, we were right, because he left you. We thought he and Anabelle would be perfect for one another, but that didn't work out, and from what we hear, Anabelle sold the Navarre Beach home she and Wiley purchased when they were a young married couple. And she has now purchased, and is living in a home in Gulf Shores on West Beach. It's time Eric and Rita got back together. She was his first love, and he was her first love. We all think it would be best if you scooted out of here and never came back."

"Scooting on out of here, Kathryn, is a fantastic idea. I think it's time to sell my property, and never come back." With that, Kristie began to make her way through the crowded back porch and into the house where she would leave through the front door.

"Wait, Kristie! You haven't had anything to eat, and we have all this food."

It was hostess, Hannah Winston.

"Hannah, what do you care if I've had something to eat or not? You weren't exactly friendly to me when we were growing up either, and Jim was almost as mean to me as Wiley, Jake, and Johnny."

"That's all in the past. We go back a long way, Kristie. Grammar school, junior high, high school, and even the University. I'm really sorry for all of that, but we were kids, and that's what kids do; be mean to those who don't fit the mold."

"Oh, and I didn't fit the mold?"

By that time, Teddy Vickers approached Kristie and Hannah. "Kristie, please don't leave or I'll cry. I was so happy when you came back to the reunion. I was really worried about you. I didn't know what you were feeling toward our classmates. I was scared you hated all of us."

"Teddy, you're one of my favorite people, and I do love you, and have treasured our friendship. Remember, you took me to my first party where people were drinking, and couples were going into the bedroom and closing the door. I was scared to death. I had never seen anything like that before. But I'm shaken. Remember, I had an encounter with the snake also. It wasn't that long, but it was fat through its middle which is a trait of water moccasins. They are also aggressive. That snake was coming after me, and I was lucky to be able push it back in the water with a paddle. I've had quite an evening, and I'm not hungry, so I think I'll slip out of here."

"Well at least take some of this food with you. Here, let's fix you some plates," said Hannah.

"That's mighty kind of you," said Kristie.

Teddy followed Kristie and Hannah into the kitchen area where folks were lined up filling their plates with barbecue ribs, honey baked ham, potato salad, coleslaw, garlic bread, steamed shrimp, West Indies salad, baked beans, grilled chicken, green bean casserole, squash casserole, and deviled eggs. The dessert table followed with fresh coconut cake, strawberry cake, key lime pie, Mississippi mud cake, blackberry cobbler, and peach cobbler.

"Sit down Kristie, you've been through a lot, we'll fix your plates," said Hannah.

Teddy and Hannah broke into the lines and loaded up the heavy plastic platters with everything on the tables. After covering the platters with foil, Hannah retrieved a large box and set them in the box.

"Now are you sure you won't stay?" asked Teddy.

"I couldn't."

"Okay then. Harold, will you take this box out to Kristie's car?"

"Sure," said Harold Phillips.

Kristie hugged Hannah and Teddy at the front door and pointed Harold in the direction of her vehicle.

"Nice convertible," said Harold. "Some people never change. I remember Jan Harpo well. She's always been a snot. I remember you too, Kristie. I never understood why people were so hard on you."

Kristie remembered Harold as being quiet and unassuming. In fact, most students at Wentworth High were okay. It was the Jan Harpo's, the Wiley Martin's, the Jake Stanley's, and even the Eric Channing's, etc. that left a bad taste for high school in everyone else's mouth.

"Thanks, Harold," replied Kristie as Harold set the box on the floorboard on the passenger side of the car.

"Be careful driving back to Birmingham."

"I will, thanks."

CHAPTER 53

With that, Kristie drove off. It was dark, and the only light on the gravel road from the Winston house to the semi-main road was provided by Kristie's headlights. This semi-main road led to the main road that would take Kristie toward Wentworth and to I-65. The tree branches were low hanging, and Kristie was glad she had chosen to leave her top up. She didn't want things falling from the trees into her car. Things she didn't want in her car. Of course, Kristie was thinking about snakes. Because she was already deathly afraid of snakes, she wondered if there would be nightmares or other issues arising out of this disastrous evening.

Suddenly the sky lit up followed by a roar of thunder. Kristie had completely forgotten the storms that were due to roll in this evening. No tornadoes were expected, but heavy rains, wind, thunder, lightning, and perhaps small hail were in the forecast.

Kristie carefully steered the car from county road to county road then onto the main highway that would take her to I-65. On the main highway, Kristie noticed how delicious the food in the floor board smelled. She was now ravenous. Would she be able to wait until she arrived at her house before diving in? Also, Kristie suddenly found herself extremely exhausted. This had been an emotional day, and one she hoped to forget soon, but knew she wouldn't.

Then there was Eric. Were Jan, Ruthie, and Kathryn attempting to get him and Rita back together? Were they already back together? She knew there would always be a special place in Eric's heart for Rita. They both lost their virginities to each other, and had plans to get married, raise a family, and live happily ever after. Guess there was no room for Kristie here. Did Eric ever really love, her or was she just someone who met his needs at the time, someone he could toss aside should something better come along?

While there was lots of thunder and lightning, the rain and wind were light, and Kristie was hoping this garden variety thunder shower would soon pass through. Because her thoughts were on Eric and Rita, she was not thinking about Jake Stanley, and how he was doing until her phone unexpectedly rang and it was Eric.

"Hi," said Eric after Kristie said hello. "Where are you?"

"A couple of miles from I-65."

"You're not at the reunion?"

"No, Jan, Kathryn, and Ruthie were all blaming me for Jake's misfortune and indicated I was not welcome in Wentworth, at least not in their clique. They admitted they were doing everything they could to hook you up with someone else other than me because they hated me."

"Now Kristie, there goes your imagination again."

"I'm not imagining anything, just ask Hannah Winston and Teddy Vickers."

"Okay, okay. So, you're driving back to Birmingham?"

"That's where I live."

"Would you like to know how Jake is?"

"Well now that you've mentioned it, how is Jake?"

"The snake put quite a bit of venom into him, but the bite to the forearm, the one closest to his heart was apparently a dry bite. Somewhere along the way, he had a heart attack, so that complicated matters. He's not out of the woods yet, but the doctor says he has a better than average chance of pulling through all of this, but it will take some time. He's looking at several weeks in the hospital. He's in ICU, but we don't know for how long."

"That's good."

"Do you really care about Jake?"

"He's not exactly my favorite person, but I certainly don't want him to die."

"When he regains consciousness, I think he would like to see you, to thank you for saving his life."

"And just how do you know that?"

"Kristie, Jake's not one hundred percent evil. He's a bad boy all right, but there's good and bad in everyone. You've said that yourself. I wanted you to talk with Wiley Martin before he died, but it didn't happen. I think if you had, things between you and my old gang would be different. In fact, I'd like for you to talk to Jake, and to Jimmy, and some of the others to clear the air."

"Why! There's no us anymore, now that you're getting back with Rita; who, by the way, is still at Jim and Hannah's. Don't forget to drive back there and get her. I'm selling the property, and after I do, I'm never having anything to do with my classmates at Wentworth again."

"Wait a minute, I'm not with Rita; she arrived at the reunion by herself."

"Oh! Well, Jan, Kathryn, and Ruthie want desperately for the two of y'all to get back together."

"Kristie, please turn around come back here to see Jake, please."

"I'll think about it."

"Okay, bye."

"Bye."

Kristie was now headed south on I-65. The storm had passed, and she was looking forward to getting home and eating some of the food Hannah and Teddy had packed up for her. She had no intention of visiting Jake Stanley and "talking things out" like Eric had suggested.

CHAPTER 54

Despite a good prognosis, Jake Stanley died on Tuesday after the reunion at Wentworth Medical Center. He never regained consciousness after the heart attack he suffered in the ambulance on the way to the hospital. Cottonmouth bites were rare in the Wentworth/Jones Lake area even though Jones Lake was infested with them. Jake's body just couldn't handle the snake bites and the heart attack. He never had a chance to meet and talk with Kristie.

There was a huge crowd at the viewing for Jake, and at his funeral and graveside services. The attendees included some rather suspicious looking characters who were probably from Jake's rather colorful past. He was the youngest of three children, having a brother and sister who were ten and twelve years older than him respectively. He also had two nephews and a niece, plus a great nephew. Because he was not affiliated with any church, the funeral service was held at the Knoll Funeral Home, the oldest and most respected funeral home in the Wentworth area, with the minister at the First Baptist Church presiding. Eric and Jimmy were pallbearers, along with Jim Winston, Dean Abercrombie, and Jake's two nephews.

Eric was disappointed Kristie didn't come back to Wentworth to see Jake while he was in ICU, but thought she would drive up for the viewing or the funeral. However, there was no Kristie for the viewing, service, or graveside. Then Eric started wondering if she even knew. He didn't bother to call her, and maybe no one else did either.

Rita McDonald Fisher was still in town, and attended the funeral and the graveside. After the graveside, Rita and Jan Harpo Franklin caught up to Eric and wanted to talk about the fun times they all had as kids and teenagers. Rita fondly remembered Jake and his girlfriend were also at the farmhouse the night she and Eric lost their virginities.

Known as the "bad boy trio" back in the day, Wiley Martin, Johnny Morton, and Jake Stanley were buried in this cemetery. All three had died in the last two years: Wiley from cancer, Johnny from AIDS, and Jake from complications due to snake bites and a heart attack. While no longer spring chickens, all three were way too young to die.

Not far away, Jimmy Harpo and Dean Abercrombie were standing beside Dean's truck making small talk. "I noticed

Kristie Tidwell didn't show up," said Jimmy. He refused to refer to her as Kristie Channing or Kristie Tidwell-Channing.

"Why would she? Jake hated her, and she hated him," replied Dean.

"She did run back to the house to get help," exclaimed Jimmy

"But how long did she wait after Jake had been bitten?"

"Dean, you're not saying Kristie might have wanted him to suffer and die?"

"Even though I was two years ahead of Kristie, I remember a lot of folks in our crowd didn't like her, mainly because she was overweight. After the scene at Jake's restaurant last fall, I looked her up in my senior yearbook. I do remember not liking her because others didn't like her. Now I kind of feel sorry for her. We all had great times in high school, but I imagine Kristie missed out on a lot of things. That can lead to a lot of pinned up hatred."

"She was actually running and was out of breath when she reached the house to tell us about Jake. Still, that doesn't necessarily mean she didn't wait for a while," Jimmy slowly remarked. "Hmm."

"Would that be considered attempted murder?" asked Dean.

"Well, there's Stu Bolen, let's ask him."

Stu was a detective for the Wentworth County Sheriff's Department. After Jake had allegedly straightened himself out, he would occasionally assist the WPD and the Sheriff's Department in catching criminals, most of which were minor drug possession cases, with the occasional dealer case thrown in. Stu was not a Wentworth native and therefore, was not involved in any drama between those who grew up in Wentworth and then stayed in Wentworth.

"Hey Stu," yelled Jimmy.

"Oh, hi guys. That was a shame about Jake, wasn't it?"

"Sure was," replied Jimmy. "But you know, there may have been a little more to his death than meets the eye. Do you know Kristie Tidwell-Channing?"

"I know she's originally from around here and still owns property not far from here. I've never met her, only seen her on cable news."

"She was married for a short time to Eric Channing, and she hated Jake. She was the only one at the boat dock when Jake was bitten. Supposedly, she knocked the snake back into the water with an oar and ran to the Winston house to get help. It's going around, though, that she delayed her run for help, and let Jake lay on the dock for a while. Could that be attempted murder?" asked Dean,

"Manslaughter, possibly, if it can be proven beyond a shadow of a doubt she purposefully delayed in seeking help in hopes that Jake would die. Were there any witnesses?"

"No," replied Dean and Jimmy simultaneously.

"And Kristie didn't bother to show up for the funeral or the viewing," replied Dean.

"She doesn't live in Wentworth," said Stu.

"But she lives in one of the southern suburbs of Birmingham," replied Jimmy, "Not far from here."

"Well, does she know about Jake's death?" questioned Stu.

"I really don't know," said Dean.

"Well guys, it's going to be hard to pin something on Kristie with no witnesses."

Stu, not wanting to continue this ridiculous conversation, turned and walked to his car. Stu was born and raised in Oneonta, Alabama, a small town in Blount County, southeast of Wentworth. He attended Auburn on a baseball scholarship, where he majored in criminology. After graduation, he accepted a job on the Birmingham Police, Force and worked there as a street cop, then as a private detective, then as a narcotics agent until corruption within the department caused him to seek other gainful employment. Stu subsequently took a job with the Wentworth County Sheriff's Department as an undercover detective ten years ago.

Stu liked Wentworth okay, but felt it was like most other smaller towns, including his own hometown. Unless you were born and raised there, you would always be an outsider. While he and his wife had met some great people, and had some wonderful friends in Wentworth, he knew he would forever remain an outsider. His children were never crazy about Wentworth, and both had graduated from college and settled in Birmingham.

While Molly, his wife, had adjusted, she still felt like an outsider and accepted it. Even though Molly had worked with the Harpo women on charity events and the like, she did not like Jan, Ruthie, and Kathryn. Molly felt that those three women had to be the queen bees of Wentworth, and only let people of their choosing into their inner circle. Ruthie Harpo and Anabelle Martin, mainly because they were married to Jimmy Harpo and the late Wiley Martin, were two rare examples of those who were not considered outsiders.

After bidding good-bye to the women, Eric got in his truck and drove the short distance to where Wiley Martin was buried. Three chums had died within two years of each other. All too young to die. Few folks in Wentworth knew about Johnny's sexual orientation until the news made it around town he had AIDS. He was extremely popular in high school and dated several girls. Eric then drove by where Johnny was buried, but didn't stop.

Suddenly, his phone rang. It was Ruthie wanting to know if he had plans for dinner that evening.

"No, not really."

"Well, why don't you come over here? Jimmy's going to grill some burgers, and I'm going to make some potato salad and baked beans. Rita's coming over here too. Even though I wasn't in high school with y'all, I just love hearing about all the stories you tell. About six-ish?"

"Sure." Eric, spending most of his time living at Gina's former house with Tanya, didn't have anything better to do, and he would love to reminisce about Jake, Wiley, and Johnny." Tanya was spending the night with her best friend since Eric didn't know what time he would get back to Birmingham after the funeral.

Because he had talked the talk, but failed to walk the walk with Kristie, he felt he had no chance with her anymore, and Rita didn't seem interested, if she ever was in her adult life. Maybe he would try to get lucky with Rita, and go back to womanizing as opposed to pursuing relationships.

Tanya was scheduled to start school at the University in August. After that, he would have Wentworth, and his house, now complete, on Jones Lake, to himself. He'd have a regular bachelor pad, and enjoy all the nubile women Wentworth had to offer. And as a booming place, Wentworth had lots of women who were looking for a fun time.

When Eric arrived at Jimmy and Ruthie's, the beer was iced down, and the daiquiris and margaritas were flowing. Rita was sitting on a bar stool sipping on a margarita, wearing white shorts and a simple light blue knit tunic. White shorts on women turned Eric on. So, he quickly grabbed a beer and hopped on the barstool next to her, loosely putting his arm on the bar behind her.

However, the conversation failed to get light and humorous. Everyone was grieving for Jake Stanley, who had died, in what they thought, was a senseless death. All agreed he shouldn't have been floating on the lake nearly drunk. If

Kristie hadn't decided to walk down to the pier, Jake might have died right there.

"Speaking of 'Little Miss Perfect,'" said Jimmy, "Did you know there are rumors already making the rounds that Kristie might possibly have waited a while, letting Jake suffer, before running to the house for help?"

"What! Jimmy…are you crazy?"

"I'm just telling you what I heard at the funeral. Stu Bolen said there was probably going to be an investigation," Jimmy lied. "Kristie could go to jail for manslaughter. She hated Jake as much as she hates Ruthie and I and all of our high school gang."

"Jimmy, you are crazy. Kristie wouldn't do that, she just wouldn't. Are you by any chance spreading these rumors? I know about your connections at the Sherriff's department. I know you have pictures, taken years ago, of Sheriff Whitt in a compromising position with a woman prisoner. What's going on?"

"Settle down, settle down. Nothing will probably come of it. Kristie will likely be investigated, but nothing will be proven. She'll be off the hook eventually."

"But until then, you and others are going to make her life miserable, perhaps even destroy her career. She's a public figure, and if this gets to the mainstream media, she may be finished."

"I never thought about that. Making Kristie miserable and ruining her life would be just as good as her being thrown in jail."

"Jimmy, I think you are really crazy. You're a psycho-dude. What's Kristie ever done to you personally?"

"Well, none of us think she's the girl for you."

"Don't you think I should be the judge of that?"

"All of us just want what's best for you. And we believe Kristie should be out of your life."

"Okay, okay, so she may not be for me. Actually, she's not for me, and we're not together, and I have no plans to ever be with Kristie again. But is that any reason to destroy her? Let's all get on with our lives, and let Kristie get on with hers."

"But she has friends up here now," said Ruthie. "She still has her property in Wentworth. From what I hear, she regularly gets together with her classmates."

"So!" exclaimed Eric.

"Well, we don't want her here," exclaimed Jimmy.

"Jimmy, this is the United States of America where people are free to travel where they wish. What's it to you if she comes up here on occasions?"

"This is our town, we run this town, and we should be able to say who we want to include and exclude. Kristie will never be welcome here."

"Just what do you three have against Kristie? Why do you hate her? Why do you want to destroy her life, have her thrown in jail for something she didn't do?

"Well," said Jimmy, "According to Jan, she was overweight and not very attractive up until the tenth grade. Then she lost the weight and was one of the prettiest girls in school."

"But Wiley, Johnny, Jake and others continued to torment her. According to what Kristie has said to me, she always longed for the day she could get out of Wentworth. When she did, her life was successful. Kristie was so unhappy as a child and teenager. However, she finally got up the nerve to attend a class reunion where she had a great time and renewed many friendships. I would think you would be happy for her."

"Once again, according to Jan, she placed high in the school beauty pageant, above all of the girls in our gang."

"And you still hate her for that?"

"Well according to Jan, some of the girls in our crowd didn't place."

"Again, you hate her for that? I can't believe what I'm hearing. Kristie always said there was something strange about y'all. I thought she was being overly sensitive, but now I see that she wasn't. You folks, folks who I considered my best friends and confidants are warped, twisted beyond anyone's imagination. I suggest you forget about this sick, sick plan of yours or you'll regret it. Remember, I know folks in this county also."

With that, Eric got up and made his way out of the house and out to his truck, with Rita following.

"Eric, can't we just have a good time and share the stories of the times we had with Jake and the gang?"

"Not tonight, honey, and probably not ever."

Eric started the truck and drove off, leaving Rita standing beside the curb alone. As he was headed toward I-65 and Birmingham, he realized he was buzzed. He'd had a couple of beers, but nothing to eat. Now that Wentworth was a booming little city, so many new eateries had sprung up. However, Eric decided to go to one of Wentworth's traditional places, one of the best barbecue restaurants on the planet. He knew the owners, in fact, he had seen the three of them at the funeral. Hopefully, at least one of them would be at the restaurant tonight, and he could have an adult conversation for a change.

CHAPTER 55

As Stu drove back to the sheriff's office, he developed an uneasy feeling about his conversation with Dean and Jimmy. Dean had a heavy foot, and had often received tickets for speeding. These tickets were always fixed. Stu also thought Jimmy, known for tipping the bottle, had been arrested for DUI, but the charges were somehow always dropped. Dean and Jimmy, along with several others had friends in the department. Maybe he should keep an eye peeled for suspicious activity by these two and others.

Kristie Tidwell-Channing was Eric Channing's ex-wife. He liked to watch Kristie on cable news. She knew her politics, and seemed genuinely nice. Eric kept company with Jimmy Harpo, Dean Abercrombie, Jake, and others, but they didn't like Kristie.

The Monday morning following Jake's Friday funeral, Stu was called into his boss's office, and told to track down Kristie Tidwell-Channing, and question her about the untimely death of Jake Stanley. His boss, Sheriff Whitt, indicated there was a possibility that Mrs. Tidwell-Channing had delayed in running for help after Mr. Stanley was bitten several times by a poisonous cottonmouth snake while at the boat dock of Jim and Hannah Winston's palatial home on Jones Lake.

"I spoke to Jimmy Harpo and Dean Abercrombie after Jake Stanley's graveside service. They asked me if Mrs. Tidwell-Channing had delayed in running for help after Mr. Stanley was bitten, could she be charged with murder. I told them manslaughter at the most, and since there were no witnesses, there couldn't possibly be any proof of a delay."

"Well, we need to get, as exact as possible, the time Kristie ran toward the Winston house, and the times calls were made to the paramedics. We also need an expert on snake bites to determine the amount of time which elapsed between the bites and Jake's admission to the hospital for treatment. That amount of time has to be compared to the other times, to determine if there had been some negligence or delay."

"Sheriff Whitt, Mrs. Tidwell-Channing is well known in Alabama and, for that matter, around the country. I think this is an exercise in futility. From what I understand, Jake's prognosis was good, but he died quite unexpectedly.

Everyone knew his recovery would be lengthy, but he wasn't supposed to die."

"Bolen, certain friends and family members of Jake Stanley feel otherwise, and want this matter looked into."

"Yes sir," said Stu as he left the sheriff's office.

CHAPTER 56

Arriving at Billy's BBQ at supper time and finding it crowded, Eric took a seat at the counter. One of the owners, Roger Sexton, working behind the counter, greeted Eric and asked what he wanted to drink. After bringing Eric an iced tea, Roger said, "It was a shame about Jake Stanley's death."

"Yeah," replied Eric. Jake and I were childhood friends. We went to elementary school, junior high, and high school together. After graduation, I used to hang out at his apartment until his escapades became too much for me to handle. But after he served his time and came back to Wentworth, semi-straightened out, we became friends again."

Eric glanced at the TV mounted on the wall, and saw Kristie, with the Birmingham skyline at her back. She was at the network's local affiliate, and appearing on one of the channel's news shows. Either the sound was turned down, or it was too noisy in the restaurant to hear what Kristie and the others participating in the segment were saying. Eric did, however, recognize Kristie's sparring partner, a slick guy whose views were diametrically opposite to hers. Eric didn't think to call Kristie and inform her of Jake's death. Would she have attended the funeral if she had known? Guess he would never know.

"Hey, isn't that…"

"Yes, it is. And I forgot to call Kristie and tell her about Jake's death. If it hadn't been for Kristie, Jake probably would have died on the dock at Jim Winston's boathouse. Kristie had wondered out to the boathouse, and Jake was in the lake floating on a truck inner tube, with a bottle of Jack or scotch. As he climbed onto the dock, a cottonmouth got hold of his leg and gave him a pretty nasty bite. According to Kristie, Jake tried to get the snake off by grabbing it by its middle. This caused the snake to bite his forearm. There were apparently a couple of other bites on him as well. When Jake threw the snake off, it landed on the dock. Kristie retrieved a paddle from the boathouse and knocked the snake back into the lake. Then she ran back to the house to get help. If Kristie hadn't been there, Jake might not have been missed by the crowd at the reunion until it was too late."

"I remember Kristie's Mom and Dad. When they were both alive, they used to come here and eat. I once asked them about Kristie. They said she lived in Birmingham, and didn't have much to do with Wentworth folks. She would come up only to see them. I could tell they were a little disturbed about it."

Eric ordered the quarter chicken, white meat, with coleslaw and potato salad, and continued to watch Kristie on the TV after Roger left to put in his order. Roger returned, seeming to want to talk to Eric. "I remember Jake, Johnny Morton, and Wiley Martin as the bad boy trio when we were in high school. I never hung out with them and their extended crowd. They were just too wild for me."

"I guess I was a part of their extended crowd. Wiley, Jake, and Johnny were wild back in the day, but Wiley was one of the best businessmen ever to come out of Wentworth. His untimely death affected me a lot, and I still miss him. I didn't hang out with Johnny that much, and wasn't really surprised to find out he was gay. Jake, though, had done some terrible things in his life. The night he sexually assaulted Julie Yarborough, I had a date with her. It was the worst evening of my life. I'll always blame Jake for Julie's downfall and death. I know Jake, after serving time, supposedly straightened himself out and was going to church, but he still had a rotten core."

Roger sensed Eric still admired his ex-wife, Kristie. So, he chose not to mention to Eric that Dean Abercrombie had been in the restaurant yesterday, telling anyone who would listen to him, that Kristie, because she hated Jake, had lingered at the dock before running for help after Jake had been bitten. And Dean was sure Kristie could be put away for manslaughter, if not murder. Roger felt this was beyond stupid, and could never be proven, but Dean Abercrombie and Jimmy Harpo seemed to always manage to get their way, and when they didn't, they threw fits. Roger also knew Jimmy and Eric were close friends.

CHAPTER 57

It wasn't difficult to get Kristie's home address, her landline number, and her cell number. He tried her landline first, and got a sleepy sounding Kristie, even though it was after 10:00 am. Guess Kristie was one of those who stayed up late and slept late.

"Kristie Channing?"

"Yes."

"I'm Detective Stu Bolen from the Wentworth County Sheriff's office, how are you this morning?"

"Just fine, thank you. What can I do for you, Detective?"

"Mrs. Channing, I would like to meet with you sometime in the next day or so to ask you some questions about Jake Stanley. I understand you were with him when he was bitten multiple times by what appeared to be a cottonmouth at Jim Winston's lake house."

"May I ask why, detective?"

"You were aware that Mr. Stanley passed away this past Tuesday and was buried this past Friday?"

"Ugh, no! I'm sorry to hear that. I thought the doctors said he would be okay."

"That's what everyone thought, but he did have a heart attack in the ambulance on the way to the hospital. Then we think another one took him out on Tuesday. Would it be possible for you to drive up here and meet with me at the Sheriff's office this afternoon?"

Kristie, now wide awake and fully coherent, replied, "Detective Bolen, I think I need to have an attorney present with me. I'll have to call you back."

"Very well, Mrs. Channing."

Stu gave Kristie the numbers where he could be reached and advised her to contact him within 48 hours.

When she hung up, her head was spinning. Jake Stanley was dead, and now the Sheriff's office was wanting to talk to her. Were they trying to say she somehow forced the snake to bite Jake? This couldn't be happening. She was glad she insisted on having a lawyer present. Kristie knew several lawyers in the Birmingham and Wentworth areas, but only one of them did criminal defense work. His name was Anthony Gross. Kristie and Anthony had worked on some political campaigns together years ago, and they were now Facebook friends.

Luck was on her side because Anthony was in his office and spoke with her. He suggested she come on over to his office as soon as she could schedule. They decided to meet at noon today.

It was slightly before 12:00 noon when Kristie walked into his simple but professional office suite in the Birmingham suburb of Hoover.

"Since it's lunchtime, why don't I have lunch brought in for us, and we can discuss your case?"

"Perfect."

Kristie was anxious to talk to someone.

She told Anthony everything that happened the afternoon and evening of the reunion. She also informed him about her relationship with Jake when they were kids, indicating they were never friends. The two of them continued to talk while eating the lunch his paralegal had ordered for them.

Anthony emphasized that it was a heads-up move by Kristie to engage an attorney before answering any questions posed by the detective, and suggested that they insist Bolen travel to his office instead of them going to Wentworth. "That way, he's on our turf."

Anthony assured Kristie this case was nothing but garbage. "You pushed the snake back into the lake then immediately ran to the Winston house to get help. Everything was done promptly, and as you say, the doctors were expecting Mr. Stanley to survive."

Anthony then called the Wentworth Sheriff's Office and spoke with Stu Bolen, making arrangements for Stu to be at his office at 9:00 am the following day.

Before Kristie left Anthony's office, she asked him about a possible wrongful death civil action.

"I handle criminal defense cases, but one of my partners handles civil actions and should one arise, he can handle that end of it for you." Anthony was thinking a civil action against Kristie would be more likely to succeed because effectuating a monetary settlement would be more appealing to the family. The family also might find a "deep pocket" with Jim Winston. His lake house sounded palatial.

At 8:00 am the following day, Kristie met with Anthony in one of the firm's conference rooms where Anthony prepared her for the questions that Stu Bolen would probably ask. It was agreed to by Anthony, Kristie, and Stu that the interrogation would be videoed and each side would receive a copy.

After the meeting with Anthony, Kristie was so shaken that she could do no work the entire day. Even though she had done what was necessary to save Jake Stanley from the venomous bites, no one, not even Eric, had bothered to notify her of Jake's passing. She probably wouldn't have attended the viewing or the service anyway.

Stu Bolen arrived at Anthony's law offices at 8:50 and was escorted to the conference room where Kristie and Anthony were already seated. Kristie looked tired and worn. Stu guessed it was a major shock she was being questioned about her incident with Jake Stanley. The inquiries he had prepared were going to be tough and intimidating, but that was his job. Kristie had done nothing wrong, but the Harpo clan had a lot of influence in Wentworth County. Anything they wanted done, got done because of Jimmy's pictures of Whitt and the woman prisoner.

Even though she looked haggard, Kristie answered the questions in a calm, cool, and collected manner; even the most intimidating of the questions where he asked Kristie if she delayed in seeking help after Jake Stanley was bitten multiple times, and was obviously in agony.

When the questioning was over, Anthony asked Stu for a few minutes for them to talk without Kristie. In the brief meeting, Stu indicated to Anthony there was absolutely no criminal case against Kristie, and he was going to recommend to the Sheriff that this matter be dropped, so Kristie wouldn't be bothered anymore. Off the record, though, Stu indicated it was a friend of the deceased's who was pushing for Kristie's arrest. Anthony then commented he felt there was a possibility of a civil suit being filed against Kristie for the wrongful death of the deceased. Stu replied he didn't think the guy who was pushing for Kristie's arrest was smart enough to think of encouraging the family to file a civil suit. All he was concerned about was seeing Kristie thrown in jail.

Stu left the law offices, and Anthony informed Kristie that Stu was going to tell the Sheriff there was nothing to this case. "I think you can go home and forget about this. If there's anything else you need, just call me."

Kristie thanked Anthony and left the law offices.

Even though Anthony had assured Kristie nothing would come of this, Kristie was uneasy. She knew there was the possibility of a wrongful death action against her by the family of Jake. But how had this possible criminal action arisen?

On her way home, Kristie burst into tears. Why was this happening to her? She had attended a high school reunion of three classes, witnessed a terrifying poisonous snake bite incident, dumped the deadly viper into the lake, then ran and got help for the bite victim. Then the victim dies, not from the snake bites, but from a series of heart attacks. She didn't do anything wrong, and there was no way a criminal action could be brought against her which could end up with a conviction. Would she have to go through a nightmare of a trial, and all the stuff taking place before the trial should a wrongful death action be filed? How much would this cost her? Kristie, again, thought of taking her own life. This was more than she could handle. While Kristie was a student of the Bible and knew God wouldn't give her any more than she could handle, she didn't want to handle any of it. Kristie wanted to die. Her parents were dead, Eric had left her, and made it abundantly clear she was not to call on him for anything. She had no reason to live, no one to live for.

Kristie had a loaded gun at the house. That would do. Should she shoot herself through the mouth or through her temple? Who would find her? Guess it would be Jennie and Phil when she didn't show up at church. Could she possibly do this to Jennie and Phil? Jennie and Phil, who had taken her in after her Mom died. Jennie and Phil, who had been there for her so many times. No, she couldn't do this to them. Kristie knew she had to wait this one out, but what a hell of a wait it was going to be.

When she arrived at her house, she logged into her laptop and onto the Internet. There, on her homepage, an Alabama news page, was a headline reading: "Birmingham area resident and well-known political analyst, Kristie Tidwell-Channing, is being investigated for manslaughter."

On cue, her cell phone rang. It was her boss at the cable news channel. "Kristie, what the hell is going on down there?"

"Hey Robert, I'm just now finding out about it myself."

After recounting the snake incident, the hiring of an attorney, and the questioning by Wentworth County detective, Stu Bolen, Robert indicated the other side was going to use this to their advantage since they hated the news organization. He also warned her to be prepared for out and out lies told by the other side with the purpose of destroying her. Then Robert uttered the final blow. He was relieving Kristie of her duties at the news organization until this mess was straightened out. Afterward, they would talk about Kristie's future with the cable channel. With that, he wished Kristie the best of luck and ended the call.

Kristie had just lost her job. She still had her blogs which were hugely popular, but would readership drop off because of the manslaughter charge? Should she issue a statement to the public? Maybe she had better call Anthony. All her life, Kristie had wanted to be someone special, someone who was semi-famous. She wanted her name to be a household word. Well, guess what, being semi-famous sucked! She remembered the tried and true saying, "Be careful what you wish for, you just might get it." This certainly applied to her life.

CHAPTER 58

After cleaning up the supper dishes with Tanya, Eric sat down at this laptop to check his email, his favorite Crimson Tide sports website, and the news. On the home page of the number one Alabama news website, Eric read one article. He stood up, and put on his shoes and socks. He then placed a call to Tanya's best friend's mother asking if Tanya could spend the night with them, and could he drop her off in about thirty minutes. Twenty minutes later, Tanya, overnight bag in hand, was leaving the house with Eric. Forty-five minutes later, Eric was headed up I-65 toward Wentworth.

Jessica Tidwell had already gone upstairs, but Barry Tidwell was still downstairs reading the news on his tablet. He had just finished reading about Crimson Tide sports and navigated to the number one Alabama news website. Barry saw a headline that made him frown, then made him furious. Turning off the laptop, Barry grabbed the keys to his truck and left the house without telling his wife, Jessica, where he was going.

On the other side of the county, Sheriff Travis Whitt was reading the news of the day on Alabama's number one news website. One of the articles, written by one of their columnists, made Whitt furious. Getting up out of his recliner, Whitt grabbed the keys to his late model SUV, kissed his wife, telling her he would be back in a couple of hours. Whitt then headed to one of the western-most points of Wentworth County from his house located in one of the eastern-most points of Wentworth County.

It was getting late, and the pornographic movie Kirk Widener was watching on his TV in his run-down shack, located in the Buzzard Hill community of Wentworth County, had just ended There was a knock on the front door. Kirk guessed it was someone who wanted someone in the county snuffed out with no trail remaining. He opened the door to a middle-aged man who had a scowl on his face. The man entered Kirk's living room where they sat down to talk. When the conversation was over, the two men got up and walked to the front door.

"Be careful where you step. I killed two copperheads in the yard this morning. One of them was a mama copperhead because about a dozen babies came out of her when I shot her in her midsection."

How much more fun can life get thought the visitor as he prayed while walking the twenty or so steps to his vehicle.

This was going to be most enjoyable, thought Kirk. He didn't that little shit who thought he owned Wentworth County. Kirk turned out the lights in what could be called the living room of the shack, shucked off his dirty clothes, and crawled into bed in his boxer shorts and wife-beater t-shirt. He had just fallen asleep when there was another knock on his door. Business is booming for a change, Kirk thought, as he turned on the lights and headed for the front door. With the services he performed, he was used to visitors in the middle of the night and happily let the next visitor into his living room. When he and visitor number two had made a deal, he showed his visitor to the door and gave him the same warning about the copperhead snakes.

Once again, Kirk crawled into his unmade bed with dirty sheets in hopes of a decent night's sleep. However, it wasn't meant to be. He was, again, abruptly awakened by a loud knock on his door. He answered the door and greeted a third visitor. Again, Kirk made a deal with this guest, warned him about the copperheads, closed the door, and turned out the living room lights, making his way back to the bedroom, smiling as he once again crawled into bed.

The three men, who had separately visited him, wanted the same little bastard snuffed out. All three were willing to pay a nice little sum of money. For snuffing out this worthless POS, he was getting paid three times. As he fell asleep, he wondered if anyone else would come to his door tonight. Unfortunately, he was unable collect any money this evening. Apparently, these guys were acting on a spur of the moment urge. He, therefore, ordered each of them to bring him half the payment tomorrow, and he assigned three different times for the guys to deliver the cash to his house. He would collect the rest of the money once the job was complete and the body of the object of their hate was deposited in one of the bottomless old wells in the backwoods of Kirk's property.

CHAPTER 59

Kristie was relieved when Anthony called her and told her the Wentworth Sheriff's department would no longer be pursuing a criminal case against her. He had spoken to Sheriff Whitt, and no one had any evidence Kristie had delayed in getting help for Jake Stanley. There were no witnesses, and the cause of death was not the snake bites, but the heart attack he suffered on the Tuesday he died. Shortly after that, Kristie's suspension from the cable news station was lifted, and she was back to doing political analysis. Her blogs were as popular as ever, receiving thousands of visitors a day, and bringing in a tidy sum of cash.

On the last business day of June, Kristie drove up to Wentworth to sign the papers for the sale of her property. For the time being, she planned to keep the money in the Wentworth Savings Bank, so she still had some interests in Wentworth, plus some of her family remained there. While Kristie had virtually made it on her own, and didn't need the proceeds from the property, it felt good to have a little nest egg.

After completing business at the bank, Kristie drove a few blocks to the Coach Restaurant, where she planned to have a few drinks at the bar and then a nice dinner. She was alone, and didn't care. Tanya had graduated high school with honors, and was headed to the University of Alabama this fall. But for the summer, she was staying with Eric at this new lake house. The last time Kristie had talked to Eric was the evening of the high school reunions after Jake Stanley had been transported to the hospital. She knew he and Tanya were living at his lake house, because Tanya told her about it in the note she wrote Kristie, thanking her for her graduation presents, which included a nice little sum of money.

After a dinner of filet mignon, blackened shrimp, steamed asparagus, garlic mashed potatoes and red wine, Kristie left the restaurant and headed south. It was still early, and it was June, so darkness wouldn't fall for another couple of hours. The Wentworth Cemetery would still be open.

Kristie drove her black convertible, top down, through the stately cemetery gates and straight to Wiley Martin's gravesite. She got out of the car, walked to the grave, stood on the grave and jumped up and down on it, muttering, "Wiley Martin, burn in hell." She then visited the graves of Johnny Morton and Jake Stanley, also jumping up and down on them, and muttering for the two of them to burn in hell, also.

Would she have time to drive by Eric's place on Jones Lake before it got dark? Probably not. She wasn't quite sure of its whereabouts, and driving around, lost, in the Jones Lake area after dark was not something she wanted to do. Maybe she would make a special trip up here just to find the house and see where Eric now lived.

On the drive down I-65, Kristie wondered if Eric was mourning Jimmy Harpo's disappearance. Jimmy went missing two or three weeks after Jake Stanley was buried. It was Jennie Stewart who told her about his disappearance, and had kept her informed on the Sheriff's investigation which appeared to only be perfunctory. No note, no body, no evidence of foul play, etc. So many of Eric's friends were gone, so who was he hanging out with? Dean Abercrombie, maybe. Kristie vaguely remembered Dean. He was two years ahead of her and Eric, was part of the wild crowd, and got his high school girlfriend pregnant after he had graduated. They were married for a brief time, but divorced. He was now married to someone else.

CHAPTER 60

Finding herself without plans on the fourth of July, Kristie got in her convertible and headed north up I-65 toward Wentworth. She had been able to get the address of Eric's new lake house, and had mapped it out on Google. The house appeared to be easier to drive to than his other house, which was close, but not on the lake. But nothing on Jones Lake was really that easy to get to by car or truck. Even though she grew up near Jones Lake, Kristie never had a desire to own a place there. In addition to the many snakes that inhabited the area, bobcats and mountain lions were known to roam the hills and hollows surrounding the treacherous finger lake.

Kristie exited I-65 at the first Wentworth exit. Then she took Trimble Road, heading toward Trimble. When Trimble Road ended, she took a left like her GPS said to do. After traveling about a mile and a half, her GPS indicated her destination was on the left. This was certainly nicer than the place he had before. The road up to the house was paved and wide enough to allow two vehicles to meet and pass each other.

She slowed down to look and observed several vehicles parked outside the house. Guess he was having a party. As she drove past the house, Kristie noticed an SUV behind her turning into Eric's. Another party guest.

The woman in the SUV parked the vehicle, grabbed the bowl of coleslaw in the seat beside her, and headed for the back of the house. "Well, guess who I followed from Trimble Road all the way out here?" said Ruthie Harpo to Eric Channing, as he held the back door open for her.

"Who?"

"Kristie. When she got close, she slowed down like she was spying or something. Then she passed the house and headed down the road."

"At some point, I guess she'll realize she missed the house and turn around and come back."

"You invited her here?"

"Yeah, Tanya misses her, and wanted her to come."

Ruthie went inside the house and put the coleslaw in the refrigerator. Several of Tanya's high school friends were there, along with Jan and Jeremy Franklin, Kathryn and Sam Harpo, Dean Abercrombie and his wife, Marianne, and others. Eric had invited a lot of the old high school gang in hopes of starting over again in Wentworth. Jimmy had been missing for almost two months. The sheriff's office had ended the investigation, and even though a body had not been found, Jimmy was presumed to be dead.

Meanwhile, Eric, Tanya, and their guests were having a great time celebrating the Fourth of July in Eric's new home. For a few minutes after Ruthie Harpo indicated she had seen Kristie, Eric was awaiting her arrival. But he soon forgot about her after a few more members of their old gang showed up. As Eric stood on his spacious screened in back porch, looking at the guests mingling outside, either on the lawn, on the dock, or in the water, his thoughts went back to when he was a teenager, and this group used to party at certain parents' houses on the lake.

Decades ago, folks would run up and down the steps from the house to the water, jump or dive off the dock with no thought to the water's depth, or to creatures lurking around. They would go boating and waterskiing without life jackets. Eric now admitted to himself he was nervous about skiing without a vest or a ski belt, but he didn't want to be called a chicken by the others.

The swimsuits the girls wore back then were brief bikinis. These same women who still had the courage to wear swimsuits now wore the kind which had skirts on them. Tanya and her friends wore the skimpy swimsuits, which didn't please Eric.

After dark at one of the parties, he recalled how he and Rita, dressed in their swimsuits, took a beach towel and went to a place behind a large bush where no one could see them. They shimmied out of their suits and lay on the towel making love. Another couple was skinny dipping in the lake, while other couples had also gone off by themselves. Alcohol was involved, and most of the guys would get drunk to the point they would throw up. Now, the women were in the kitchen, and the men were standing on the dock. While alcohol was still being consumed, the old gang members had grown up and were pacing themselves.

"A penny for your thoughts."

Startled, Eric saw Ruthie Harpo standing beside him, smiling up at him.

"Oh, hi, Ruthie. I was just reminiscing about the great times we had at various places on Jones Lake when we were teenagers. This was before you and Jimmy met."

"Jimmy has told me about the things y'all used to do. I admit I was a little jealous of the gang members when we first started going out, but y'all welcomed me into the group with open arms. And we had some good times together as adults as well. And we still do. I remember when you and Gina were together. I also remember Wiley and Anabelle, and Jake. I don't think I ever met Johnny Morton. He graduated from Auburn, and left Wentworth for bigger and better things. He found them, and then he died of AIDS. It really hurt Jimmy when Johnny came out of the closet."

"Wiley and Jake weren't happy about it either. They had gym classes together, worked out together, skinny dipped together, etc. I was never that close to Johnny."

"Did Kristie ever show up? It's been a while since she drove past the house."

"No. Hey, Tanya, did Kristie say she would come when you called her?"

Tanya suddenly gasped. "I didn't call her. I guess I got busy and forgot."

"Well," said Ruthie, "She must have heard about our party and decided to come stalking."

"I doubt Kristie would drive up here just to drive by the house. I'm sure she has plans of her own today. Ruthie are you sure that was her in the car ahead of you?"

"Well, the woman ahead of me was driving a black convertible. I didn't catch the make. She had a University of Alabama license plate, and her long dark hair was blowing in the breeze."

"She sounds a lot like Kristie, but it must not have been her, guess we had better fire up the grills." replied Eric.

Kristie continued to drive down the county road looking at all the lake houses. Some were palatial, and some were little more than cottages. The road ended at Jones Lake Park where there was a marina and a restaurant. The restaurant was obviously open because folks were going in and out. In the park, many of the picnic tables, all covered by sheds were occupied by families or groups of friends.

Because she was beginning to get hungry, Kristie decided to get something to eat at the restaurant before she headed back to Wentworth. Eric was not spending the fourth alone, he had friends over, and she wasn't invited. Did she expect to be invited? Of course not.

Kristie entered the restaurant, but because it was crowded, decided to take a seat at the bar. The menu was primarily barbecue, but there was also a selection of steak and seafood entrees. Since it was the fourth of July, Kristie ordered a half slab of baby back ribs with collards, mac and cheese, cornbread, and sweet tea. Guess she was hungrier than she thought because she finished everything on her plate, but declined to order dessert. Could she drive home without falling asleep?

Walking out to her car, she was reminded of how nice a day this was. Even though this was Alabama in July, the high was supposed to be only in the upper eighties, and the humidity was expected to be below normal. While most of the tables in the park were taken, Kristie decided to grab a quilt and a beach chair she always kept in the convertible. She also had a bag containing a couple of books. She would spread her quilt in a shady area and read for a while before heading back to her house.

On this beautiful Fourth of July day, Kristie began reading her book, but couldn't keep her eyes open and nodded off. When she woke up, the sun was getting low on the horizon. Looking at her watch, Kristie realized she had been asleep for about two and a half hours. Even though it was a while before darkness would fall, she was anxious to pack up and head back to Wentworth. She checked her purse to make sure nothing had been taken from it while she was asleep. Everything was in place, including her cell phone which she hadn't checked all day. She had missed three calls. One was from Eric, who didn't leave a message. The other two were from two separate friends who invited Kristie to spend the Fourth with them. One invited her over for dinner, and then to watch the fireworks, sponsored by one of the Birmingham area's radio stations, beginning at 9:00 pm. She would have plenty of time to get to Birmingham, and join these friends for the fireworks. She texted back she would be at their house shortly, and asked if she could bring anything.

As Kristie was putting her things in the backseat of the convertible, a silver pickup truck pulled up beside her. It was Eric in the driver's seat, and Ruthie Harpo in the passenger's seat.

"Kristie! What are you doing here?"

"It's a free country, I can go anywhere I please within its borders."

Rolling his eyes, Eric replied, "Yeah, yeah, yeah, let's start over. Hi Kristie, how are you?"

"I'm fine and you."

"Very well, thank you. I tried to call you earlier, to invite you up here. We're having a party at my place. It's mostly the old gang."

"Your call was placed after 1:00 pm, you must not have wanted me at your party that bad."

Ruthie Harpo got out of the truck, and walked over to the driver's side where Kristie and Eric were talking. "Ruthie, will you excuse us please." Eric got out of the truck, and took Kristie by the arm, and steered her several yards away from where their vehicles were parked.

"I'll go in and get the ice," said Ruthie.

"Kristie, I know this looks bad, and I do apologize. Tanya wanted to invite you, and I told her she could. However, I forgot to follow up with Tanya, and she forgot to call you. She's all wrapped up in preparing for college and gets absent-minded. That's no excuse, and I had some words with her about it, and I intend to have some more words with her after everyone leaves later this evening. I messed up also. I should have followed up with her, and then with you, but I didn't. For that, I apologize with all my heart. Please come over and have ice cream with us. Also, there's plenty of real food left, you can have all you want and take some home."

"Thanks, Eric, but I've already accepted an invitation to dinner and to watch the fireworks."

"Well call them and say something's come up, and you can't make it. I'm sure they won't care. There's supposed to be a fireworks show out here on the lake tonight. I'm sure some of us will drive over here to watch it."

"I hate to do that when I've already said I would join them."

"Just call them or text them."

"Who all is over at your house?"

"The people you don't like, but you don't have to talk to them. Just talk to Tanya and her friends. Two of her girlfriends are spending the Fourth with her up here. And talk to me, stay with me. Not for the night, not with Tanya and her friends here. Just stay beside me."

"I'm not sure I can find my way out after dark."

"Sure you can. You can also follow some of the guests as they head back to Wentworth. You can follow them to Trimble Road then to the Highway and back to I-65. You know this part of the country. Everyone's a little down after Jimmy's disappearance. You knew about that, didn't you?"

"Yes. Well, Ruthie seems all right. It looks like she has her sights set on you."

"She's not all right, believe me."

"Look, no one is going to be hateful to you. I'm not going to let that happen."

"What if they start blaming me for Jimmy's disappearance? They sure didn't hesitate to blame me for Jake's death."

"No one blamed you for Jake's death," Eric lied.

"Bull shit! I was questioned by Stu Bolen, had to hire an attorney, and was suspended from the news channel until the charges were dropped."

"I didn't know all of that."

"Well, now you do. I went through some of the worst shit I've ever been through in my life"

Of course, Eric knew Jimmy was speculating that Kristie had lingered on the dock after Jake was bitten, instead of immediately running for help. He also knew Kristie had been suspended by the news channel, but was quickly reinstated. He thought it best if he plead ignorance.

"Hey, what's keeping y'all?" yelled Ruthie. "This ice is going to melt."

"Come on Kristie, I need to get back to the house. Please follow us back and stay for a while. We'll talk about the things we've been trying to talk about for a while. Of course, I want you to see the new house, also."

"Okay, but just for a little while."

EPILOGUE

The minister and his wife were hurrying down I-65 as fast as he felt comfortable driving. The sun was to set on this lovely early October evening at 6:45 pm and the two of them had to be in Orange Beach by at least 6:00.

A couple, who were good friends of the bride, were in their hotel room drinking wine and watching the Weather Channel. A late season hurricane was churning in the Gulf of Mexico, southwest of Orange Beach. The medium strength storm was projected to make landfall somewhere on the Mississippi Coast in the wee hours of the morning. While the Alabama Coast would not take a direct hit, the Coast would be on the east side of the storm, which was generally the "bad side." The waves were high, and there were rip currents. By tomorrow morning, it would be raining and windy in the lovely Alabama beach town. No damage was expected, but residents were asked to monitor the weather because tornadoes were a possibility in the northeast quadrant of the storm.

Eric and his daughter, Tanya Channing, were in another hotel room, also watching the Weather Channel, but flipping back and forth to the Auburn game. Alabama had this Saturday off, so this was the only weekend when a fall wedding was possible. Walking out on the balcony Eric saw a brilliant crimson sun in the western sky. Underneath the sun, gunmetal gray clouds were forming to the southwest. What would the sky look like at 6:45? Would there be any sun or just looming darkness? Either way was okay, because he knew the direction in which he was taking his life, was the right direction. He had never been as sure of himself as he was now. Eric was at peace.

Tanya looked nothing short of beautiful in her over-sized sweatshirt and leggings. Her long dark hair was streaming down her back. Eric didn't know how Tanya would fix her hair for this special occasion, but he knew it would be beautiful. Tanya was getting a new Mom, a Mom who already loved her very much. Even though Tanya was already in college, she still needed the guidance that only a mother can give a daughter.

Tanya suddenly stood up, went to the closet, and pulled out a deep red dress, went into the hotel room bathroom, and shut the door. In less than five minutes she emerged from the bathroom wearing the simple deep red dress with an empire waist and a white sash. She then retrieved a pair of strappy white flat sandals from her suitcase, and put them carefully on her feet.

"Honey, you look absolutely beautiful," exclaimed Eric. "You look so much like your mother. Even though our marriage didn't last, she was nonetheless a beautiful woman."

"Thanks, Daddy. Shouldn't you be getting ready?"

"I guess I should."

Eric, already showered and shaved, grabbed a pair of white slacks, and a deep red polo shirt, and retreated to the bathroom. When he emerged, he put on a pair of white socks and some brown top-siders.

"Let's take a selfie," said Tanya after Eric was fully dressed.

Tanya took several pictures of her and her Dad. They all turned out beautiful. But shouldn't all wedding photos be beautiful?

The minister and his wife pulled up in the hotel parking lot right at 6:00. By 6:10, they were checked into the hotel room Eric had reserved for them. Both quickly changed clothes as the minister rehearsed the wedding vows. Just before the sun began to set, he was supposed to be saying,

"By the power invested in me by the state of Alabama and the Lord Jesus Christ I now pronounce…"

"I hope this works out," said the minister. "Some folks may be upset with me for marrying these two."

"Eric has said he's never been as sure of anything in his life. He knows there's going to be some angst, but he's willing to live with that," replied the minister's wife.

"I'm going to go on down to the pool, and wait for the rest of the party," said the minister.

The wedding party was to gather at the pool and he was going to lead the procession onto the beach to within about ten feet of the shore.

"Okay, I'll go get the bride, and we'll see you down there."

A minute or so after the minister arrived at the pool area, the bride's best friends joined him. Next, Eric and Tanya joined the group. There were hugs and handshakes all around. Everyone lined up behind the minister, Eric and Tanya, arm in arm, followed by the bride's friends.

At 6:30 sharp, the door from the hotel lobby to the pool area opened, and walking onto the pool area was the most beautiful woman Eric had ever seen in his life, clutching the hand of the minister's wife. Kristie, wearing a long casual white dress, accentuated at its empire waist with a deep red sash, waved as she and Jennie walked toward the group.

When Kristie and Jennie were lined up, Phil turned to the wedding party and offered a prayer. Then he led the group down the boardwalk and onto the white sands of Orange, Beach, Alabama. Stopping about ten yards from the shoreline, Phil turned around and opened his book while Tanya and Eric, and Kristie and Jennie made their way toward Phil. Jennie then let go of Kristie's hand and gave her a big hug. Tanya let go of Eric's hand and gave him a big hug. Then she gave Kristie a big hug.

Phil performed the ceremony flawlessly, uttering the words, "By the power invested in me by the state of Alabama and the Lord Jesus Christ, I now pronounce Eric Channing and Kristie Tidwell-Channing husband and wife, and what God hath joined together, let no one put asunder." After briefly kissing his bride, Eric took Tanya by the hand and steered her to where she stood between him and Kristie.

"Tanya, please repeat after me," said Phil. "I, Tanya Channing, take Kristie Channing as my Mom, and I promise to love her forever." And Tanya did.

"Kristie, please repeat after me," said Phil, once again. "I, Kristie Channing, take Tanya Channing as my daughter, and I promise to love her forever." Kristie repeated the vow.

"Tanya Channing and Kristie Channing, through the eyes of the Lord Jesus Christ, you are mother and daughter. Tanya Channing, you may now hug your Mom."

Both women hugged one another and cried for what was about a half minute. Phil then ended the ceremony by introducing Mr. and Mrs. Eric Channing and daughter Tanya to the remainder of the wedding party and a small gathering of onlookers.

The wedding party then turned to face west as the crimson sun, surrounded by gun metal gray clouds, slipped into the shimmering waters of the Gulf of Mexico.

Once the sun had set, everyone clapped again and hugged.

"Is anyone around here hungry, I'm about to starve," exclaimed Eric.

Nothing had been planned for after the wedding.

"Want to go across the road to Wolf Bay?" asked Natalie. It was one of her and Tim's favorite restaurants.

"Sure, let's go," said Eric.

The small group made its way up the beach and onto the boardwalk. Tim, Eric, and Phil were leading the group. Jennie and Natalie were walking behind them. And bringing up the rear were Kristie and Tanya, walking together with their arms around one another. Kristie had a daughter, and Tanya had a mother. This was the happiest day of their lives.

Kristie looked ahead and saw Eric engaged in conversation with Phil and Tim. They were laughing and having fun, anticipating a scrumptious dinner. That was her Eric. He was one of a kind, and she loved him so much.

Smiling, she whispered to herself, "Sorry girls, he's taken."

****

Hi everyone,

I sure hope you enjoyed Sunsets. An author's success depends largely on what others think of his or her work. Thus, I would greatly appreciate your taking the time to post a review on Amazon.com.

Also, if you haven't read the first book in the "Kristie and Eric" series, For Best and Worst, please do so. Even though I wrote Sunsets with enough back story that reading FBAW was not necessary, I think you will like it.

While I included some favorite recipes with FBAW, not much cooking took place in Sunsets. The characters went out to eat a lot, though. So, here are some links to some of the restaurants mentioned.

Cullman, Alabama:

All Steak Restaurant (Inspiration for The Coach):
https://www.allmenus.com/al/cullman/412257-all-steak-restaurant/menu/

Johnny's Bar-B-Q (Inspiration for Billy's Bar-B-Q):
http://johnnysbarbq.com/

Alabama/Florida/Mississippi Gulf Coast

Felix's Fish Camp, Mobile, Al:
http://www.felixsfishcamp.com
Snapper's Seafood, Biloxi, Ms:
http://www.snappersseafoodbiloxi.com/home/html
Lambert's Café, Foley, Al: http://www.throwedrolls.com
Bahama Bob's Beachside Café, Gulf Shores, Al.:
http://www.bamahamabobs.com
Wolf Bay Lodge, Orange Beach, Al:
http://www.wolfbaylodge.com
Hazel's Seafood Restaurant, Orange Beach, Al.:
http://www.hazelsseafoodrestaurant.com
Cosmo's Restaurant and Bar, Orange Beach, Al:
http://www.cosmosrestaurantandbar.com
Big Fish Restaurant and Bar, Orange Beach, Al:
http://www.bigfishrestaurantandbar.com
Tacky Jack's, various locations:
http://www.tackyjacks.com
Original Oyster House, Gulf Shores, Al:
http://www.originaloysterhouse.com
Captain Anderson's, Panama City, Fl:
http://www.captaindersons.com
Kitty's Kafe, Gulf Shores, Al: http://www.kittyskafe.com
Flora-Bama Yacht Club, Alabama/Florida line:
http://www.florabamayachtclub.com

While not in the book, the Flora-Bama Yacht Club has become one of your author's favs. It's across the road from the infamous Flora-Bama.

New York City (Midtown Manhattan):

La Bonne Soupe: http://labonnesoupe.com/
Tommy Bahama Restaurant:
http://www.tommybahama.com/restaurants/new-york-city
Wolfgang's Steakhouse:
http://www.wolfgangssteakhouse.net/
Le Parisien: http://www.leparisiennyc.com/
Joe Allen: http://www.joeallenrestaurant.com/

Franklin, Tennessee:
Puckett's Grocery: https://puckettsgro.com/franklin/

My next novel will be entitled, "Meandering the Eastern Shore." Like "Sunsets" and "For Best and Worst," it will be southern contemporary romance. So, visit my website often: http://www.marienicoleharper.com.

Love Y'all,
Marie

www.ingramcontent.com/pod-product-compliance
Lightning Source LLC
Chambersburg PA
CBHW051510250626
47156CB00001B/42